HARD TIMES

Published by Priory Books,
© Peter Haddock Publishing,
United Kingdom, YO16 6BT.

HARD TIMES

BOOK I

CHAPTER 1

"Now, what I want is, Facts. Teach these boys and girls nothing but Facts. Facts alone are wanted in life. Plant nothing else, and root out everything else. You can only form the minds of reasoning animals upon Facts: nothing else will ever be of any service to them. This is the principle on which I bring up my own children, and this is the principle on which I bring up these children. Stick to Facts, sir!"

The scene was a bare vault of a schoolroom, and the speaker's square forefinger emphasised his observations by underscoring every sentence with a line on the schoolmaster's sleeve. The emphasis was helped by the speaker's square wall of a forehead, with eyebrows for its base, while his eyes seemed as if in two dark caves, overshadowed by the wall. It was helped by the speaker's mouth, which was wide, thin, and hard set. It was helped by the speaker's voice, which was dry, and dictatorial. It was helped by the speaker's hair, which bristled on the skirts of his bald head. The speaker's obstinate carriage, square coat, square legs, square shoulders, all helped the emphasis.

"In this life, we want nothing but Facts, sir!"

The speaker, the schoolmaster and the third grown person present, all backed a little, and glanced across the vessels then and there arranged, ready to have imperial gallons of facts poured into them.

CHAPTER 2

Thomas Gradgrind, sir. A man of facts and calculations. A man who proceeds upon the principle that two and two are four, and nothing over, and who is not to be talked into allowing for anything over. With a rule and a pair of scales, and the multiplication table always in his pocket, sir, ready to weigh and measure any parcel of human nature, and tell you exactly what it comes to. It is a mere question of figures, a case of simple arithmetic. Thomas Gradgrind now presented Thomas Gradgrind to the little pitchers before him, who were to be filled full of facts.

"Girl number twenty," said Mr Gradgrind, squarely pointing with his square forefinger, "Who is that girl?"

"Sissy Jupe, sir," explained number twenty, blushing, standing up, and curtseying.

"Sissy is not a name," said Mr Gradgrind. "Don't call yourself Sissy. Call yourself Cecilia."

"It's father as calls me Sissy, sir," returned the young girl in a trembling voice, with another curtsey.

"Then he has no business to," said Mr Gradgrind. "Tell him he mustn't. Cecilia Jupe. Let me see. What is your father?"

"He belongs to the horse-riding, if you please, sir."

Mr Gradgrind frowned, and waved off the objectionable calling with his hand.

"Your father breaks horses, don't he?"

"If you please, sir, when they can get any to break, they do break horses in the ring, sir."

"You mustn't tell us about the ring here. He doctors sick horses, I dare say?"

"Oh yes, sir."

"Very well. He is a veterinary surgeon, a farrier and horsebreaker. Give me your definition of a horse."

This threw Sissy Jupe into the greatest alarm.

"Girl number twenty unable to define a horse!" said Mr Gradgrind. "Girl number twenty possessed of no facts, in reference to one of the commonest of animals! Some boy's definition of a horse. Bitzer, yours."

The square finger lighted suddenly on Bitzer, perhaps because he happened to sit in the same ray of sunlight that lit up Sissy. The boys and girls sat in two compact bodies, divided up the centre by a narrow interval. Sissy, at the corner of a row on the sunny side, came in for the beginning of a sunbeam, while Bitzer, on the other side, a few rows ahead, caught the end. But, whereas the girl was dark-eyed and dark-haired, and seemed to receive a more lustrous colour from the sunshine, the boy was so light-eyed and light-haired that the same rays appeared to take away what little colour he possessed. His skin was so unwholesomely deficient in the natural tinge, that he looked as though, if he were cut, he would bleed white.

"Bitzer," said Thomas Gradgrind. "Your definition of a horse."

"Quadruped. Graminivorous. Forty teeth, namely twenty-four grinders, four eye-teeth, and twelve incisive. Sheds coat in the spring; in marshy countries, sheds hoofs, too. Hoofs hard, but requiring to be shod with iron. Age known by marks in mouth."

"Now girl number twenty," said Mr Gradgrind. "You know what a horse is."

She curtseyed again, and would have blushed deeper, if she could have. Bitzer blinked at Thomas Gradgrind with both eyes at once, put his knuckles to his freckled forehead, and sat down again.

The third gentleman now stepped forth. He was a government officer, and a professed pugilist; always in training, always ready to fight all England. To continue in fistic phraseology, he had a genius for coming up to the scratch, wherever and whatever it was, and proving himself an ugly customer. He would go in and damage any subject whatever with his right, follow up with his left, stop, exchange, counter, bear his opponent to the ropes, and fall upon him neatly. He was certain to knock the wind out of common sense, and render that unlucky adversary deaf to the call of time.

"Very well," said this gentleman, briskly smiling, and folding his arms. "That's a horse. Now, let me ask you, girls and boys. Would you paper a room with representations of horses?"

After a pause, half of the children cried in chorus, "Yes, sir!" Upon which the other half, seeing in the gentleman's face that Yes was wrong, cried out in chorus, "No, sir!"

"Of course not. Why wouldn't you?"

A pause.

"I'll explain to you, then," said the gentleman, "why you wouldn't paper a room with representations of horses. Do you ever see horses walking up and down the sides of rooms in reality?"

"Yes, sir!" from one half. "No, sir!" from the other.

"Of course no," said the gentleman with an indignant look at the wrong half. "Why, then, you are not to see anywhere, what you don't see in fact; you are not to have anywhere, what you don't have in fact. What is called Taste, is only another name for Fact." Thomas Gradgrind nodded his approbation.

"This is a new principle, a great discovery," said the gentleman. "Now, I'll try you again. Suppose you were going to carpet a room. Would you use a carpet having a representation of flowers?"

There being a general conviction by this time that "No, sir!" was always the right answer to this gentleman, the chorus of NO was very strong. Only a few said Yes; among them Sissy Jupe.

"Girl number twenty," said the gentleman, smiling in the calm strength of knowledge.

Sissy blushed, and stood up.

"So you would carpet your room with representations of flowers, would you?" said the gentleman. "Why?"

"If you please, sir, I am very fond of flowers," returned the girl.

"And is that why you would put tables and chairs upon them, and have people walking over them with heavy boots?"

"It wouldn't hurt them, sir. They wouldn't crush and wither, if you please, sir. They would be the pictures of something very pretty and pleasant, and I would fancy – "

"Ay! But you mustn't fancy," cried the gentleman, quite elated by coming so happily to his point. "That's it! You are never to fancy."

"You are not, Cecilia Jupe," Thomas Gradgrind solemnly repeated, "to do anything of that kind."

"Fact, fact, fact!" said the gentleman.

And "Fact, fact, fact!" repeated Thomas Gradgrind.

"You are to be in all things governed," said the gentleman, "by fact. We hope to have, before long, a board of fact, composed of commissioners of fact, who will force the people to be a people of fact, and of nothing but fact. You must discard the word Fancy altogether. You are not to have, in any object of use or ornament, what would be a contradiction in fact. You don't walk upon flowers in fact; you cannot walk upon flowers in carpets. You don't find foreign birds perching upon your crockery; you cannot paint foreign birds upon your crockery. You never meet with quadrupeds going up and down walls; you must not have quadrupeds represented upon walls. You must use," said the gentleman, "for all these purposes, combinations and modifications (in primary colours) of mathematical figures that are susceptible of proof and demonstration. This is the new discovery. This is fact. This is taste."

The girl curtseyed, and sat down. She was very young, and looked worried by the matter-of-fact prospect the world afforded.

"Now, if Mr M'Choakumchild," said the gentleman, "will proceed to give his first lesson here, Mr Gradgrind, I shall be happy, at your request, to observe his mode of procedure."

Mr Gradgrind was much obliged. "Mr M'Choakumchild, we only wait for you."

So, Mr M'Choakumchild began in his best manner. He and some one hundred and forty other schoolmasters, had been lately turned at the same time, in the same factory, on the same principles, like so many pianoforte legs. He had been put through an immense variety of paces, and had answered volumes of head-breaking questions. Orthography, etymology, syntax, and prosody, biography, astronomy, geography, and general cosmography, the sciences of compound proportion, algebra, land-surveying and levelling, vocal music, and drawing from models, were all at the ends of his ten chilled fingers. He had worked his stony way into Her Majesty's most Honourable Privy Council's Schedule B, and had taken the bloom off the higher branches of mathematics and physical science, French, German, Latin, and Greek. He knew all about all the Water Sheds of all the world (whatever they are), and all the histories of all the peoples, and all the names of all the rivers and mountains, and all the productions, manners, and customs of all the countries, and all their boundaries and bearings on the two and thirty points of the compass. If he had only learnt a little less, how infinitely better he might have taught much more!

He went to work in this preparatory lesson, not unlike Morgiana in the Forty Thieves: looking into all the vessels ranged before him, one after another, to see what they contained

CHAPTER 3

Mr Gradgrind walked home from the school, fairly satisfied. It was his school, and he intended it to be a model. He intended every child in it to be a model – just as the young Gradgrinds were all models.

There were five young Gradgrinds. They had been lectured at from their tenderest years. Almost as soon as they could run alone, they had been made to run to the lecture-room. The first object with which they had any remembrance was a large blackboard with an Ogre chalking ghastly white figures on it.

Not that they knew, by name or nature, anything about an Ogre. Fact forbid!

No little Gradgrind had ever seen a face in the moon. No little Gradgrind had ever learnt the nursery rhyme, Twinkle, twinkle, little star! No little Gradgrind had ever known wonder on the subject, as each little Gradgrind had at five years old dissected the Great Bear. No little Gradgrind had ever associated a cow in a field with that famous cow with the crumpled horn that tossed the dog who worried the cat who killed the rat who ate the malt. It had never heard of those celebrities, and had only been introduced to a cow as a ruminating quadruped with several stomachs.

To his matter of fact home, which was called Stone Lodge, Mr Gradgrind directed his steps. He had virtually retired from the wholesale hardware trade before he built Stone Lodge, and was now looking about for a suitable opportunity of making an arithmetical figure in Parliament. Stone Lodge was situated on a moor within a mile or two of a great town, Coketown.

Stone Lodge was a great square house, with a heavy portico darkening the principal windows. A calculated, cast up, balanced, and proved house. Six windows on this side of the door, six on that side; a total of twelve in this wing, a total of twelve in the other wing; four-and-twenty carried over to the back wings. A lawn and garden and an infant avenue, all ruled straight. Gas and ventilation, drainage and water-service, all of the best quality. Fire-proof from top to bottom; mechanical lifts for the housemaids, with all their brushes and brooms; everything that could be desired.

Everything? Well, the little Gradgrinds had cabinets in various departments of science too. They had a little conchological cabinet, and a little metallurgical cabinet, and a little mineralogical cabinet. All specimens were arranged and labelled.

Their father walked on in a hopeful and satisfied frame of mind. He was an affectionate father, after his manner; but he would probably have described himself as "an eminently practical" father. He had a particular pride in the phrase eminently practical. Whatever the public meeting held in Coketown, and whatever the subject of such meeting, some Coketowner was sure to seize the occasion of alluding to his eminently practical friend Gradgrind. This always pleased the eminently practical friend. He knew it to be his due.

He had reached the neutral ground upon the outskirts of the town when his ears were invaded by the sound of music. The clashing and banging band attached to the horse-riding establishment, which had set up a wooden pavilion was in full bray. A flag proclaimed to mankind that it was "Sleary's Horse-riding". Sleary himself, a stout modern statue with a money-box at its elbow, took the money. Miss Josephine Sleary, the printed bill announced, was then inaugurating the entertainments with her graceful equestrian Tyrolean flower-act. Signor Jupe was that afternoon to "elucidate the diverting accomplishments of his highly trained performing dog Merrylegs." The same Signor Jupe was to "enliven the varied performances at frequent intervals with his chaste Shakespearean quips." Lastly, he was to wind them up by appearing in his favourite character of Mr William Button, of Tooley Street, in "the highly novel and laughable hippo-comedietta of The Tailor's Journey to Brentford."

Thomas Gradgrind took no heed of these trivialities of course, but passed by as a practical man ought to pass by, either brushing the noisy insects from his thoughts, or consigning them to the House of Correction. But, the road took him by the back of the booth, where a number of children gathered, striving to peep in at the hidden glories of the place.

This brought him to a stop. "Just think of these vagabonds," said he, "attracting the young rabble from a model school."

He took his eyeglass from his waistcoat to look for any child he knew by name. Lo and behold, what did he see but his own metallurgical Louisa, peeping with all her might through a hole, and his own mathematical Thomas lying on the ground to catch but a hoof of the graceful equestrian Tyrolean flower-act!

Dumb with amazement, Mr Gradgrind crossed to where his family was thus disgraced, laid his hand upon each erring child, and said: "Louisa!! Thomas!!"

Both stood, red and disconcerted. But, Louisa looked at her father more

9

boldly than Thomas did. Indeed, Thomas did not look at him, but gave himself up to be taken home.

"In the name of idleness, and folly!" said Mr Gradgrind, leading each away by a hand. "What do you do here?"

"Wanted to see what it was like," returned Louisa, shortly.

There was an air of jaded sullenness in them both, and particularly in the girl: yet, struggling through the dissatisfaction of her face, there was a light with nothing to rest upon, a fire with nothing to burn, a starved imagination keeping life in itself somehow, which brightened its expression. Not with the brightness natural to cheerful youth, but with uncertain, eager, doubtful flashes.

She was a child now, of fifteen or sixteen; but would soon become a woman. Her father thought so as he looked at her. She was pretty. Would have been self-willed (he thought in his eminently practical way) but for her upbringing.

"Thomas, I find it difficult to believe that you have brought your sister to a scene like this."

"I brought him, father," said Louisa, quickly. "I asked him to come."

"I am very sorry indeed to hear it. It makes Thomas no better, and it makes you worse, Louisa."

She looked at her father again, but no tear fell down her cheek.

"Thomas and you, to whom the circle of the sciences is open; Thomas and you, who may be said to be replete with facts; Thomas and you, here!" cried Mr Gradgrind. "In this degraded position! I am amazed."

"I was tired, father. I have been tired a long time," said Louisa.

"Tired? Of what?" asked the astonished father.

"I don't know of what – of everything I think."

"Say not another word," returned Mr Gradgrind. "You are childish. I will hear no more." He did not speak again until they had walked some half-a-mile in silence, when he gravely broke out with: "What would your best friends say, Louisa? Do you attach no value to their good opinion? What would Mr Bounderby say?"

At the mention of this name, his daughter stole a look at him, intense and searching. He saw nothing of it, for before he looked at her, she had again cast down her eyes!

"What," he repeated presently, "would he say?" All the way home, he repeated at intervals, "What would Mr Bounderby say!"

CHAPTER 4

Mr Bounderby was as near being Mr Gradgrind's bosom friend, as a man perfectly devoid of sentiment can approach that spiritual relationship towards another man also devoid of sentiment.

He was a rich man: banker, merchant, manufacturer. A big, loud man. A man made out of a coarse material, which seemed to have been stretched to make so much of him. A man with a great puffed head and forehead, swelled veins in his temples, and such a strained skin to his face that it seemed to hold his eyes open, and lift his eyebrows up. A man who always proclaimed in that brassy speaking trumpet of a voice of his, of his old ignorance and poverty. The Bully of humility.

A year or two younger than his eminently practical friend, Mr Bounderby looked older; his seven or eight and forty might have had the seven or eight added to it again, without surprising anybody. He had not much hair.

In the formal drawing room of Stone Lodge, standing on the hearthrug, warming himself before the fire, Mr Bounderby told Mrs Gradgrind that it was his birthday. He stood before the fire, partly because it was a cool spring afternoon, and partly because he took up a commanding position, thus subduing Mrs Gradgrind.

"I hadn't a shoe to my foot. I passed the day in a ditch, and the night in a pigsty. That's the way I spent my tenth birthday. Not that a ditch was new to me, for I was born in a ditch."

Mrs Gradgrind, a thin, white, pink-eyed bundle of shawls, of surpassing feebleness, mental and bodily, hoped it was a dry ditch?

"No! A foot of water in it," said Mr Bounderby.

"Enough to give a baby cold," Mrs Gradgrind considered.

"Cold? For years, ma'am, I was one of the most miserable little wretches ever seen," returned Mr Bounderby. "I was so sickly, that I was always moaning. I was so ragged and dirty, you wouldn't have touched me with a pair of tongs."

Mrs Gradgrind faintly looked at the tongs.

"How I fought through it, I don't know," said Bounderby. "I was determined, I suppose. I have been a determined character in later life, and I suppose I was then. Here I am, Mrs Gradgrind, anyhow, and nobody to thank for my being here, but myself."

Mrs Gradgrind meekly and weakly hoped that his mother –

"My mother? Bolted, ma'am!" said Bounderby.

Mrs Gradgrind, stunned as usual, collapsed and gave it up.

"My mother left me to my grandmother," said Bounderby; "and, to the best of my remembrance, my grandmother was the wickedest old woman that ever lived. If I got a little pair of shoes by any chance, she would take 'em and sell 'em for drink. Why, I have known that grandmother of mine lie in her bed and drink her fourteen glasses of liquor before breakfast!"

Mrs Gradgrind weakly smiled.

"She kept a chandler's shop," pursued Bounderby, "and kept me in an egg-box. That was the cot of my infancy – an old egg-box. As soon as I was big enough to run away, of course I ran away. Then I became a young vagabond; and instead of one old woman knocking me about and starving me, everybody knocked me about and starved me. They were right. I was a nuisance, an incumbrance, and a pest."

His pride in having achieved such a great social distinction as to be a nuisance, an incumbrance, and a pest, was only to be satisfied by three repetitions of the boast.

"I pulled through it, though nobody threw me out a rope. Vagabond, errand-boy, vagabond, labourer, porter, clerk, chief manager, small partner. Josiah Bounderby of Coketown learnt his letters from the outsides of the shops, Mrs Gradgrind, and was first able to tell the time upon a dial-plate, from studying the steeple clock of St Giles's Church, London, under the direction of a drunken cripple. Tell Josiah Bounderby of your district schools and model schools, your training schools, and whole kettle-of-fish of schools; and Josiah Bounderby of Coketown tells you plainly, he hadn't such advantages – and the education that made him won't do for everybody, he knows."

Josiah Bounderby of Coketown stopped just as his eminently practical friend, still accompanied by the two young culprits, entered the room. His eminently practical friend, on seeing him, stopped also, and gave Louisa a reproachful look that plainly said, "Behold your Bounderby!"

"Well!" blustered Mr Bounderby, "what is young Thomas in the dumps about?"

He spoke of young Thomas, but he looked at Louisa.

"We were peeping at the circus," muttered Louisa, haughtily, without lifting up her eyes, "and father caught us."

"And Mrs Gradgrind," said her husband in a lofty manner, "I should as soon have expected to find my children reading poetry."

"Dear me," whimpered Mrs Gradgrind. "I wonder at you. I declare you're enough to make one regret ever having had a family at all. I have a great mind to say I wish I hadn't. Then what would you have done, I should like to know."

Mr Gradgrind did not seem favourably impressed by these remarks, and frowned impatiently.

"As if, with my head in its present throbbing state, you couldn't go and look at the shells and minerals and things provided for you, instead of circuses!" said Mrs Gradgrind. "You know, as well as I do, no young people have circus masters or keep circuses in cabinets, or attend lectures about circuses. What can you possibly want to know of circuses? I am sure you have enough to do. With my head in its present state, I couldn't remember the mere names of half the facts you have got to attend to."

"That's the reason!" pouted Louisa.

"Don't tell me that's the reason, because it can be nothing of the sort," said Mrs Gradgrind. "Go and be somethingological directly." Mrs Gradgrind was not a scientific character, and usually dismissed her children to their studies with this general injunction to choose their pursuit.

In truth, Mrs Gradgrind's stock of facts in general was woefully defective; but Mr Gradgrind had married her for two reasons. Firstly, she was most satisfactory as a question of figures; and, secondly, she had "no nonsense" about her, and by nonsense he meant fancy.

Being left alone with her husband and Mr Bounderby, was sufficient to stun this lady. She once more died away, and nobody minded.

"Bounderby," said Mr Gradgrind, drawing a chair to the fireside, "you are always so interested in my young people, particularly Louisa, so I don't mind saying to you I am very much vexed by this discovery. I have devoted myself (as you know) to the education of the reason of my family. The reason is (as you know) the only faculty to which education should be addressed. And yet, Bounderby, it would appear from this unexpected circumstance of today, though in itself trifling, as if something had crept into Thomas's and Louisa's minds which is – or rather which has never been intended to be developed."

"Then comes the question," continued the eminently practical father, "where does this vulgar curiosity come from?"

"In idle imagination."

"I hope not," said the eminently practical. "I confess, however, that the misgiving has crossed me on my way home."

"In idle imagination, Gradgrind," repeated Bounderby. "Bad enough for anybody, but a cursed bad thing for a girl like Louisa."

"Could a servant or anybody have suggested something," said Mr Gradgrind, pondering with his hands in his pockets. "Could Louisa or Thomas have been reading anything? Can, in spite of all precautions, an idle story-book have got into the house? Because, in minds that have been practically formed by rule and line from the cradle upwards, this is so curious, so incomprehensible."

"Stop a bit!" cried Bounderby, who all this time had been standing on the hearth. "You have one of those strollers' children in the school."

"Cecilia Jupe, by name," said Mr Gradgrind, with something of a stricken look at his friend.

"How did she come there?" asked Bounderby.

"Why, the fact is, this is the first time I saw the girl myself. She specially applied here at the house to be admitted, as not regularly belonging to our town, and – yes, you are right, Bounderby."

"Louisa saw her when she came?" cried Bounderby, once more.

"Louisa certainly did, for she mentioned the application to me. But she saw her, I have no doubt, in Mrs Gradgrind's presence."

"Pray, Mrs Gradgrind," said Bounderby, "what passed?"

"Oh, my!" returned Mrs Gradgrind. "The girl wanted to come to the school, and Mr Gradgrind wanted girls to come to the school, and Louisa and Thomas both said that the girl wanted to come, and that Mr Gradgrind wanted girls to come. How was it possible to contradict them when such was the fact!"

"Turn this girl out," said Mr Bounderby. "And there's an end."

"I am much of your opinion."

"Do it at once," said Bounderby.

"Are you walking?" asked his friend. "I have the father's address. You would not mind walking with me?"

"Not in the least," said Mr Bounderby, "as long as you do it at once!"

So, Mr Bounderby threw on his hat. While waiting in the hall a moment while Mr Gradgrind went upstairs for the address, he opened the door of the children's study and looked into that serene floor-clothed apartment. Louisa leaned upon the window looking out, without looking at anything, while young Thomas stood sniffing revengefully at the fire. Adam Smith and Malthus, two younger Gradgrinds, were out at lecture; and little Jane, after manufacturing a good deal of moist pipe-clay on her face with slate-pencil and tears, had fallen asleep over vulgar fractions.

"It's all right now, Louisa, young Thomas," said Mr Bounderby. "You won't do so any more. I'll answer for it's being all over with father. Well, Louisa, that's worth a kiss, isn't it?"

"You can take one, Mr Bounderby," returned Louisa, when she had coldly paused, and slowly walked across the room, and ungraciously raised her cheek towards him, with her face turned away.

"Always my pet, ain't you, Louisa?" said Mr Bounderby. "Good bye, Louisa!"

He went his way, but she stood still, rubbing the cheek he had kissed with her handkerchief, until it was burning red. She was still doing this, five minutes later.

"What are you about, Loo?" her brother asked. "You'll rub a hole in your face."

"You may cut the piece out with your penknife if you like, Tom. I wouldn't cry!"

CHAPTER 5

Coketown, to which Messrs Bounderby and Gradgrind now walked, was a triumph of fact – it had no greater taint of fancy in it than Mrs Gradgrind herself. It was a town of red brick, or of brick that would have been red if the smoke and ashes had allowed it.

It was a town of machinery and tall chimneys, from which interminable serpents of smoke rose.

It had a black canal in it, and a river that ran purple with ill-smelling dye, and vast piles of building full of windows where there was a rattling and a trembling all day long, and where the piston of the steam-engine worked monotonously up and down. It contained several large streets all very like one another, and many small streets, inhabited by people equally like one another, who all went in and out at the same hours, with the same sound upon the same pavements, to do the same work, and to whom every day was the same as yesterday and tomorrow.

There was nothing in Coketown but what was severely utilitarian. If the members of a religious persuasion built a chapel there – as the members of eighteen religious persuasions had done – they made it a pious warehouse of red brick, with sometimes, a bell in a birdcage on the top of it. The solitary exception was the New Church, a stuccoed edifice with a square steeple over the door, terminating in four short pinnacles like florid wooden legs. All the public inscriptions in the town were painted alike, in severe characters of black and white. The jail might have been the infirmary, the infirmary might have been the jail, the town hall might have been either, both, or anything else. Fact, fact, fact, everywhere in the material aspect of the town; fact, fact, fact, everywhere in the immaterial. Everything was fact between the lying-in hospital and the cemetery.

Along came Mr Gradgrind and Mr Bounderby walking through Coketown.

"This man lives at Pod's End, and I don't quite know Pod's End," said Mr Gradgrind. "Which is it, Bounderby?"

Mr Bounderby knew it was somewhere down town, but knew no more. So they stopped for a moment, looking about.

Almost as they did so, there came running round the corner at a quick pace and with a frightened look, a girl whom Mr Gradgrind recognised. "Halloa!" said he. "Stop! Where are you going? Stop!" Girl number twenty stopped then, and made him a curtsey.

"Why are you tearing about the streets," said Mr Gradgrind, "in this improper manner?"

"I was – I was run after, sir," the girl panted, "and I wanted to get away."

"Who would run after you?" asked Mr Gradgrind.

The question was unexpectedly and suddenly answered, by the colourless boy, Bitzer, who came round the corner with such blind speed and so little anticipating a stoppage on the pavement, that he brought himself up against Mr Gradgrind's waistcoat and rebounded into the road.

"What do you mean, boy?" said Mr Gradgrind. "What are you doing? How dare you dash against – everybody – in this manner?"

Bitzer picked up his cap, and backing, and knuckling his forehead, pleaded that it was an accident.

"Was this boy running after you, Jupe?" asked Mr Gradgrind.

"Yes, sir," said the girl reluctantly.

"No, I wasn't, sir!" cried Bitzer. "Not till she run away from me. But the horse-riders never mind what they say, sir; they're famous for it. It's as well known in the town as – please, sir, as the multiplication table isn't known to the horse-riders." Bitzer tried Mr Bounderby with this.

"He frightened me," said the girl, "with his cruel faces!"

"Oh!" cried Bitzer. "Oh! An't you one of the rest! An't you a horse-rider! I never looked at her, sir. I asked her if she would know how to define a horse tomorrow, and offered to tell her again, and she ran away, and I ran after her, sir, that she might know how to answer when she was asked."

"Her calling seems to be pretty well known among 'em," observed Mr Bounderby. "You'd have had the whole school peeping in a week."

"Truly, I think so," returned his friend. "Bitzer, take yourself home. Jupe, stay a moment. If I hear of your running in this manner any more, boy, you will hear of me through the master of the school. You understand. Go along."

The boy stopped in his rapid blinking, knuckled his forehead again, glanced at Sissy, turned about, and retreated.

"Now, girl," said Mr Gradgrind, "take this gentleman and me to your father's – we are going there. What is in that bottle?"

"Gin," said Mr Bounderby.

"Dear, no, sir! It's the nine oils."

"The what?" cried Mr Bounderby.

"The nine oils, sir. To rub father with."

Then said Mr Bounderby, with a loud short laugh, "Why the devil do you rub your father with nine oils?"

"It's what our people use, sir, when they get any hurts in the ring," replied the girl. "They bruise themselves, very bad sometimes."

"Serve 'em right," said Mr Bounderby, "for being idle." She glanced up at his face, with mingled astonishment and dread.

"By George!" said Mr Bounderby, "when I was younger than you, I had worse bruises upon me than ten oils, twenty oils, forty oils, would have rubbed off. I got 'em by being banged about."

Mr Gradgrind was by no means so rough a man as Mr Bounderby. His character was not unkind, all things considered; it might have been a very kind one indeed, if he had only made some round mistake in the arithmetic that balanced it, years ago. He said, in what he meant for a reassuring tone, as they turned down a narrow road, "And this is Pod's End; is it, Jupe?"

"This is it, sir, and – if you wouldn't mind, sir – this is the house."

She stopped, at twilight, at the door of a mean little public-house, with dim red lights in it.

"It's only across the bar, sir, and up the stairs, if you wouldn't mind waiting a moment. I'll get a candle. If you should hear a dog, sir, it's only Merrylegs, and he only barks."

"Merrylegs and nine oils, eh!" said Mr Bounderby, entering last. "Pretty well this, for a self-made man!"

CHAPTER 6

The name of the public house was the Pegasus's Arms. Underneath the winged horse upon the signboard, the name was inscribed in Roman letters.

Framed and glazed upon the wall behind the dingy little bar, was another Pegasus – a theatrical one -- with real gauze for his wings, golden stars stuck on all over him, and a harness of red silk.

As it had grown too dusky to see the sign, and as it was not light enough inside to see the picture, Mr Gradgrind and Mr Bounderby received no offence from these images. They followed the girl up some steep corner-stairs without meeting any one, and waited while she went on for a candle. They expected to hear Merrylegs, but the highly trained performing dog had not barked when the girl and the candle appeared.

"Father is not in our room, sir," she said, in great surprise. "If you wouldn't mind walking in, I'll find him directly."

They walked in, and Sissy set two chairs for them, then sped away with a quick step. It was a shabbily furnished room, with a bed in it. The white night-cap, embellished with two peacock's feathers, in which Signor Jupe had that very afternoon enlivened the varied performances with his chaste Shakespearean quips and retorts, hung upon a nail; but no other item of his wardrobe, or hint of his pursuits, was to be seen anywhere. There was no sign of Merrylegs.

They heard the doors of rooms above, opening and shutting as Sissy went from one to another, and presently they heard voices expressing surprise. She came bounding down again in a great hurry, opened a battered and mangy old hair trunk, found it empty, and looked round with her hands clasped and her face full of terror.

"Father must have gone down to the Booth, sir. He must be there; I'll bring him in a minute!" She was gone directly, without her bonnet, her long, dark, childish hair streaming behind her.

"Back in a minute?" said Mr Gradgrind. "It's more than a mile off."

Before Mr Bounderby could reply, a young man appeared at the door, introducing himself with the words, "By your leaves, gentlemen!" He walked in with his hands in his pockets. His face, close-shaven, thin, and sallow was shaded by a great quantity of dark hair, brushed into a roll all round his head, and parted up the centre. His legs were very robust, but short. His chest and back were as much too broad, as his legs were too short. He was dressed in a Newmarket coat and tight-fitting trousers and wore a shawl round his neck. He smelt of lamp oil, straw, orange-peel, horses' provender, and sawdust. This gentleman was Mr E.W.B. Childers, justly celebrated for his daring vaulting act as the Wild Huntsman of the North American Prairies. In this popular performance, a diminutive boy with an old face, who now accompanied him, assisted as his infant son. Made up with curls, wreaths, wings, white bismuth, and carmine, this hopeful young person soared into so pleasing a Cupid as to constitute the chief delight of the maternal part of the spectators. However in private, where his characteristics were a precocious cutaway coat and an extremely gruff voice, he became of the Turf, turfy.

"By your leaves, gentlemen," said Mr E.W.B. Childers, glancing round the room. "It was you, I believe, that were wishing to see Jupe!"

"It was," said Mr Gradgrind. "His daughter has gone to fetch him, but I can't wait. I will leave a message with you."

"You see, my friend," Mr Bounderby put in, "we are the kind of people who know the value of time, and you are the kind of people who don't know the value of time."

"I have not," retorted Mr Childers, after surveying Bounderby from head to foot, "the honour of knowing you. But if you mean that you can make more money of your time than I can of mine, I should judge from your appearance, that you are about right."

"And when you have made it, you can keep it," said Cupid.

"Kidderminster, stow that!" said Mr Childers. (Master Kidderminster was Cupid's mortal name.)

"What does he come here cheeking us for, then?" cried Master Kidderminster.

"Kidderminster," said Mr Childers, raising his voice, "stow that! – Sir," to Mr Gradgrind, "I was addressing myself to you. You may or you may not be aware, that Jupe has missed his tip often, lately."

"Has – what has he missed?" asked Mr Gradgrind, glancing at Bounderby for assistance.

"Didn't do what he ought to do. Was short in his leaps and bad in his tumbling," Mr Childers interpreted.

"Oh!" said Mr Gradgrind, "that is tip, is it?"

"In a general way that's missing his tip," Mr E.W.B. Childers answered. "You were going to give me a message?"

"Yes, I was."

"Then," continued Mr Childers, quickly, "my opinion is, he will never receive it. Do you know much of him?"

"I never saw the man in my life."

"I doubt if you ever will see him now. It's pretty obvious, he's off."

"Do you mean that he has deserted his daughter?"

"Ay! I mean," said Mr Childers, with a nod, "that he has cut. He was goosed last night, he was goosed the night before last, he was goosed today and he can't stand it."

"Why has he been – so very much – Goosed?" asked Mr Gradgrind, forcing the word out.

"His joints are turning stiff, and he is getting used up," said Childers. "He has his points as a Cackler still, but he can't get a living out of them."

"A Cackler!" Bounderby repeated. "Here we go again!"

"A speaker, if the gentleman likes it better," said Mr E.W.B. Childers, throwing the interpretation over his shoulder, and accompanying it with a shake of his long hair. "Now, it's a remarkable fact, sir, that it cut that man deeper, to know that his daughter knew of his being goosed, than to go through with it."

"This is good, Gradgrind!" interrupted Mr Bounderby. "A man so fond of his daughter, that he runs away from her! This is devilish good! Ha! Ha! Now, I'll tell you what, young man. I haven't always occupied my present station of life. You may be surprised to hear it, but my mother ran away from me."

E.W.B. Childers replied he was not at all surprised.

"Very well," said Bounderby. "I was born in a ditch and my mother ran away from me. Do I excuse her for it? No. Have I ever excused her for it? Not I. What do I call her for it? I call her probably the very worst woman that ever lived in the world, except my drunken grandmother. I call a spade a spade; and I call the mother of Josiah Bounderby, without any fear or any favour, what I should call her if she were the mother of Dick Jones of Wapping. The same for this man. He is a runaway rogue and a vagabond, that's what he is, in English."

"It's all the same to me what he is, whether in English or in French," retorted Mr E.W.B. Childers. "I am telling your friend the facts."

Eyeing Mr Bounderby from head to foot again, he turned from him to Mr Gradgrind.

"Jupe sent his daughter out on an errand not an hour ago, and then was seen to slip out, his hat over his eyes, and a bundle tied up under his arm. She will never believe it of him but he has left her."

"Pray," said Mr Gradgrind, "why will she never believe it of him?"

"Because those two were one, they were never apart. Because, up to this time, he seemed to dote upon her," said Childers, taking a step or two to look into the empty trunk. Both Mr Childers and Master Kidderminster walked in a curious manner – their legs wider apart than the general run of men. This walk was common to all the male members of Sleary's company, and was understood to express that they were always on horseback.

"Poor Sissy! He had better have apprenticed her," said Childers, giving his hair another shake, as he looked up from the empty box. "Now, he leaves her with nothing to take to."

"It is creditable to you, who have never been apprenticed, to express that opinion," returned Mr Gradgrind, approvingly.

"I never apprenticed? I was apprenticed when I was seven year old."

"Oh! Indeed?" said Mr Gradgrind, rather resentfully, as if cheated of his good opinion. "I was not aware of its being the custom to apprentice young persons to – "

"Idleness," Mr Bounderby put in with a loud laugh. "No, by the Lord Harry! Nor I!"

"Her father always had it in his head," resumed Childers, ignoring Mr Bounderby, "that she was to be taught the deuce-and-all of education. How it got into his head, I can't say. He has been picking up a bit of reading for her, here – and a bit of writing for her, there – and a bit of ciphering for her, somewhere else – these seven years."

Mr E.W.B. Childers took one of his hands out of his pockets, stroked his face and chin, and looked with a good deal of doubt and a little hope at Mr Gradgrind. From the first he had sought to conciliate that gentleman, for the sake of the deserted girl.

"When Sissy got into the school here," he pursued, "her father was as pleased as Punch. I couldn't make out why, as we were not stationary here, being but comers and goers anywhere. But I suppose he had this move in his mind and considered her provided for. If you were looking in tonight, for the purpose of telling him that you were going to do her any little service," said Mr Childers, stroking his face again, repeating his look, "it would be very fortunate and well-timed."

"On the contrary," returned Mr Gradgrind. "I came to tell him that her connections made her not an object for the school, and that she must not attend any more. Still, if her father really has left her, without any connivance on her part – Bounderby, let me have a word with you."

Upon this, Mr Childers politely betook himself, with his equestrian walk, to the landing outside the door, and there stood stroking his face, and softly whistling. Here he overheard such phrases in Mr Bounderby's voice as "No. I say no. I advise you not." While, from Mr Gradgrind, he heard in his much lower tone the words, "But as an example to Louisa, of what this pursuit which has been the subject of a vulgar curiosity, leads to and ends in. Think of it, Bounderby, from that point of view."

Meanwhile, the various members of Sleary's company gradually gathered together from the upper regions, where they were quartered,

22

and, from standing about, talking in low voices to one another and to Mr Childers, gradually insinuated themselves and him into the room. There were two or three handsome young women among them, with their two or three husbands, and their two or three mothers, and their eight or nine little children, who did the fairy business when required. The father of one of the families was in the habit of balancing another father on the top of a great pole; the father of a third family often made a pyramid of both those fathers, with Master Kidderminster for the apex, and himself for the base. All the mothers could (and did) dance, upon the slack wire and the tight rope, and perform rapid acts on bare-backed steeds. None were at all bothered at showing their legs; and one of them, alone in a Greek chariot, drove six in hand into every town they came to. They all assumed to be mighty rakish and knowing, they were not very tidy in their private dresses, they were not at all orderly in their domestic arrangements, and the combined literature of the whole company would have produced but a poor letter on any subject. Yet there was a remarkable gentleness and childishness about these people, a special inaptitude for any kind of sharp practice, and an untiring readiness to help one another.

Last of all appeared Mr Sleary, a stout man as already mentioned, with one fixed eye, and one loose eye, a voice like the efforts of a broken old pair of bellows, a flabby surface, and a muddled head which was never sober and never drunk.

"Thquire!" said Mr Sleary, who was troubled with asthma, and whose breath came far too thick and heavy for the letter s, "Your thervant! Thith ith a bad piethe of bithnith, thith ith. You've heard of my Clown and hith dog being thuppothed to have morrithed?"

He addressed Mr Gradgrind, who answered "Yes."

"Well, Thquire," he returned, taking off his hat, and rubbing the lining with his pocket-handkerchief, which he kept inside for the purpose. "Ith it your intenthion to do anything for the poor girl, Thquire?"

"I have something to propose to her when she returns," said Mr Gradgrind.

"Glad to hear it, Thquire. Not that I want to get rid of the child. I'm willing to take her prentith, though at her age ith late. My voithe ith a little huthky, Thquire, and not eathy heard by them ath don't know me; but if you'd been chilled and heated, heated and chilled, chilled and heated in

23

the ring when you wath young, ath often ath I have been, your voithe wouldn't have lathted out, Thquire, no more than mine."

"I dare say not," said Mr Gradgrind.

"What thall it be, Thquire, while you wait? Thall it be Therry? Give it a name, Thquire!" said Mr Sleary, with hospitable ease.

"Nothing for me, I thank you," said Mr Gradgrind.

"Don't thay nothing, Thquire. What doth your friend thay? If you haven't took your feed yet, have a glath of bitterth."

Here his daughter Josephine – a pretty fair-haired girl of eighteen, who had been tied on a horse at two years old, and had made a will at twelve, which she always carried about with her, expressive of her dying desire to be drawn to the grave by the two piebald ponies – cried, "Father, hush! She has come back!" Then came Sissy Jupe, running into the room as she had run out of it. And when she saw them all assembled, and saw their looks, and saw no father there, she broke into a most deplorable cry, and took refuge on the bosom of the most accomplished tight-rope lady who knelt down on the floor to nurse her, and to weep over her.

"Ith an internal thame, upon my thoul it ith," said Sleary.

"O my dear father, where are you gone? You are gone to try to do me some good, I know! You are gone away for my sake, I am sure! And how miserable and helpless you will be without me, poor father, until you come back!" She said many things of this kind, with her face turned upward, and her arms stretched out as if she were trying to stop his departing shadow.

Mr Bounderby (growing impatient) took the case in hand. "Now, good people all," said he, "this is wanton waste of time. Let the girl understand the fact. Let her take it from me, if you like, who have been run away from myself. Here, what's your name? Your father has deserted you and you mustn't expect to see him again as long as you live."

They cared so little for plain Fact, these people, and were in that advanced state of degeneracy on the subject, that instead of being impressed by the speaker's strong common sense, they took it in extraordinary dudgeon. The men muttered "Shame!" and the women "Brute!" and Sleary, in some haste, communicated the following hint, apart to Mr Bounderby.

"I tell you what, Thquire. To thpeak plain to you, my opinion ith that you had better cut it thort, and drop it. They're a very good natur'd people, my people, but they're accuthtomed to be quick in their movementh; and if you don't act upon my advithe, I'm damned if I don't believe they'll puth you out o' winder."

Mr Bounderby being restrained by this mild suggestion, Mr Gradgrind found an opening.

"It is of no moment," said he, "whether this man is expected back at any time, or not. He is gone, and there is no present expectation of his return. That, I believe, is agreed on all hands."

"Thath agreed, Thquire. Thtick to that!" From Sleary.

"Well then. I came here to inform the father of the poor girl, Jupe, that she could not be received at the school any more due to practical objections, into which I need not enter, to having children of persons so employed. I am prepared in these altered circumstances to make a proposal. I am willing to take charge of you, Jupe, and to educate you, and provide for you. The only condition, over and above your good behaviour, is that you decide now, at once, whether to accompany me or stay. Also, that if you accompany me now, it is understood that you communicate no more with any of your friends here. That is my proposal."

"At the thame time," said Sleary, "I mutht put in my word, Thquire, tho that both thides of the banner may be equally theen. If you like, Thethilia, to be prentitht, you know the natur of the work and you know your companionth. Emma Gordon, in whothe lap you're a lying at prethent, would be a mother to you, and Joth'phine would be a thithter to you. I never did a horthe a injury yet, no more than thwearing at him went, and that I don't expect I thall begin otherwithe at my time of life, with a rider. I never wath much of a Cackler, Thquire, and I have thed my thay."

The latter part of this speech was addressed to Mr Gradgrind, who received it with a grave inclination of his head, and then remarked:

"The only observation I will make to you, Jupe, in the way of influencing your decision, is, that it is highly desirable to have a sound practical education. Your father himself seems, on your behalf, to have known and felt that much."

The last words had a visible effect upon her. She stopped in her wild crying, detached herself from Emma Gordon, and turned her face full upon her patron. The whole company perceived the force of the change, and drew a long breath together, that plainly said, "she will go!"

"Be sure you know your own mind, Jupe," Mr Gradgrind cautioned her. "I say no more. Be sure you know your own mind!"

"When father comes back," cried the girl, bursting into tears again after a moment, "how will he ever find me if I go away!"

"You may be quite at ease," said Mr Gradgrind, calmly, working out the whole matter like a sum, "on that score. In such a case, your father, I apprehend, must find Mr – "

"Thleary. Thath my name, Thquire. Not athamed of it. Known all over England, and alwayth paythe ith way."

"Must find Mr Sleary, who would then let him know where you went. I should have no power of keeping you against his wish, and he would have no difficulty, at any time, in finding Mr Thomas Gradgrind of Coketown. I am well known."

"Well known," assented Mr Sleary, rolling his loose eye.

There was another silence and then she exclaimed, sobbing with her hands before her face, "Oh, give me my clothes, and let me go before I break my heart!"

The women sadly bestirred themselves to get the clothes together – it was soon done, for they were not many. Sissy sat all the time, upon the ground, still sobbing. Mr Gradgrind and his friend Bounderby stood near the door, ready to take her away. Mr Sleary stood in the middle of the room, with the male members of the company about him, exactly as if he were in the centre of the ring during his daughter Josephine's performance. He wanted nothing but his whip.

The basket packed in silence, they brought her bonnet to her, and smoothed her disordered hair, and put it on. Then they pressed about her, and bent over her in very natural attitudes, kissing and embracing her. They brought the children to take leave of her and were a tenderhearted, simple, foolish set of women altogether.

"Now, Jupe," said Mr Gradgrind. "If you are quite determined, come!"

But she had to take her farewell of the male part of the company yet, and every one of them had to unfold his arms and give her a parting. Mr Sleary was reserved until the last. Opening his arms wide he took her by both her hands, and she stood before him crying.

"Good bye, my dear!" said Sleary. "You'll make your fortun, I hope, and none of our poor folkth will ever trouble you. I with your father hadn't taken hith dog with him; ith a ill-conwenienth to have the dog out of the billth. But on thecond thoughth, he wouldn't have performed without hith mathter, tho ith ath broad ath ith long!"

With that he regarded her attentively with his fixed eye, surveyed his company with his loose one, kissed her, shook his head, and handed her to Mr Gradgrind.

"There the ith, Thquire," he said, "and the'll do you juthtithe. Good bye, Thethilia!"

"Good bye, Cecilia!" "Good bye, Sissy!" "God bless you, dear!" In a variety of voices from all the room.

But the riding-master eye had observed the bottle of the nine oils in her bosom, and he now interposed with "Leave the bottle, my dear; ith large to carry; it will be of no uthe to you now."

"No, no!" she said, in another burst of tears. "Oh, no! Pray let me keep it for father! He will want it when he comes back. He hadn't thought of going away, when he sent me. I must keep it for him, please!"

"Tho be it, my dear. (You thee how it ith, Thquire!) Farewell, Thethilia! My latht wordth to you ith thith, Thtick to the termth of your engagement, be obedient to the Thquire, and forget uth. But if, when you're grown up and married and well off, you come upon any horthe-riding ever, don't be hard upon it, don't be croth with it, give it a Bethpeak if you can, and think you might do wurth. People mutht be amuthed, Thquire, thomehow," continued Sleary, rendered more pursy than ever, by so much talking; "they can't be alwayth a working, nor yet they can't be alwayth a learning. Make the betht of uth; not the wurtht. I've got my living out of the horthe-riding all my life, I know; but I conthider that I lay down the philothophy of the thubject when I thay to you, Thquire, make the betht of uth: not the wurtht!"

The Sleary philosophy was propounded as they went downstairs; and the fixed eye of Philosophy – and its rolling eye, too – soon lost the three figures and the basket in the darkness of the street.

27

CHAPTER 7

Mr Bounderby being a bachelor, an elderly lady presided over his establishment. Mrs Sparsit was this lady's name and she was a prominent figure in attendance on Mr Bounderby as he rolled along in triumph.

For, Mrs Sparsit was highly connected. She had a great aunt living in these very times called Lady Scadgers. Mr Sparsit, deceased, had been by the mother's side what Mrs Sparsit still called "a Powler." Strangers of limited information were sometimes observed not to know what a Powler was, and even to appear uncertain whether it might be a business, or a political party, or a profession of faith. The better class of minds, however, did not need to be informed that the Powlers were an ancient stock.

The late Mr Sparsit, being by the mother's side a Powler, married this lady, being by the father's side a Scadgers. Lady Scadgers, an immensely fat old woman, with a huge appetite for butchers' meat, and a mysterious leg that had now refused to get out of bed for fourteen years, contrived the marriage, when Sparsit was just of age. He inherited a fair fortune from his uncle, but owed it all before he came into it, and spent it twice over immediately afterwards. He died at twenty-four in Calais and he did not leave his widow, from whom he had been separated soon after the honeymoon, in affluent circumstances. That bereaved lady, fifteen years older than he, fell presently at deadly feud with her only relative, Lady Scadgers; and, partly to spite her ladyship, and partly to maintain herself, went out at a salary. And here she was now, in her elderly days, making Mr Bounderby's tea as he took his breakfast.

"Mr Bounderby," said Mrs Sparsit, "you are unusually slow sir, with your breakfast this morning."

"Why, ma'am," he returned, "I am thinking about Tom Gradgrind's whim of bringing up the tumbling-girl."

"The girl is now waiting to know," said Mrs Sparsit, "whether she is to go straight to the school, or up to the Lodge."

"She must wait, ma'am," answered Bounderby, "till I know myself. We shall have Tom Gradgrind down here presently. If he wishes her to remain here a day or two longer, of course she can, ma'am."

"Of course she can if you wish it, Mr Bounderby."

"I told him I would give her a shake-down here, last night, in order that he might sleep on it before he decided to let her have any association with Louisa."

"Indeed, Mr Bounderby. Very thoughtful of you!"

"It's clear to me," said Bounderby, "that the little puss can get very little out of such companionship."

"Are you speaking of young Miss Gradgrind, Mr Bounderby?"

"Yes, ma'am, I'm speaking of Louisa."

"Your observation being limited to 'little puss,'" said Mrs Sparsit, "and there being two little girls in question, I did not know which might be indicated by that expression."

"Louisa," repeated Mr Bounderby.

"You are quite another father to Louisa, sir." Mrs Sparsit took a little more tea.

"If you had said I was another father to Tom – young Tom, I mean, not my friend Tom Gradgrind – you might have been nearer the mark. I am going to take young Tom into my office. Going to have him under my wing ma'am."

"Indeed? Rather young for that, is he not, sir?" Mrs Sparsit's "sir," in addressing Mr Bounderby, was a word of ceremony, rather exacting consideration for herself in the use than honouring him.

"I'm not going to take him at once; he is to finish his educational cramming before then," said Bounderby. "He'd open his eyes, that boy would, if he knew how empty of learning my young maw was, at his time of life." Which he probably did know, for he had heard of it often enough.

Mr and Miss Gradgrind were then announced, and he received the former with a shake of the hand, and the latter with a kiss.

"Can Jupe be sent here, Bounderby?" asked Mr Gradgrind.

Certainly. So Jupe was sent there. She curtseyed to Mr Bounderby, and to his friend Tom Gradgrind, and also to Louisa. She was waved over by the master of the house to Mr Gradgrind. She stood looking intently at him, and Louisa stood coldly by, with her eyes upon the ground, while he proceeded.

"Jupe, I have decided to take you into my house and, when you are not at the school, to employ you about Mrs Gradgrind, who is rather an invalid. I have explained to Miss Louisa – this is Miss Louisa – the miserable but natural end of your late career; and you are to expressly understand that the whole of that subject is not to be referred to any more. From this time you begin your history. You are, at present, ignorant, I know."

"Yes, sir, very," she answered, curtseying.

"I shall have the satisfaction of causing you to be strictly educated and you will be a living proof to all who come into communication with you, of the advantages of the training you will receive. You will be reclaimed and formed. You have been in the habit of reading to your father, and those people I found you among, I dare say?" said Mr Gradgrind, beckoning her nearer to him before he said so, and dropping his voice.

"Only to father and Merrylegs, sir."

"Never mind Merrylegs, Jupe," said Mr Gradgrind, with a frown. "I don't ask about him. I understand you used to read to your father?"

"O yes, sir, thousands of times. They were the happiest – O, of all the happy times we had together, sir!"

It was only now when her sorrow broke out, that Louisa looked at her.

"And what," asked Mr Gradgrind, in a still lower voice, "did you read to your father, Jupe?"

"About the Fairies, sir, and the Dwarf, and the Hunchback, and the Genies," she sobbed out. "And about – "

"Hush!" said Mr Gradgrind, "that is enough. Never breathe a word of such destructive nonsense any more. Bounderby, this is a case for rigid training, and I shall observe it with interest."

"Well," returned Mr Bounderby, "I have given you my opinion already, and I wouldn't do as you do. But since you are bent upon it, very well!"

So, Mr Gradgrind and his daughter took Cecilia Jupe off with them to Stone Lodge, and on the way Louisa never spoke one word, good or bad. And Mr Bounderby went about his daily pursuits. And Mrs Sparsit meditated all the evening.

CHAPTER 8

When she was six years younger, Louisa had been overheard to begin a conversation with her brother one day, by saying "Tom, I wonder" – upon which Mr Gradgrind, who was the person overhearing, stepped up and said, "Louisa, never wonder!"

Never wonder. By means of addition, subtraction, multiplication, and division, settle everything somehow, and never wonder. Bring to me, says M'Choakumchild, yonder baby just able to walk, and I will engage that it shall never wonder.

"I am sick of my life, Loo. I hate it altogether, and I hate everybody except you," said the unnatural young Thomas Gradgrind in the hair-cutting chamber at twilight.

"You don't hate Sissy, Tom?"

"I hate to be obliged to call her Jupe. And she hates me," said Tom, moodily.

"No, she does not, Tom, I am sure!"

"She must," said Tom. "She must just hate and detest the whole set-up. They'll bother her head off, I think, before they have done with her. Already she is as pale as wax, and as heavy as – I am."

Young Thomas expressed these sentiments sitting astride a chair before the fire, with his arms on the back, and his sulky face on his arms. His sister sat in the darker corner by the fireside, now looking at him, now looking at the bright sparks as they dropped upon the hearth.

"As to me," said Tom, tumbling his hair all manner of ways with his sulky hands, "I am a Donkey, that's what I am. I am as obstinate as one, I am more stupid than one, I get as much pleasure as one, and I should like to kick like one."

"Not me, I hope, Tom?"

"No, Loo; I wouldn't hurt you. I made an exception of you at first. I don't know what this – jolly old – Jaundiced Jail," Tom paused to find an expressive name for the parental roof, "would be without you."

"Indeed, Tom? Do you really and truly say so?"

"Why, of course I do. What's the use of talking about it!" returned Tom, rubbing his face on his coat-sleeve.

"Because, Tom," said his sister, after silently watching the sparks

31

awhile, "as I get older, and nearer growing up, I often sit wondering here, and think how unfortunate it is for me that I can't make home feel better for you than I am able to do. I don't know what other girls know. I can't play or sing to you. I can't talk to you so as to enlighten your mind, for I never see any amusing sights or read any amusing books that it would be a pleasure or a relief to you to talk about, when you are tired."

"Well, no more do I for I am as bad as you in that respect. I am a Mule too, which you're not. If father was determined to make me either a Prig or a Mule, and I am not a Prig, why, it stands to reason, I must be a Mule," said Tom, desperately.

"It's a great pity," said Louisa, after another pause, and speaking thoughtfully out of her dark corner. "It's a great pity, Tom. It's very unfortunate for both of us."

"Oh! You," said Tom, "you are a girl, Loo, and a girl comes out of it better than a boy does. I don't miss anything in you. You are the only pleasure I have – you can brighten even this place."

"You are a dear brother, Tom; and while you think I can do such things, I don't so much mind knowing better. Though I do know better, Tom, and am very sorry for it." She came and kissed him and went back into her corner again.

"I wish I could collect all the Facts we hear so much about," said Tom, spitefully setting his teeth, "and all the Figures, and all the people who found them out, and I wish I could put a thousand barrels of gunpowder under them, and blow them all up together! However, when I go to live with old Bounderby, I'll have my revenge."

"Your revenge, Tom?"

"I mean, I'll enjoy myself a little, and go about and see something, and hear something. I'll recompense myself for the way in which I have been brought up."

"But don't disappoint yourself beforehand, Tom. Mr Bounderby thinks like father, and is a great deal rougher, and not half so kind."

"Oh," said Tom, laughing, "I don't mind that. I shall very well know how to manage and smooth old Bounderby!"

"What is your great mode of smoothing and managing, Tom? Is it a secret?"

"Oh!" said Tom, "if it is a secret, it's not far off. It's you. You are his little pet, you are his favourite, he'll do anything for you. When he says

32

to me what I don't like, I shall say to him, 'My sister Loo will be hurt and disappointed, Mr Bounderby. She always used to tell me she was sure you would be easier with me than this.' That'll bring him about, or nothing will."

After waiting for some answering remark, and getting none, Tom wearily relapsed into the present time, until he suddenly looked up, and asked, "Have you gone to sleep, Loo?"

"No, Tom. I am looking at the fire."

"You seem to find more to look at in it than ever I could find," said Tom. "Another of the advantages, I suppose, of being a girl."

"Tom," inquired his sister, slowly, and in a curious tone, as if she were reading what she asked in the fire, and it were not quite plainly written there, "do you look forward with any satisfaction to this move to Mr Bounderby's?"

"Why, there's one thing to be said," returned Tom, pushing his chair away, and standing up, "it will be getting away from home."

"There is one thing to be said of it," Louisa repeated in her former curious tone, "it will be getting away from home. Yes."

"But I shall be very unwilling, both to leave you, Loo, and to leave you here. But I must go, you know, whether I like it or not. But I may as well go where I can take with me some advantage of your influence. Don't you see?"

"Yes, Tom."

The answer was so long in coming, though there was no indecision in it, that Tom went and leaned on the back of her chair, to contemplate the fire which so engrossed her, from her point of view, and see what he could make of it.

"Except that it is a fire," said Tom, "it looks to me as stupid and blank as everything else looks. What do you see in it?"

"I don't see anything much, Tom. But since I have been looking, I have been wondering about you and me, grown up."

"Wondering again!" said Tom.

"I have such unmanageable thoughts," returned his sister, "that they will wonder."

"Then I beg of you, Louisa," said Mrs Gradgrind, who had opened the door without being heard, "to do nothing of that description, for goodness' sake, you inconsiderate girl, or I shall never hear the last of it from your father. And, Thomas, it is really shameful, with my poor head continually wearing me out, that a boy brought up as you have been should be found encouraging his sister to wonder, when he knows his father has expressly forbidden it."

Louisa denied Tom's participation in the offence; but her mother stopped her with the conclusive answer, "Louisa, don't tell me, in my state of health; for unless you had been encouraged, it is morally and physically impossible that you could have done it."

"I was encouraged by nothing, mother, but by looking at the red sparks dropping out of the fire, and whitening and dying. It made me think, after all, how short my life would be, and how little I could hope to do in it."

"Nonsense!" said Mrs Gradgrind, rendered almost energetic. "Don't stand there and tell me such stuff, Louisa, when you know very well that if it was ever to reach your father's ears I should never hear the last of it. After all the trouble that has been taken with you! After the lectures you have attended, and the experiments you have seen! After I have heard you myself, when the whole of my right side has been benumbed, going on with your master about combustion, and calcination, and calorification, and I may say every kind of ation that could drive a poor invalid distracted, to hear you talking in this absurd way about sparks and ashes! I wish," whimpered Mrs Gradgrind, taking a chair, "yes, I really do wish that I had never had a family, and then you would have known what it was to do without me!"

CHAPTER 9

Sissy Jupe had not an easy time of it, and was sorely tempted in the first months of her probation, to run away. There was one restraint.

This restraint was the result of no arithmetical process, was self-imposed in defiance of all calculation, and went dead against any table of probabilities that any Actuary would have drawn up from the premises. The girl believed that her father had not deserted her; she lived in the hope that he would come back, and in the faith that he would be happier by her remaining where she was.

34

The wretched ignorance with which Jupe clung to this consolation, rejecting the superior comfort of knowing, on a sound arithmetical basis, that her father was an unnatural vagabond, filled Mr Gradgrind with pity. Yet, what was to be done? M'Choakumchild reported that she had a very dense head for figures; that, once possessed with a general idea of the globe, she took the smallest conceivable interest in its exact measurements; that she was extremely slow in the acquisition of dates, unless some pitiful incident happened to be connected therewith; that she would burst into tears on being required (by the mental process) immediately to name the cost of two hundred and forty-seven muslin caps at fourteen-pence half-penny; that she was as low down, in the school, as low could be.

Mr Gradgrind observed, shaking his head, that all this was very bad, that it showed the necessity of infinite grinding at the mill of knowledge, as per system, schedule, blue book, report, and tabular statements A to Z, and that Jupe "must be kept to it." So Jupe was kept to it, and became low-spirited, but no wiser.

"It would be a fine thing to be you, Miss Louisa!" she said, one night, when Louisa had endeavoured to make her perplexities for next day something clearer to her.

"Do you think so?"

"I should know so much, Miss Louisa. All that is difficult to me now, would be so easy then."

"You might not be the better for it, Sissy."

Sissy submitted, after a little hesitation, "I should not be the worse, Miss Louisa."

To which Miss Louisa answered, "I don't know that."

There had been so little communication between these two – both because life at Stone Lodge went monotonously round like a piece of machinery which discouraged human interference, and because of the prohibition relative to Sissy's past career – that they were still almost strangers. Sissy, with her dark eyes wonderingly directed to Louisa's face, was uncertain whether to say more or to remain silent.

"You are more useful to my mother, and more pleasant with her than I can ever be," Louisa resumed.

Louisa stood looking at the pretty modest head, as it drooped abashed before her, until it was raised again to glance at her face. Then she asked:

"Did your father know so much himself, that he wished you to be well taught too, Sissy?"

Sissy hesitated before replying, plainly feeling that they were entering on forbidden ground. Louisa added, "No one hears us, and if any one did, I am sure there is no harm in such an innocent question."

"No, Miss Louisa," answered Sissy upon this encouragement, shaking her head. "Father knows very little indeed. It's as much as he can do to write and it's more than people in general can do to read his writing. Though it's plain to me."

"Your mother!"

"Father says she was quite a scholar. She died when I was born. She was," Sissy made the terrible communication nervously, "she was a dancer."

"Did your father love her?" Louisa asked these questions with a strong, wild, wandering interest peculiar to her; an interest gone astray like a banished creature, and hiding in solitary places.

"O yes! As dearly as he loves me. Father loved me for her sake. He carried me about with him when I was quite a baby. We have never been asunder from that time."

"Yet he leaves you now, Sissy?"

"Only for my good. Nobody knows him as I do. When he left me for my good – he never would have left me for his own – I know he was almost broken-hearted. He will not be happy for a single minute, till he comes back."

"Tell me more about him," said Louisa, "I will never ask you again. Where did you live?"

"We travelled about the country, and had no fixed place to live in. Father's a – " Sissy whispered the awful word, "a clown."

"To make the people laugh?" said Louisa, with a nod of intelligence.

"Yes. But they wouldn't laugh sometimes, and then father cried. Lately, they very often wouldn't laugh, and he used to come home despairing. Father's not like most. Those who didn't know him as well as I do might believe he was not quite right. Sometimes they played tricks upon him, never knowing how much he felt them, and shrunk up, when he was alone with me. He was far more timid than they thought!"

"And you were his comfort through everything?"

She nodded, with the tears rolling down her face. "I hope so, and father said I was. It was because he grew so scared and trembling, and because he felt himself to be a poor, weak, ignorant, helpless man – those were his words – that he wanted me so much to know a great deal, and be different from him. I used to read to him to cheer his courage, and he was very fond of that. They were wrong books – I am never to speak of them here – but we didn't know there was any harm in them."

"And he liked them?" said Louisa, with a searching gaze on Sissy all this time.

"O very much! They kept him, many times, from what did him real harm. And often of a night, he used to forget all his troubles in wondering whether the Sultan would let the lady go on with the story, or would have her head cut off before it was finished."

"And your father was always kind? To the last?" asked Louisa, contravening the great principle, and wondering very much.

"Always, always!" returned Sissy, clasping her hands. "Kinder than I can tell. He was angry only one night, and that was not to me, but Merrylegs. Merrylegs," she whispered the awful fact, "is his performing dog."

"Why was he angry with the dog?" Louisa demanded.

"Father, after the performance, told Merrylegs to jump up on the backs of the two chairs and stand across them – which is one of his tricks. He looked at father, and didn't do it at once. Everything of father's had gone wrong that night, and he hadn't pleased the public at all. He cried out that the very dog knew he was failing. Then he beat the dog, and I was frightened, and said, 'Father, father! Pray don't hurt the creature that is so fond of you! O Heaven forgive you, father, stop!' And he stopped, and the dog was bloody, and father lay down crying on the floor with the dog in his arms, and the dog licked his face."

Louisa saw that she was sobbing; and going to her, kissed her, took her hand, and sat down beside her.

"Finish by telling me how your father left you, Sissy. Now that I have asked you so much, tell me the end. The blame, if there is any, is mine, not yours."

"Dear Miss Louisa," said Sissy, covering her eyes, and sobbing yet. "I came home from the school that afternoon, and found poor father just come home too, from the booth. And he sat rocking himself over the fire, as if he was in pain. And I said, 'Have you hurt yourself, father?' He did sometimes. He said, 'A little, my darling.' And when I came to stoop down and look up at his face, I saw that he was crying. The more I spoke to him, the more he hid his face. At first he shook all over, and said nothing but 'My darling,' and 'My love!'"

Here Tom came lounging in, and stared at the two.

"I am asking Sissy a few questions, Tom," observed his sister. "You don't have to go away, but don't interrupt us, Tom dear."

"Oh! Very well!" returned Tom. "Only father has brought old Bounderby home, and I want you to come into the drawing room. Because if you come, there's a good chance old Bounderby'll ask me to dinner; and if you don't, there's none."

"I'll come directly."

"I'll wait for you," said Tom, "to make sure."

Sissy resumed in a lower voice. "At last poor father said that he had given no satisfaction again, and never gave satisfaction now, and that he was a shame and disgrace, and I should have done better without him all along. I said all the affectionate things to him that came into my heart, and presently he was quiet and I sat down by him. When I said no more, he put his arms round my neck, and kissed me a great many times. Then he asked me to fetch some of the stuff he used, for the little hurt he had had, and to get it at the best place, which was at the other end of town from there. After kissing me again, he let me go. When I had gone downstairs, I turned back that I might be a little bit more company to him yet, and looked in at the door, and said, 'Father dear, shall I take Merrylegs?' He shook his head and said, 'No, Sissy, no, take nothing that's known to be mine, my darling.' I left him sitting by the fire. Then the thought must have come upon him, poor, poor father, of going away to try something for my sake. When I came back, he was gone."

"I say! Look sharp for old Bounderby, Loo!" Tom remonstrated.

"There's no more to tell, Miss Louisa. I keep the nine oils ready for him. I know he will come back. Every letter that I see in Mr Gradgrind's hand takes my breath away and blinds my eyes, for I think it comes from father, or from Mr Sleary about father. Mr Sleary promised to write as soon as ever father should be heard of, and I trust to him to keep his word."

"Do look sharp for old Bounderby, Loo!" said Tom, with an impatient whistle. "He'll be off if you don't look sharp!"

After this, whenever Sissy dropped a curtsey to Mr Gradgrind in front of his family, and said in a faltering way, "I beg your pardon, sir, for being troublesome – but – have you had any letter yet about me?" Louisa would suspend the occupation of the moment, and look for the reply as earnestly as Sissy did. And when Mr Gradgrind regularly answered, "No, Jupe, nothing of the sort," the trembling of Sissy's lip would be repeated in Louisa's face, and her eyes would follow Sissy with compassion to the door. Mr Gradgrind usually remarked, when she was gone, that if Jupe had been properly trained from an early age she would have realised the baselessness of these fantastic hopes.

This observation must be limited exclusively to his daughter. Tom was becoming that not unprecedented triumph of calculation that is usually at work on number one.

CHAPTER 10

In the hardest working part of Coketown, lived a certain Stephen Blackpool, forty years of age.

Stephen looked older, but he had had a hard life. It is said that every life has its roses and thorns; there seemed, however, to have been a mistake in Stephen's case, whereby somebody else had received his roses, and he had in return the same somebody else's thorns in addition to his own.

He had known, to use his words, a peck of trouble. A rather stooping man, with a knitted brow, a pondering expression of face, and a hard-looking head sufficiently capacious, on which his iron-grey hair lay long and thin. He was a good power-loom weaver, and a man of perfect integrity. What more he was, or what else he had in him, if anything, let him show for himself.

The lights in the great factories, which looked, when they were illuminated, like Fairy palaces, were all extinguished. The bells had rung for knocking off for the night, and had ceased again. The Hands – men and women, boy and girl – were clattering home. Stephen stood in the street.

"Yet I don't see Rachael, still!" said he.

It was a wet night, and many young women passed him, with their shawls drawn over their bare heads and held close under their chins. A glance at any one of these groups was sufficient to show him that she was not there. At last, there were no more to come and he turned away, saying in a tone of disappointment, "Why, then, ha' missed her!"

But, he had not gone the length of three streets, when he saw another of the shawled figures before him. He darted on until he was very near this figure, and called "Rachael!"

She turned, being then in the brightness of a lamp; and raising her hood a little, showed a quiet oval face, dark and rather delicate, irradiated by a pair of very gentle eyes, and further set off by the perfect order of her shining black hair. It was not a face in its first bloom; she was a woman five-and-thirty years of age.

"Ah, lad! 'Tis thou?" When she had said this, she replaced her hood again, and they went on together.

"I thought thou wast ahind me, Rachael?"

"No."

"Early t'night, lass?"

"Times I'm a little early, Stephen! 'times a little late. I'm never to be counted on, going home."

"Nor going t'other way, neither, 'tseems to me, Rachael?"

"No, Stephen."

He looked at her with some disappointment in his face, but with a respectful and patient conviction that she must be right in whatever she did. The expression was not lost upon her; she laid her hand lightly on his arm a moment as if to thank him for it.

"We are such true friends, lad, and such old friends, and getting to be such old folk, now. T'hide a word of honest truth fro' one another would be a sin and a pity. 'Tis better not to walk too much together."

"'Tis hard, anyways, Rachael."

"Try to think not; and 'twill seem better."

"I've tried a long time, and 'tan't got better. But thou'rt right; 'tmight mak fok talk, even of thee. Thou hast been that to me, Rachael, through so many years. Thou hast done me so much good, and heartened me in that cheering way, that thy word is law to me. Ah, lass, and a bright good law! Better than some real ones."

"Never fret about them, Stephen," she answered quickly, and not without an anxious glance at his face. "Let the laws be."

"Yes," he said, with a slow nod or two. "Let 'em be. Let everything be. Let all sorts alone. "'Tis a muddle, and that's aw."

"Always a muddle?" said Rachael, with another gentle touch upon his arm. The touch had its instantaneous effect. He turned a smiling face upon her, and said, as he broke into a good-humoured laugh, "Ay, Rachael, lass, awlus a muddle. That's where I stick. I come to the muddle many times, and I never get beyond it."

They had walked some distance, and were near their own homes. The woman's was the first reached. She stopped at the corner, and putting her hand in his, wished him good night.

"Good-night, dear lass; good-night!"

She went, with her neat figure and her sober womanly step, down the dark street, and he stood looking after her until she turned into one of the small houses.

When she was lost to his view, he pursued his homeward way, glancing up sometimes at the sky, where the clouds were sailing fast and wildly. But, they were broken now, and the rain had ceased, and the moon shone. The man seemed to have brightened with the night, as he went on.

His home, in such another street as the first, was over a little shop. He took his end of candle from a shelf, lighted it at another end of candle on the counter, without disturbing the mistress of the shop who was asleep in her little room, and went upstairs into his lodging.

It was neat, at present, as such a room could be. A few books and writings were on an old bureau in a corner, the furniture was decent and sufficient, and, though the atmosphere was tainted, the room was clean.

Going to the hearth to set the candle down upon a round three-legged table standing there, he stumbled against something. As he recoiled, looking down at it, it raised itself up into the form of a woman in a sitting attitude.

"Heaven's mercy, woman!" he cried, moving back. "Hast thou come back again?"

Such a woman! A disabled, drunken creature, barely able to retain her sitting position by steadying herself with one begrimed hand on the floor, while the other was so purposeless in trying to push away her tangled hair from her face, that it only blinded her the more with the dirt upon it. A creature so foul to look at, in her tatters, stains and splashes, but so much fouler than that in her moral infamy, that it was a shameful thing even to see her.

After an impatient oath or two, and some stupid clawing of herself with the hand not necessary to her support, she got her hair away from her eyes sufficiently to see him. Then she sat swaying to and fro, and making gestures, which seemed intended as the accompaniment to a fit of laughter, though her face was stolid and drowsy.

"Eigh, lad? What, yo'r there?" Some hoarse sounds meant for this, came mockingly out of her at last; and her head drooped forward.

"Back agen?" she screeched, after some minutes, as if he had that moment said it. "Yes! And back agen. Back agen ever and ever so often. Back? Yes, back. Why not?"

Roused by the unmeaning violence with which she cried it out, she scrambled up, and leant against the wall, dangling in one hand by the string, a dunghill-fragment of a bonnet, and trying to look scornfully at him.

"I'll sell thee off again, and I'll sell thee off a score of times!" she cried, with something between a furious menace and an effort at a defiant dance. "Come awa' from th' bed!" He was sitting on the side of it, with his face hidden in his hands. "Come awa' from 't. 'Tis mine, and I've a right to 't!"

As she staggered to it, he avoided her with a shudder, and passed to the opposite end of the room. She threw herself upon the bed heavily, and soon was snoring hard. He sunk into a chair, and moved but once all that night to throw a covering over her.

CHAPTER 11

The fairy palaces burst into illumination before pale morning showed the monstrous serpents of smoke trailing over Coketown

Stephen bent over his loom, quiet, watchful, and steady. A special contrast, as every man was in the forest of looms where Stephen worked, to the crashing, smashing, tearing piece of mechanism at which he laboured.

So many hundred Hands in this Mill; so many hundred horse Steam Power. It is known, to the force of a single pound weight, what the engine will do, but, not all the calculators of the National Debt can tell me the capacity for good or evil, for love or hatred, for patriotism or discontent, for the decomposition of virtue into vice, or the reverse, at any single moment in the soul of one of these its quiet servants. There is no mystery in it, whereas there is an unfathomable mystery in the meanest of them.

The day grew strong, and showed itself outside, even against the flaming lights within. The lights were turned out, and the work went on. The rain fell, and the Smoke-serpents, submissive to the curse of all that tribe, trailed themselves upon the earth. In the waste-yard outside, the steam from the escape pipe, the litter of barrels and old iron, the shining heaps of coals, the ashes everywhere, were shrouded in a veil of mist and rain.

The work went on, until the noon-bell rang. A clattering of clogs upon the pavements. The looms, and wheels, and Hands all out of gear for an hour.

Stephen came out of the hot mill into the damp wind and cold wet streets, haggard and worn. He turned from his own class and his own quarter, taking nothing but a little bread as he walked along, towards the hill on which his principal employer lived, in a red house with black outside shutters, green inside blinds, a black street door, up two white steps, BOUNDERBY (in letters very like himself) upon a brazen plate, and a round brazen door-handle underneath it.

Mr Bounderby was at his lunch. So Stephen had expected. Would his servant say that one of the Hands begged leave to speak to him? Message in return required name of such Hand. Stephen Blackpool. There was nothing troublesome against Stephen Blackpool; yes, he might come in.

Stephen Blackpool in the parlour. Mr Bounderby sat at lunch on chop and sherry. Mrs Sparsit netting at the fireside, in a side saddle attitude, with one foot in a cotton stirrup. It was a part, at once of Mrs Sparsit's dignity and service, not to lunch. She supervised the meal but implied that in her own stately person she considered lunch a weakness.

"Now, Stephen," said Mr Bounderby, "what's the matter with you?"

Stephen made a bow. Not a servile one – these Hands will never do that! Lord bless you, sir, you'll never catch them at that, if they have been

43

with you twenty years – as a complimentary toilet for Mrs Sparsit, he tucked his neckerchief ends into his waistcoat.

"Now, you know," said Mr Bounderby, taking some sherry, "we have never had any difficulty with you, and you have never been unreasonable. Now, you don't expect to be set up in a coach and six, and to be fed on turtle soup and venison, with a gold spoon, as a good many of 'em do!" Mr Bounderby always represented this as the sole, immediate, and direct object of any Hand who was not entirely satisfied; "and therefore I know already that you have not come here to make a complaint. Now, you know, I am certain of that, before-hand."

"No, sir, sure I ha' not coom for nowt o' th' kind."

Mr Bounderby seemed agreeably surprised. "Very well," he returned. "You're a steady Hand, and I was not mistaken. Now, let me hear what it's all about. What have you got to say? Out with it, lad!"

Stephen happened to glance towards Mrs Sparsit. "I can go, Mr Bounderby, if you wish it," said that self-sacrificing lady, making a feint of taking her foot out of the stirrup.

Mr Bounderby stayed her, holding a mouthful of chop in suspension before swallowing it, and putting out his left hand. Then, withdrawing his hand and swallowing his mouthful of chop, he said to Stephen:

"Now you know, this good lady is a born lady, a high lady. You are not to suppose because she keeps my house for me, that she hasn't been very high up the tree! Now, if you have anything to say that can't be said before a born lady, this lady will leave the room. If what you have got to say can be said before a born lady, this lady will stay where she is."

"Sir, I hope I never had nowt to say, not fitten for a born lady to year, sin' I were born mysen," was the reply, accompanied with a slight flush.

"Very well," said Mr Bounderby, pushing away his plate, and leaning back. "Fire away!"

"I ha' coom," Stephen began, raising his eyes from the floor, after a moment's consideration, "to ask yo yor advice. I need't overmuch. I were married on Eas'r Monday nineteen year sin, long and dree. She were a young lass wi' good accounts of herseln. Well! She went bad soon. Not along of me. Gonnows I were not a unkind husband to her."

"I have heard all this before," said Mr Bounderby. "She took to drinking, left off working, sold the furniture, pawned the clothes, and played old Gooseberry."

"I were patient wi' her."

"The more fool you, I think," muttered Mr Bounderby into his wineglass.

"I were very patient wi' her. I tried to wean her fra't ower and ower agen. I tried this, I tried that, I tried t'other. I ha' gone home, many's the time, and found all vanished as I had in the world, and her without a sense left to bless herseln lying on bare ground. I ha' dun't not once, not twice, twenty time!"

Every line in his face deepened as he said it, and put in its affecting evidence of the suffering he had undergone. "From bad to worse, from worse to worsen. She left me. She disgraced herseln everyways, bitter and bad. She coom back, she coom back, she coom back. What could I do t' hinder her? I ha' walked the streets nights long, ere ever I'd go home. I ha' gone t' th' brigg, minded to fling myseln ower, and ha' no more on't. I ha' bore that much, that I were owd when I were young."

Mrs Sparsit, easily ambling along with her netting-needles, raised and shook her head, as if as to say, "The great know trouble as well as the small. Please to turn your humble eye in my direction."

"I ha' paid her to keep awa' fra' me. These five year I ha' paid her. I ha' gotten decent fewtrils about me agen. I ha' lived hard and sad, but not ashamed and fearfo' a' the minnits o' my life. Last night, I went home. There she lay upon my har-stone! There she is!"

In the strength of his misfortune, and the energy of his distress, he fired for the moment like a proud man. A moment later, he stood as he had stood all the time – his usual stoop upon him. His pondering face addressed to Mr Bounderby, a curious expression on it, half shrewd, half perplexed, his hat held tight in his left hand, which rested on his hip; his right arm, with a rugged propriety and force of action, very earnestly emphasising what he said, and stopping, a little bent but not withdrawn, as he paused.

"I was acquainted with all this," said Mr Bounderby, "except the last clause, long ago. It's a bad job; that's what it is. You were better never to have married. However, it's too late to say that."

"Was it an unequal marriage, sir, in point of years?" asked Mrs Sparsit.

"You hear what this lady asks. Was it an unequal marriage in point of years, this unlucky job of yours?" said Mr Bounderby.

"Not so. I were one-and-twenty myseln; she were twenty nighbut."

"Indeed, sir?" said Mrs Sparsit to her Chief, with great placidity. "I inferred, from its being so miserable a marriage, that it was probably an unequal one in point of years."

Mr Bounderby looked very hard at the good lady in a sidelong way that had an odd sheepishness about it. He fortified himself with a little more sherry.

"Well? Continue," he then said, turning rather irritably on Stephen Blackpool.

"I ha' coom to ask yo, sir, how I am to be ridded o' this woman." Stephen infused a yet deeper gravity into the mixed expression of his attentive face. Mrs Sparsit uttered a gentle ejaculation, as having received a moral shock.

"What do you mean?" said Bounderby, getting up to lean his back against the chimney-piece. "You took her for better for worse."

"I mun' be ridden o' her. I cannot bear 't nommore. I ha' lived under 't so long, but I ha' had the pity and comforting words o' th' best lass living or dead. Haply, but for her, I should ha' gone hottering mad."

"He wishes to be free, to marry the female of whom he speaks, I fear, sir," observed Mrs Sparsit in an undertone, and much dejected by the immorality of the people.

"I do. The lady says what's right. I were a coming to 't. I ha' read i' th' papers that great folk are not bonded together for better for worst so fast, but that they can be set free fro' their misfortnet marriages, an' marry ower agen. When they dunnot agree, for that their tempers is ill-sorted, they has rooms o' one kind an another in their houses, above a bit, and they can live asunders. We fok ha' only one room, and we can't. When that won't do, they ha' gowd an other cash, an' they can say 'This for yo' an that for me,' an they can go their separate ways. We can't. Spite o' all that, they can be set free for smaller wrongs than mine. So, I mun' be ridden o' this woman, and I want t' know how?"

"No how," returned Mr Bounderby.

"If I do her any hurt, sir, there's a law to punish me?"

"Of course there is."

"If I flee from her, there's a law to punish me?"

"Of course there is."

"If I marry t'oother dear lass, there's a law to punish me?"

"Of course there is."

"If I was to live wi' her an' not marry her - saying such a thing could be, which it never could or would, an her so good - there's a law to punish me, in every innocent child belonging to me?"

"Of course there is."

"Now, a' God's name," said Stephen Blackpool, "show me the law to help me!"

"Hem! There's a sanctity in this relation of life," said Mr Bounderby, "and it must be kept up."

"No no, dunnot say that, sir. 'Tan't kep' up that way. Not that way. 'Tis kep' down that way. I'm a weaver, I were in a fact'ry when a chilt, but I have eyes to see wi' and eern to hear wi'. I read in th' papers every 'Sizes, every Sessions – and you read too – I know it! – with dismay – how th' supposed impossibility o' ever getting unchained from one another, at any price, on any terms, brings blood upon this land, and brings many common married fok to battle, murder, and sudden death. Let us ha' this, right understood. Mine's a grievous case, and I want – if yo will be so good – t' know the law that helps me."

"Now, I tell you what!" said Mr Bounderby, putting his hands in his pockets. "There is such a law."

Stephen, never wandering in his attention, gave a nod.

"But it's not for you at all. It costs money. It costs a mint of money."

"How much might that be?" Stephen calmly asked.

"Why, you'd have to go to Doctors' Commons with a suit, and you'd have to go to a court of Common Law with a suit, and you'd have to go to the House of Lords with a suit, and you'd have to get an Act of Parliament to enable you to marry again, and it would cost you I suppose from a thousand to fifteen hundred pound," said Mr Bounderby. "Perhaps twice the money."

"There's no other law?"

"Certainly not."

"Why then, sir," said Stephen, turning white, and motioning with his right hand as if he gave everything to the four winds, "'tis a muddle. 'Tis just a muddle a'toogether, an the sooner I am dead, the better."

"Pooh, pooh! Don't talk nonsense, my good fellow," said Mr Bounderby, "about things you don't understand; and don't you call the Institutions of your country a muddle, or you'll get yourself into a real muddle one of these fine mornings You took your wife for better for worse. If she has turned out worse – why, all we have got to say is, she might have turned out better."

"'Tis a muddle," said Stephen, shaking his head as he moved to the door. "'Tis a' a muddle!"

"Now, I'll tell you what!" Mr Bounderby resumed, as a valedictory address. "Your unhallowed opinions have quite shocked this lady, who, as I have already told you, is a born lady. But I have not already told you, she has had her own marriage misfortunes to the tune of tens of thousands of pounds – tens of Thousands of Pounds!" (he repeated it with great relish). "Now, you have always been a steady Hand hitherto, but my opinion is, that you are turning into the wrong road. You have been listening to some mischievous stranger and the best thing you can do is to come out of that. Now you know;" here his countenance expressed marvellous acuteness; "I can see as far into a grindstone as another man, farther than many, perhaps. I see traces of the turtle soup, and venison, and gold spoon in this. Yes, I do!" cried Mr Bounderby, shaking his head with obstinate cunning. "By the Lord Harry, I do!"

With a very different shake of the head and deep sigh, Stephen said, "Thank you, sir, I wish you good day." So he left Mr Bounderby swelling at his own portrait on the wall.

CHAPTER 12

Stephen descended the two white steps, shutting the black door with the aid of the brazen door-handle, to which he gave a parting polish with the sleeve of his coat, observing that his hot hand clouded it. He crossed the street with his eyes bent upon the ground, and thus was walking sorrowfully away, when he felt a touch upon his arm.

It was not the touch he needed most at such a moment – the touch that could calm the wild waters of his soul – yet it was a woman's hand too. It was an old woman, tall and shapely still, though withered by time on whom his eyes fell when he stopped and turned. She was very cleanly and plainly dressed, and had country mud upon her shoes. The flutter of her manner, in the noise of the streets; the spare shawl, carried unfolded on her arm; the heavy umbrella, and little basket; all bespoke an old woman from the country, in her plain holiday clothes, come into Coketown on a rare trip. Remarking this at a glance, with the quick observation of his class, Stephen Blackpool bent his attentive face the better to hear what she asked him.

"Pray, sir," said the old woman, "didn't I see you come out of that gentleman's house?" pointing back to Mr Bounderby's. "I believe it was you, unless I have had the bad luck to mistake the person in following?"

"Yes, missus," returned Stephen, "it were me."

"Have you – you'll excuse an old woman's curiosity – have you seen the gentleman?"

"Yes, missus."

"And how did he look, sir? Was he portly, bold, outspoken, and hearty?" As she straightened her own figure, and held up her head in adapting her action to her words, the idea crossed Stephen that he had seen this old woman before, and had not quite liked her.

"O yes," he returned, observing her more attentively, "he were all that."

"And healthy?" said the old woman.

"Yes," returned Stephen. "He were ett'n and drinking – as large and as loud as a Hummobee."

"Thank you!" said the old woman, with infinite content.

He certainly never had seen this old woman before. Yet there was a vague remembrance in his mind, as if he had dreamed of someone like her.

She walked along at his side, and he said Coketown was a busy place, was it not? To which she answered "Eigh sure! Dreadful busy!" Then he said, she came from the country, he saw? To which she answered in the affirmative.

"I come once a year," she said. "I spend my savings so, once every year. I come regular, to tramp about the streets, and see the gentlemen."

"Only to see 'em?" returned Stephen.

"That's enough for me," she replied, with great earnestness. "I ask no more! I have been standing about, to see that gentleman," turning her head back towards Mr Bounderby's again, "come out. But, he's late this year, and I have not seen him. You came out instead. Now, if I am obliged to go back without a glimpse of him – I only want a glimpse – well! I have seen you, and you have seen him, and I must make that do." Saying this, she looked at Stephen as if to fix his features in her mind, and her eye was not so bright as it had been.

This seemed so extraordinary a source of interest to take so much trouble about, that it perplexed him. But they were passing the church now – his eye caught the clock and he quickened his pace.

He was going to his work? the old woman said, quickening hers, too, quite easily. Yes, time was nearly out. On his telling her where he worked, the old woman became a more singular old woman than before.

"An't you happy?" she asked him.

'Why – there's awmost nobbody but has their troubles, missus." He answered evasively, because the old woman appeared to take it for granted that he would be very happy indeed, and he had not the heart to disappoint her.

"Ay, ay! You have your troubles at home, you mean?" she said.

"Times. Just now and then," he answered, slightly.

"But, working under such a gentleman, they don't follow you to the Factory?"

No, no; they didn't follow him there, said Stephen. All correct there.

They were now in the black by-road near the place, and the Hands were crowding in. The bell was ringing, and the Serpent was a Serpent of many coils. The strange old woman was delighted with the very bell. It was the beautifullest bell she had ever heard, she said, and sounded grand!

She asked him, when he stopped good-naturedly to shake hands with her before going in, how long he had worked there?

"A dozen year," he told her.

"I must kiss the hand," said she, "that has worked in this fine factory for a dozen year!" And she lifted it, though he would have prevented her, and put it to her lips. What harmony, besides her age and her simplicity, surrounded her, he did not know, but even in this fantastic action, there was a something which it seemed as if nobody else could have made as serious, or done with such a natural and touching air.

He had been at his loom full half an hour, thinking about this old woman, when, having occasion to move round the loom for its adjustment, he glanced through a window in his corner, and saw her still looking up at the pile of building, lost in admiration. Heedless of the smoke and mud and wet, and of her two long journeys, she was gazing at it, as if the heavy thrum that issued from its many stories were proud music to her.

She was gone by-and-by, and the day went after her, and the lights sprung up again. Long before then his thoughts had gone back to the dreary room above the little shop, and to the shameful figure heavy on the bed, but heavier on his heart.

Machinery slackened, throbbing feebly like a fainting pulse, stopped. The bell again, the glare of light and heat dispelled, and the factories, looming heavy in the black wet night.

He had spoken to Rachael only last night, it was true, and had walked with her a little way, but he had this new misfortune and there was no one else he could turn to, and for this, and knowing that no other could soften his anger he decided to wait for her again. He waited, but she had eluded him. She was gone. On no other night in the year was he so desperate to see her.

O! Better to have no home, than to have a home and dread to go there. He ate and drank, for he was exhausted – but he little knew or cared what; and he wandered about in the chill rain, thinking and thinking, and brooding.

No word of a new marriage had ever passed between them; but Rachael had taken great pity on him years ago, and to her alone he had opened his closed heart all this time, on the subject of his miseries; and he knew very well that if he were free to ask her, she would take him. He thought of the different home he might at that moment have been seeking with pleasure and pride; of the different man he might have been that night. He thought of the waste of the best part of his life, of the change it made in his character for the worse every day, of the dreadful nature of his existence, bound to a dead woman, and tormented by a demon in her shape. He thought of Rachael, how young when they were first brought together in these circumstances, how mature now, how soon to grow old. He thought of the many girls and women she had seen marry, who now had grown, how she had contentedly pursued her own lone quiet path – for him – and how he had sometimes seen a shade of melancholy on her blessed face. This struck him with remorse and despair. He set the picture of her up, beside the infamous image of last night. Could it be, he thought, that the whole earthly course of one so gentle, good, and self-denying, was dependent on such a wretch!

Filled with these thoughts, he went home for shelter.

51

CHAPTER 13

A candle faintly burned in the window.

From the outside of his home he gloomily stepped inside, with suspended breath and with a slow footstep. He went up to his door, opened it, and so into the room.

Quiet and peace were there. Rachael was there, sitting by the bed.

She turned her head, and the light of her face shone in upon the midnight of his mind. She sat by the bed, watching and tending his wife. That is to say, he saw that someone lay there, and he knew it must be she; but Rachael had put a curtain up, so that she was screened from his eyes. Her disgraceful garments were removed, and some of Rachael's were in the room. Everything was in its place. It appeared to him that he saw all this in Rachael's face, and looked at nothing besides. While looking at it, it was lost from his view by the softened tears that filled his eyes; but not before he had seen how earnestly she looked at him, and how her own eyes were filled too.

She turned again towards the bed, and satisfying herself that all was quiet there, spoke in a low, calm, cheerful voice.

"I am glad you have come at last, Stephen. You are very late."

"I ha' been walking up an' down."

"I thought so. But 'tis too bad a night for that. The rain falls very heavy, and the wind has risen."

The wind? True. It was blowing hard. Hark to the thundering in the chimney! To have been out in such a wind, and not to have known it was blowing!

"I have been here once before, today, Stephen. Landlady came round for me at dinnertime. There was someone here that needed looking to, she said. And 'deed she was right. All wandering and lost, Stephen. Wounded too, and bruised."

He slowly moved to a chair and sat down, drooping his head before her.

"I came to do what little I could, Stephen. First, because we worked together when we were girls, and that you courted her and married her when I was her friend – "

He laid his furrowed forehead on his hand, with a low groan.

"And next, I know your heart, and am certain that 'tis far too merciful

52

to let her die, or even so much as suffer, for want of aid. Thou knowest who said, 'Let him who is without sin among you cast the first stone at her!' There have been plenty to do that. Thou art not the man to cast the last stone, Stephen, when she is brought so low."

"O Rachael, Rachael!"

"Thou hast suffered cruelly, Heaven reward thee!" she said, in compassionate accents. "I am thy poor friend, with all my heart."

The wounds of which she had spoken seemed to be about the neck of the self-made outcast. She dressed them now. She steeped a piece of linen in a basin, into which she poured some liquid from a bottle, and laid it with a gentle hand upon the sore. The three-legged table had been drawn close to the bedside, and on it there were two bottles. This was one.

Stephen, following her hands with his eyes, could read what was printed on it in large letters. He turned of a deadly hue, and a sudden horror seemed to fall upon him.

"I will stay here, Stephen," said Rachael, quietly resuming her seat, "till the bells go Three. 'Tis to be done again at three, and then she may be left till morning."

"But thy rest before tomorrow's work, my dear."

"I slept sound last night. I can wake many nights, when I am put to it. 'Tis thou who art in need of rest – so white and tired. Try to sleep in the chair there, while I watch. Thou hadst no sleep last night, I can well believe. Tomorrow's work is far harder for thee than for me."

It seemed to him that his late angry mood was trying to get at him. She had cast it out; she would keep it out; he trusted to her to defend him from himself.

"She don't know me, Stephen; she just drowsily mutters and stares. I have spoken to her, but she don't notice! 'Tis as well so. When she comes to her right mind once more, I shall have done what I can, and she never the wiser."

"How long, Rachael, will she be so?"

"Doctor said she would haply come to her mind tomorrow."

His eyes fell again on the bottle, and a tremble passed over him, causing him to shiver in every limb. She thought he was chilled with the wet. "No," he said, "it was not that." He had had a fright.

"A fright?"

"Ay, ay! Coming in. When I were walking. When I were thinking.

53

When I – " It seized him again; and he stood up, holding the mantel-shelf, shaking in every limb.

"Stephen!"

She was coming to him, but he stretched out his arm to stop her.

"No! Don't, please don't. Let me see thee setten by the bed. Let me see thee, a' so good, and so forgiving. Let me see thee as I see thee when I coom in. I can never see thee better than so. Never, never!"

He had a violent fit of trembling, and then sunk into his chair. After a time he controlled himself, and, resting with an elbow on one knee, and his head upon that hand, could look towards Rachael. Seen across the dim candle with his moistened eyes, she looked as if she had a glory shining round her head. He believed she had, as the noise outside shook the window, rattled at the door below, and went about the house clamouring and lamenting.

"When she gets better, Stephen, we can hope she'll leave thee to thyself again, and do thee no more hurt. And now I shall keep silence, for I want thee to sleep."

He closed his eyes, more to please her than to rest his weary head, but, by slow degrees as he listened to the great noise of the wind, he ceased to hear it, or it changed into the working of his loom, or even into the voices of the day; and at last, he dreamed a long, troubled dream.

He thought that he, and someone on whom his heart had long been set – surprisingly, she was not Rachael – stood in the church being married. While the ceremony was performing, and while he recognised among the witnesses some whom he knew to be living, and many whom he knew to be dead, darkness came on, succeeded by the shining of a tremendous light. It broke from one line in the table of commandments at the altar, and illuminated the building with the words. They were sounded through the church, too, as if there were voices in the fiery letters. Upon this, the whole appearance before him and around him changed, and nothing was left as it had been, but himself and the clergyman. They stood in the daylight before a crowd so vast, that if all the people in the world could have been brought together into one space, they could not have looked, he thought, more numerous; and they all abhorred him, and there was not one pitying or friendly eye among the millions that were fastened on his face. He stood on a raised stage, under his own loom; and, looking up at the shape the loom took, and hearing the burial service distinctly read, he knew that he was there to suffer death. In an instant what he stood on fell below him, and he was gone.

Out of what mystery he came back to his usual life, and to places that he knew, he was unable to consider; but he was back in those places by some means, and condemned never, in this world or the next, through all the unimaginable ages of eternity, to look on Rachael's face or hear her voice. Wandering to and fro, without hope, searching for he knew not what (he only knew that he was doomed to seek it), he was the subject of a nameless, horrible dread, a mortal fear of one particular shape that everything took. Whatsoever he looked at grew into that form sooner or later. The object of his miserable existence was to prevent its recognition by any one among the various people he encountered. Hopeless labour! If he led them out of rooms where it was, if he shut up drawers and closets where it stood, if he drew the curious from places where he knew it to be secreted, and got them out into the streets, the very chimneys of the mills assumed that shape, and round them was the printed word.

The wind was blowing again, the rain was beating on the housetops, and he was once again within the four walls of his room. Saving that the fire had died, it was as his eyes had closed upon it. Rachael seemed to have fallen into a doze, in the chair by the bed. She sat wrapped in her shawl, perfectly still. The table stood in the same place, close by the bedside, and on it, in its real proportions and appearance, was the shape so often repeated.

He thought he saw the curtain move. He looked again, and he saw a hand come forth and grope about a little. Then the curtain moved more perceptibly, and the woman in the bed put it back, and sat up.

With her woeful eyes, so haggard and wild, so heavy and large, she looked all round the room, passing the corner where he slept. Her eyes returned to that corner, and she put her hand over them as a shade, while she looked into it. Again they went all round the room, scarcely heeding Rachael, and returned to that corner. He thought, as she once more shaded them – not so much looking at him, as looking for him knowing that he was there – that no single trace was left in those debauched features, or in the mind that went along with them, of the woman he had married eighteen years before. But that he had seen her come to this by inches, he never could have believed her to be the same.

All this time, as if a spell were on him, he was motionless and powerless, except to watch her.

She sat for a little while with her hands at her ears, and her head resting on them. Presently, she resumed her staring round the room. And then her eyes stopped at the table with the bottles on it.

Straightway she looked back to his corner, with the defiance of last night, and moving very cautiously, stretched out her greedy hand. She drew a mug into the bed, and sat for a while considering which of the two bottles she should choose. Finally, she laid her insensate grasp upon the bottle containing swift and certain death, and, before his eyes, pulled out the cork with her teeth.

Dream or reality, he had no voice, nor had he power to stir. If this be real, and her allotted time is not yet come, wake, Rachael!

She thought of that, too, looking at Rachael, and very slowly, poured out the contents. The draught was at her lips. A moment and she would be past all help. But in that moment Rachael started up with a soft cry. The creature struggled, struck her, seized her by the hair, but Rachael had the cup.

Stephen broke out of his chair. "Rachael, am I wakin' or dreamin' this dreadfo' night?"

"'Tis all well, Stephen. I have been asleep, myself. 'Tis near three. Hush! I hear the bells."

The wind brought the sounds of the church clock to the window. They listened, and it struck three. Stephen looked at her, saw how pale she was, noted the disorder of her hair, and the red marks of fingers on her forehead, and knew that his senses of sight and hearing had been awake. She held the cup in her hand even now.

"I thought it must be near three," she said, calmly pouring from the cup into the basin, and steeping the linen as before. "I am thankful I stayed. There! And now she's quiet again. The few drops in the basin I'll pour away, for 'tis bad stuff to leave about." As she spoke, she drained the basin into the ashes of the fire, and broke the bottle on the hearth.

She had nothing to do, then, but to cover herself with her shawl before going out into the wind and rain.

"Thou'lt let me walk wi' thee at this hour, Rachael?"

"No, Stephen. 'Tis but a minute, and I'm home."

"Thou'rt not fearfo';" he said it in a low voice, as they went out at the door, "to leave me alone wi' her!"

As she looked at him, saying, "Stephen?" he went down on his knee before her, and put an end of her shawl to his lips.

"Thou art an Angel. Bless thee, bless thee!"

"I am, as I have told thee, Stephen, thy poor friend. Angels are not like me. Between them, and a working woman fu' of faults, there is a deep gulf. My little sister is among them, but she is changed."

She raised her eyes for a moment as she said the words, and then they fell again, in all their gentleness, on his face.

"Thou changest me from bad to good. Thou mak'st me humbly wishfo' to be more like thee, and fearfo' to lose thee when this life is ower. Thou'rt an Angel. Thou hast saved my soul alive!"

She looked at him, on his knee at her feet, with her shawl still in his hand, and the reproof on her lips died away when she saw the working of his face.

"I coom home desp'rate, and mad wi' thinking that when I said a word o' complaint I was reckoned a onreasonable Hand. I told thee I had had a fright. It were the Poison-bottle on table. I never hurt a livin' creetur; but happenin' so suddenly upon 't, I thowt, 'How can I say what I might ha' done to myseln, or her, or both!'"

She put her two hands on his mouth, with a face of terror, to stop him from saying more. He caught them in his free hand, and holding them, while clasping the border of her shawl, said hurriedly: "But I see thee, Rachael, setten by the bed. I ha' seen thee, aw this night. In my troublous sleep I ha' known thee still to be there. Evermore I will see thee there. I nevermore will see her or think o' her, but thou shalt be beside her. I nevermore will see or think o' anything that angers me, but thou, so much better than me, shalt be by th' side. And so I will try t' trust t' th' time, when thou and me at last shall walk together far awa', beyond the deep gulf, in th' country where thy little sister is."

He kissed the border of her shawl again, and let her go. She bade him good-night in a broken voice, and went out into the street.

The wind blew from the quarter where the day would soon appear, and still blew strongly. It had cleared the sky before it, and the stars were bright. He stood bareheaded in the road, watching her quick disappearance. As the shining stars were to the heavy candle in the window, so was Rachael, in the rugged fancy of this man, to the common experiences of his life.

57

CHAPTER 14

"Louisa is becoming," said Mr Gradgrind, "almost a young woman."

Time worked away, not minding what anybody said, and presently turned out young Thomas a foot taller than when his father had last taken particular notice of him.

"Thomas is becoming," said Mr Gradgrind, "almost a young man."

Time passed Thomas on in the mill, while his father was thinking about it, and there he stood in a long-tailed coat and a stiff shirt-collar.

"Really," said Mr Gradgrind, "now Thomas ought to go to Bounderby."

Time, sticking to him, passed him on into Bounderby's bank, made him an inmate of Bounderby's house, necessitated the purchase of his first razor, and exercised him diligently in his calculations relative to number one.

The same great manufacturer, always with an immense variety of work on hand, in every stage of development, passed Sissy onward in his mill, and worked her up into a very pretty article indeed.

"I fear, Jupe," said Mr Gradgrind, "that your continuance at the school any longer would be useless."

"I am afraid it would, sir," Sissy answered with a curtsey. "Yet I have tried hard, sir."

"Yes," said Mr Gradgrind, "I believe you have tried hard. I have observed you, and I can find no fault in that respect."

"Thank you, sir. I have thought sometimes," Sissy very timidly suggested, "that perhaps I tried to learn too much, and that if I had asked to be allowed to try a little less, I might have – "

"No, Jupe, no," said Mr Gradgrind, shaking his head. "The course you pursued, you pursued according to the system and there is no more to be said about it. I can only suppose that the circumstances of your early life were too unfavourable to the development of your reasoning powers, and that we began too late. Still, as I have said already, I am disappointed."

"I wish I could have made a better acknowledgement, sir, of your kindness to a poor forlorn girl who had no claim upon you, and of your protection of her."

"Don't shed tears," said Mr Gradgrind. "You are an affectionate, earnest, good young woman and we must make that do."

"Thank you, sir, very much," said Sissy, with a grateful curtsey.

"You are useful to Mrs Gradgrind, and a help to the whole family also, as I understand from Miss Louisa, and, indeed, so I have observed myself. I therefore hope," said Mr Gradgrind, "that you can make yourself happy in those relations."

"I should have nothing to wish, sir, if – "

"I understand," said Mr Gradgrind, "you still refer to your father. I heard from Miss Louisa that you still preserve that bottle. Well! If your training in the science of arriving at exact results had been more successful, you would have been wiser on these points. I will say no more."

He really liked Sissy too well to have a contempt for her. Somehow or other, he had become possessed by an idea that there was something in this girl which could hardly be set forth in a tabular form.

In some stages of his manufacture of the human fabric, the processes of Time are very rapid. Young Thomas and Sissy being both at such a stage of their working up, these changes were effected in a year or two; while Mr Gradgrind himself seemed stationary in his course, and underwent no alteration.

Except one; time hustled him into a little noisy and rather dirty machinery, and made him Member of Parliament for Coketown.

All this while, Louisa had been passing on, so quiet and reserved, and so much given to watching the bright ashes at twilight as they fell into the grate, and became extinct, that from the period when her father had said she was almost a young woman – which seemed but yesterday – she had scarcely attracted his notice again, when he found her quite a young woman.

"Quite a young woman," said Mr Gradgrind, musing. "Dear me!"

Soon after this discovery, he became more thoughtful than usual for several days, and seemed much engrossed by one subject. One night, when he was going out, and Louisa came to bid him goodbye before his journey, he held her in his arms, looking at her in his kindest manner, and said: "My dear Louisa, you are a woman!"

She answered with the old, quick, searching look of the night when she was found at the Circus, then cast down her eyes. "Yes, father."

"My dear," said Mr Gradgrind, "I must speak with you alone and seriously. Come to my room after breakfast tomorrow, will you?"

"Yes, father."

"Your hands are rather cold, Louisa. Are you not well?"

"Quite well, father."

"And cheerful?"

She looked at him again, and smiled in her peculiar manner. "I am as cheerful, father, as I usually am, or usually have been."

"That's well," said Mr Gradgrind. So, he kissed her and went away; and Louisa looked again at the short-lived sparks that so soon subsided into ashes.

"Are you there, Loo?" said her brother, looking in at the door. He was quite a young gentleman of pleasure now, and not quite a prepossessing one.

"Dear Tom," she answered, rising and embracing him, "how long it is since you have been to see me!"

"Why, I have been otherwise engaged, Loo, in the evenings; and in the daytime old Bounderby has been keeping me at it rather. But I touch him up with you when he comes it too strong, and so we preserve an understanding. I say! Has father said anything particular to you today or yesterday, Loo?"

"No, Tom. But he told me that he wishes to do so in the morning."

"Ah! That's what I mean," said Tom. "Do you know where he is tonight?"

"No."

"Then I'll tell you. He's with old Bounderby. They are having a regular confab together up at the Bank. Why at the Bank, do you think? To keep Mrs Sparsit's ears off it, I expect."

With her hand upon her brother's shoulder, Louisa still stood looking at the fire. Her brother glanced at her face with greater interest than usual, and, encircling her waist with his arm, drew her coaxingly to him.

"You are very fond of me, an't you, Loo?"

"Indeed I am, Tom, though you do let such long intervals go by without coming to see me."

"Well, sister of mine," said Tom, "when you say that, you are near my thoughts. We might be so much oftener together – mightn't we? Always together, almost – mightn't we? It would do me a great deal of good if you were to make up your mind to I know what, Loo. It would be a splendid thing for me!"

Her thoughtfulness baffled his cunning scrutiny. He could make nothing of her face. He pressed her in his arm, and kissed her cheek. She returned the kiss, but still looked at the fire.

"I say, Loo! I thought I'd come, and just hint to you what was going on: though I expect you'd most likely guess. I can't stay but you won't forget how fond you are of me?"

"No, dear Tom, I won't forget."

"That's a capital girl," said Tom. "Good-bye, Loo."

She gave him an affectionate goodnight, and went out with him to the door, whence the fires of Coketown could be seen, making the sky glow. She stood there listening to his departing steps. They retreated quickly, as glad to get away from Stone Lodge; and she stood there yet, when he was gone and all was quiet.

CHAPTER 15

Mr Gradgrind's room was quite a blue chamber due to its abundance of blue books. A window looked towards Coketown, and when Louisa sat down near the table, she saw the high chimneys and the long tracts of smoke looming in the heavy distance.

"My dear Louisa," said her father, "I prepared you last night to give me your serious attention in the conversation we are now going to have together. You have been so well trained that I have perfect confidence in your good sense. You are not impulsive, you are not romantic, you are accustomed to view everything from the strong dispassionate ground of reason and calculation. From that ground alone, I know you will view and consider what I am going to communicate."

He waited, as if he might be glad that she said something. But she said never a word.

"Louisa, my dear, you are the subject of a proposal of marriage that has been made to me."

Again he waited, and again she answered not one word. So he gently repeated, "a proposal of marriage, my dear."

To which she returned, without any visible emotion whatever: "I hear you, father. I am attending, I assure you."

"Well!" said Mr Gradgrind, breaking into a smile, after being at a momentary loss, "you are even more dispassionate than I expected, Louisa. Or, perhaps, you are not unprepared for what I have to say?"

"I cannot say that, father, until I hear it. Prepared or unprepared, I wish to hear you state it to me, father."

Strangely, Mr Gradgrind was not so collected at this moment as his daughter was. He took a paperknife in his hand, turned it and looked at it, considering how to go on.

"What you say, my dear Louisa, is perfectly reasonable. I have undertaken then to let you know that – in short, that Mr Bounderby has told me that he has long watched your progress with particular interest and pleasure. He has long hoped that the time might ultimately arrive when he should offer you his hand in marriage. That time, to which he has so long, and certainly with great constancy, looked forward, is now come. Mr Bounderby has made his proposal of marriage to me, and has entreated me to make it known to you, and to express his hope that you will take it into your favourable consideration."

Silence. The clock ticked hollowly. The distant smoke rose very black and heavy.

"Father," said Louisa, "do you think I love Mr Bounderby?"

Mr Gradgrind had not expected this question. "Well, my child," he returned, "I – really – cannot take upon myself to say."

"Father," pursued Louisa in exactly the same tone, "do you ask me to love Mr Bounderby?"

"My dear Louisa, no. I ask nothing."

"Father," she still pursued, "does Mr Bounderby ask me to love him?"

"Really, my dear," said Mr Gradgrind, "it is difficult to answer your question – "

"Difficult to answer it. Yes or No, father?"

"Certainly, my dear. Because," here was something to demonstrate, and it set him up again; "because the reply depends so materially, Louisa, on the sense in which we use the expression. Now, Mr Bounderby does not do you the injustice, and does not do himself the injustice, of pretending to anything fanciful, fantastic, or (I am using synonymous terms) sentimental. Mr Bounderby would have seen you grow up under his eyes, to very little purpose, if he could so far forget what is due to your good sense, not to say to his, as to address you from any such ground.

Therefore, perhaps the expression itself – I merely suggest this to you, my dear – may be a little misplaced."

"What would you advise me to use in its stead, father?"

"Why, my dear Louisa," said Mr Gradgrind, completely recovered by this time, "I would advise you, since you ask, to consider this question, as you have been accustomed to consider every other question, simply as one of tangible Fact. Now, what are the Facts of this case? You are, we will say in round numbers, twenty years of age; Mr Bounderby is, we will say in round numbers, fifty. There is some disparity in your ages, but in your means and positions there is none – on the contrary, there is a great suitability. So the question arises, is this one disparity a sufficient bar to such a marriage? In considering this question, it is not unimportant to take into account the statistics of marriage, so far as they have yet been obtained, in England and Wales. I find, on reference to the figures, that a large proportion of these marriages are contracted between parties of very unequal ages, and that the elder of these contracting parties is, in rather more than three-fourths of these instances, the bridegroom."

"What do you recommend, father," asked Louisa again, "that I should substitute for the term I used just now? For the misplaced expression?"

"Louisa," returned her father, "it seems that nothing can be plainer. Confining yourself rigidly to Fact, the question of Fact you state to yourself is: Does Mr Bounderby ask me to marry him? Answer: Yes, he does. The sole remaining question then is: Shall I marry him? I think nothing can be plainer than that."

"Shall I marry him?" repeated Louisa, with great deliberation.

"Precisely. And it is satisfactory to me, as your father, my dear Louisa, to know that you do not come the consider that question with the previous habits of mind, and habits of life, that belong to many young women."

"No, father," she returned, "I do not."

"I now leave you to judge for yourself," said Mr Gradgrind. "I have stated the case, as such cases are usually stated among practical minds; I have stated it, as the case of your mother and myself was stated in its time. The rest, my dear Louisa, is for you to decide."

From the beginning, she had sat staring at him. As he now leaned back in his chair, and gazed at her in his turn, perhaps he might have seen one wavering moment in her, when she was impelled to throw herself upon his breast, and tell him what she felt in her heart. But, to see it, he must have leaped over the artificial barriers he had for many years been erecting, between himself and all those subtle essences of humanity. The barriers were too many and too high for such a leap. With his unbending, utilitarian, matter-of-fact face, he hardened her again; and the moment shot away into the plumbless depths of the past, to mingle with all the lost opportunities that are drowned there.

Removing her eyes from him, she sat so long looking silently towards the town, that he said, at length: "Are you consulting the chimneys of the Coketown works, Louisa?"

"There seems to be nothing there but monotonous smoke. Yet when the night comes, fire bursts out, father!" she answered, turning quickly.

"Of course I know that, Louisa, though I do not see the application of the remark." To do him justice he did not, at all.

She passed it away with a slight motion of her hand, and concentrating her attention upon him again, said, "Father, I have often thought that life is very short." – This was so distinctly one of his subjects that he interposed.

"It is short, no doubt, my dear. Still, the average duration of human life is proved to have increased of late years. The calculations of various life assurance and annuity offices, among other figures which cannot go wrong, have established the fact."

"I speak of my own life, father."

"Oh indeed? Still," said Mr Gradgrind, "I need not point out to you, Louisa, that it is governed by the laws which govern lives in the aggregate."

"While it lasts, I would wish to do the little I can, and the little I am fit for. What does it matter?"

Mr Gradgrind seemed rather at a loss to understand the last four words, replying, "How, matter? What matter, my dear?"

"Mr Bounderby," she went on in a steady way, without regarding this, "asks me to marry him. The question I have to ask myself is, shall I marry him? That is so, father, is it not?"

"Certainly, my dear."

"Let it be so. Since Mr Bounderby likes to take me thus, I accept his proposal. Tell him, father, as soon as you please, that this was my answer. Repeat it, word for word, if you can, because I should wish him to know what I said."

64

"It is quite right, my dear," retorted her father approvingly, "to be exact. I will observe your very proper request. Have you any wish in reference to the period of your marriage, my child?"

"None, father. What does it matter!"

Mr Gradgrind had drawn his chair a little nearer to her, and taken her hand. But, her repetition of these words seemed to strike with some little discord on his ear. He paused to look at her, and, still holding her hand, said:

"Louisa, I have not considered it essential to ask you one question, because the possibility implied in it appeared to me to be too remote. But perhaps I ought to do so. You have never entertained in secret any other proposal?"

"Father," she returned, almost scornfully, "what other proposal can have been made to me? Whom have I seen? Where have I been? What are my heart's experiences?"

"My dear Louisa," returned Mr Gradgrind, reassured and satisfied. "You correct me justly. I merely wished to discharge my duty."

"What do I know, father," said Louisa quietly, "of tastes and fancies; of aspirations and affections; of all that part of my nature in which such light things might have been nourished? What escape have I had from problems that could be demonstrated, and realities that could be grasped?" As she said it, she unconsciously closed her hand, as if upon a solid object, and slowly opened it as though releasing dust or ash.

"My dear," assented her eminently practical parent, "quite true."

"Why father," she pursued, "what a strange question to ask me! The baby-preference that even I have heard of as common among children, has never had its innocent resting-place in my breast. You have been so careful of me, that I never had a child's heart. You have trained me so well, that I never dreamed a child's dream. You have dealt so wisely with me, father, from my cradle to this hour, that I never had a child's belief or a child's fear."

Mr Gradgrind was quite moved by his success, and by this testimony to it. "My dear Louisa," said he, "you abundantly repay my care. Kiss me, my dear girl."

So, his daughter kissed him. Detaining her in his embrace, he said, "I may assure you now, my favourite child, that I am made happy by the sound decision at which you have arrived. Mr Bounderby is a very remarkable man; and what little disparity can be said to exist between you – if any – is more than counterbalanced by the tone your mind has acquired. It has always been my object so to educate you, as that you might, even at an early age, be (if I may so express myself) considered any age. Kiss me once more, Louisa. Now, let us go and find your mother."

Accordingly, they went down to the drawing room, where the esteemed lady was recumbent as usual, while Sissy worked beside her. She gave some feeble signs of returning animation when they entered, and presently the faint transparency was presented in a sitting attitude.

"Mrs Gradgrind," said her husband, who had waited for the achievement of this feat with some impatience, "allow me to present to you Mrs Bounderby."

"Oh!" said Mrs Gradgrind, "so you have settled it! Well, I'm sure I hope your health may be good, Louisa. I give you joy, my dear – and I hope you may now turn all your ological studies to good account! I must give you a kiss of congratulation, Louisa; but don't touch my right shoulder, for there's something running down it all day long. And now you see," whimpered Mrs Gradgrind, adjusting her shawls after the affectionate ceremony, "I shall be worrying myself, morning, noon, and night, to know what I am to call him!"

"Mrs Gradgrind," said her husband, solemnly, "what do you mean?"

"Whatever do I call him, Mr Gradgrind, when he is married to Louisa! I must call him something. It's impossible," said Mrs Gradgrind, "to be constantly addressing him and never giving him a name. I cannot call him Josiah. You yourself wouldn't hear of Joe. Am I to call my own son-in-law, Mister. Not, I believe, unless the time has arrived when, as an invalid, I am to be trampled upon by my relations. Then, what am I to call him!"

Nobody present having any suggestion to offer, Mrs Gradgrind departed this life for the time being, after delivering the following codicil to her remarks already executed:

"As to the wedding, all I ask, Louisa, is, – and I ask it with a fluttering in my chest, which extends to the soles of my feet, – that it may take place soon. Otherwise, I know it is one of those subjects I shall never hear the last of."

When Mr Gradgrind had presented Mrs Bounderby, Sissy had

suddenly turned her head, and looked, in wonder, in pity, in sorrow, in doubt, in a multitude of emotions, towards Louisa. Louisa had known it, and seen it, without looking at her. From that moment she was impassive, proud and cold – held Sissy at a distance -- changed to her altogether.

CHAPTER 16

Mr Bounderby's first worry on hearing of his happiness was how to tell Mrs Sparsit. On his way home, on the evening he set aside for this momentous purpose, he took the precaution of stepping into a chemist's shop and buying a bottle of the very strongest smelling salts.

"By George!" said Mr Bounderby, "if she takes to fainting, I'll have the skin off her nose with this!" But, in spite of being thus forearmed, he entered his own house with anything but a courageous air and appeared before the object of his misgivings, like a dog who was conscious of coming direct from the pantry.

"Good evening, Mr Bounderby!"

"Good evening, ma'am, good evening." He drew up his chair, and Mrs Sparsit drew back hers, as if to say, "Your fireside, sir."

"Don't go to the North Pole, ma'am!" said Mr Bounderby.

"Thank you, sir," said Mrs Sparsit, and returned, though short of her former position.

Mr Bounderby sat looking at her, as, with the points of a stiff, sharp pair of scissors, she picked out holes for some inscrutable ornamental purpose, in a piece of cambric. She was so steadfastly occupied, that many minutes elapsed before she looked up from her work. When she did so Mr Bounderby bespoke her attention with a hitch of his head.

"Mrs Sparsit, ma'am," said Mr Bounderby, putting his hands in his pockets, and assuring himself with his right hand that the cork of the little bottle was ready for use, "I must say that you are a devilish sensible woman. What I say now is going to astonish you."

"Yes, sir?" returned Mrs Sparsit in the most tranquil manner possible.

"I am going, ma'am," said Bounderby, "to marry Tom Gradgrind's daughter."

"Yes, sir," returned Mrs Sparsit. "I hope you may be happy, Mr Bounderby." And she said it with such great condescension as well as with such great compassion for him, that Bounderby, – far more disconcerted than if she had thrown her work-box at the mirror, or swooned on the hearthrug, – corked up the smelling-salts tight in his pocket, and thought, "Now confound this woman, who could have ever guessed that she would take it in this way!"

"I wish with all my heart, sir," said Mrs Sparsit, in a highly superior manner; somehow she seemed in a moment, to have established a right to pity him ever afterwards; "that you may be in all respects very happy."

"Well, ma'am," returned Bounderby, with some resentment in his tone, "I am obliged to you. I hope I shall be."

"Do you, sir!" said Mrs Sparsit, with great affability. "But of course you do."

A very awkward pause on Mr Bounderby's part succeeded. Mrs Sparsit sedately resumed her work and occasionally gave a small cough.

"Well, ma'am," resumed Bounderby, "under these circumstances, I imagine it would not be agreeable to a character like yours to remain here, though you would be very welcome here."

"Oh, dear no, sir, I could on no account think of that!" Mrs Sparsit shook her head, still in her highly superior manner, and a little changed the small cough.

"However, ma'am," said Bounderby, "there are apartments at the Bank, where a born and bred lady, as keeper of the place, would be rather a catch than otherwise; and if the same terms – "

"I beg your pardon, sir. You were so good as to promise that you would always substitute the phrase, annual compliment."

"Well, ma'am, if the same annual compliment would be acceptable there, why, I see nothing to part us, unless you do."

"Sir," returned Mrs Sparsit. "The proposal is like yourself, and if the position I shall assume at the Bank is one that I could occupy without descending lower in the social scale – "

"Why, of course it is," said Bounderby. "If it was not, ma'am, you don't suppose that I should offer it to a lady who has moved in the society you have moved in. Not that I care for such society, you know! But you do."

"Mr Bounderby, you are very considerate."

"You'll have your own private apartments, and you'll have your coals and your candles, and all the rest of it, and you'll have your maid to attend upon you, and you'll have your light porter to protect you, and you'll be what I take the liberty of considering precious comfortable," said Bounderby.

"Sir," rejoined Mrs Sparsit, "say no more. In yielding up my trust here, I shall not be freed from the necessity of eating the bread of dependence, and I would rather receive it from your hand, than from any other. Therefore, sir, I accept your offer gratefully, and with many sincere acknowledgements for past favours. And I hope, sir," said Mrs Sparsit, concluding in an impressively compassionate manner, "I fondly hope that Miss Gradgrind may be all you desire, and deserve!"

Nothing moved Mrs Sparsit from that position any more. Bounderby blustered in vain to assert himself in any of his explosive ways; Mrs Sparsit was resolved to have compassion on him, as a Victim. She was polite, cheerful, hopeful; but, the more polite, the more cheerful, the more hopeful, the more exemplary altogether, she; the forlorner Sacrifice and Victim, he.

Meanwhile the marriage was arranged to be solemnised in eight weeks' time, and Mr Bounderby went every evening to Stone Lodge as an accepted wooer. Love was made on these occasions in the form of bracelets; and, on all occasions during the period of betrothal, took a manufacturing aspect. Dresses were made, jewellery was made, cakes and gloves were made, settlements were made. The business was all Fact, from first to last.

So the day came, as all other days come to people who will only stick to reason; and when it came, there were married in the church of the florid wooden legs – that popular order of architecture – Josiah Bounderby Esquire of Coketown, to Louisa eldest daughter of Thomas Gradgrind Esquire of Stone Lodge, M.P. for that borough. And when they were united in holy matrimony, they went home to breakfast at Stone Lodge.

There was an improving party assembled on the auspicious occasion, who knew what everything they had to eat and drink was made of, and how it was imported or exported, and in what quantities, and in what bottoms, whether native or foreign, and all about it. The bridesmaids, down to little Jane Gradgrind, were, in an intellectual point of view, fit helpmates for the calculating boy; and there was no nonsense about any of the company.

After breakfast, the bridegroom addressed them in the following terms:

"Ladies and gentlemen, I am Josiah Bounderby of Coketown. Since you have done my wife and myself the honour of drinking our healths and happiness, I suppose I must acknowledge the same; though, as you all know me, and know what I am, and what my extraction was, you won't expect a speech from a man who, when he sees a Post, says 'that's a Post,' and when he sees a Pump, says 'that's a Pump'. If you want a speech this morning, my friend and father-in-law, Tom Gradgrind, is a Member of Parliament, and you know where to get it. I am not your man. However, if I feel a little independent when I look around this table today, and reflect how little I thought of marrying Tom Gradgrind's daughter when I was a ragged street-boy, I hope I may be excused. So, I hope you like my feeling independent. If you don't, I can't help it. I do feel independent. Now I have mentioned, and you have mentioned, that I am this day married to Tom Gradgrind's daughter. I am very glad to be so. It has long been my wish to be so. I have watched her bringing-up, and I believe she is worthy of me. At the same time – not to deceive you – I believe I am worthy of her. So, I thank you, on both our parts, for the goodwill you have shown towards us; and the best wish I can give the unmarried part of the present company, is this: I hope every bachelor may find as good a wife as I have found. And I hope every spinster may find as good a husband as my wife has found."

Shortly after which oration, as they were going on a nuptial trip to Lyons, in order that Mr Bounderby might take the opportunity of seeing how the Hands got on in those parts, and whether they, too, required to be fed with gold spoons; the happy pair departed for the railroad. The Bride, in passing downstairs, dressed for her journey, found Tom waiting for her – flushed, either with his feelings or the vinous part of the breakfast.

"What a game girl you are, to be such a first-rate sister, Loo!" whispered Tom.

She clung to him as she should have clung to some far better nature that day, and was a little shaken in her reserved composure for the first time.

"Old Bounderby's quite ready," said Tom. "Time's up. Good bye! I shall be on the lookout for you, when you come back. I say, my dear Loo! *An't* it uncommonly jolly now!"

BOOK 2

CHAPTER 1

A sunny midsummer day. There was such a thing sometimes, even in Coketown.

Seen from a distance in such weather, Coketown lay shrouded in a haze of its own. You only knew the town was there, because you knew there could have been no such sulky blotch upon the prospect without a town. Coketown in the distance was suggestive of itself, though not a brick of it could be seen.

There was a stifling smell of hot oil everywhere. The steam-engines shone with it, the dresses of the Hands were soiled with it, the mills throughout their many stories oozed and trickled it.

Mrs Sparsit sat in her afternoon apartment at the Bank, on the shadier side of the frying street. Office-hours were over, and at that period of the day, in warm weather, she usually embellished with her genteel presence, a managerial boardroom over the public office. Her own private sitting-room was a storey higher, at the window of which post of observation she was ready, every morning, to greet Mr Bounderby, as he came across the road, with the sympathising recognition appropriate to a Victim. He had been married now a year and Mrs Sparsit had never released him from her determined pity a moment.

The Bank was another red brick house, with black outside shutters, green inside blinds, a black street-door up two white steps, a brazen door-plate, and a brazen door-handle full-stop. It was a size larger than Mr Bounderby's house, as other houses were from a size to half a dozen sizes smaller; in all other particulars, it was strictly according to pattern.

Mrs Sparsit was conscious that by coming during the evening among the desks and writing implements, she shed a feminine, not to say also aristocratic, grace upon the office. Seated, with her needlework, at the window, she felt she corrected, by her ladylike deportment, the rude business aspect of the place. Mrs Sparsit considered herself, in some sort, the Bank Fairy. The townspeople who, in their passing and repassing, saw her there, regarded her as the Bank Dragon keeping watch over the treasures.

A deaf serving-woman and the light porter completed Mrs Sparsit's empire. Mrs Sparsit's tea was just set for her on a pert little table close to the stern, leathern-topped, long board-table that bestrode the middle of the room. The light porter placed the tea tray on it, knuckling his forehead as a form of homage.

"Thank you, Bitzer," said Mrs Sparsit.

"Thank you, ma'am," returned the light porter. He was a very light porter indeed; as light as in the days when he blinkingly defined a horse, for girl number twenty.

"All is shut up, Bitzer?" said Mrs Sparsit.

"All is shut up, ma'am."

"And what," said Mrs Sparsit, pouring out her tea, "is the news of the day? Anything?"

"Well, ma'am, I can't say that I have heard anything particular."

"What are the restless wretches doing now?" asked Mrs Sparsit.

"Merely going on in the old way, ma'am. Uniting, and leaguing, and engaging to stand by one another."

"It is much to be regretted," said Mrs Sparsit, "that the united masters allow of any such class-combinations."

"Yes, ma'am," said Bitzer.

"Being united themselves, they ought one and all to set their faces against employing any man who is united with any other man," said Mrs Sparsit.

"They have done that, ma'am," returned Bitzer; "but it rather fell through, ma'am."

"I do not pretend to understand these things," said Mrs Sparsit, with dignity, "my lot having been signally cast in a widely different sphere. Mr Sparsit, as a Powler, was quite out of the pale of any such dissensions. I only know that these people must be conquered, and that it's high time it was done, once for all."

"Yes, ma'am," returned Bitzer, with a demonstration of great respect for Mrs Sparsit's oracular authority. "You couldn't put it clearer, I am sure, ma'am."

As this was his usual hour for having a little confidential chat with Mrs Sparsit, and as he realised that she was going to ask him something, he made a pretence of arranging the rulers, inkstands, and so forth, while that lady went on with her tea, glancing through the open window, down into the street.

"Has it been a busy day, Bitzer?" asked Mrs Sparsit.

"Not a very busy day, my lady. About an average day." He now and then slid into my lady, instead of ma'am, as an involuntary acknowledgment of Mrs Sparsit's personal dignity and claims to reverence.

"The clerks," said Mrs Sparsit, carefully brushing an imperceptible crumb of bread and butter from her left-hand mitten, "are trustworthy, punctual, and industrious, of course?"

"Yes, ma'am, pretty fair, ma'am. With the usual exception."

He held the respectable office of general spy and informer in the establishment, for which volunteer service he received a present at Christmas, over and above his weekly wage. He had grown into an extremely clear-headed, cautious, prudent young man, who was safe to rise in the world. His mind was so exactly regulated, that he had no affections or passions. All his proceedings were the result of the nicest and coldest calculation. Having satisfied himself, on his father's death, that his mother had a right of settlement in Coketown, this young economist had asserted that right for her with such a steadfast adherence to the principle of the case, that she had been shut up in the workhouse ever since.

"Pretty fair, ma'am. With the usual exception, ma'am," repeated Bitzer.

"Ah-h!" said Mrs Sparsit, shaking her head over her tea-cup, and taking a long gulp.

"Mr Thomas, ma'am, I don't like his ways at all."

"Bitzer," said Mrs Sparsit, in a very impressive manner, "do you recollect my having said anything to you respecting names?"

"I beg your pardon, ma'am. It's quite true that you did object to names being used, and they're always best avoided."

"Please to remember that I have a charge here," said Mrs Sparsit. "I hold a trust here, Bitzer, under Mr Bounderby. However improbable both Mr Bounderby and myself might have deemed it years ago, that he would ever become my patron, making me an annual compliment, I cannot but regard him in that light. From Mr Bounderby I have received every acknowledgement of my social station, and every recognition of my family descent, that I could possibly expect. Therefore, to my patron I would be scrupulously true. And I do not consider, I will not consider, I cannot consider," said Mrs Sparsit, with a most extensive stock on hand of honour and morality, "that I should be scrupulously true, if I allowed names to be mentioned under this roof, that are unfortunately – most unfortunately – no doubt of that – connected with his."

Bitzer knuckled his forehead again, and again begged pardon.

"No, Bitzer," continued Mrs Sparsit, "say an individual, and I will hear you; say Mr Thomas, and you must excuse me."

"With the usual exception, ma'am," said Bitzer, trying again, "of an individual."

"Ah-h!" Mrs Sparsit repeated the ejaculation, the shake of the head over her tea-cup, and the long gulp, as taking up the conversation again at the point where it had been interrupted.

"An individual, ma'am," said Bitzer, "has never been what he ought to have been, since he first came into the place. He is a dissipated, extravagant idler. He is not worth his salt, ma'am. He wouldn't get it either, if he hadn't a friend and relation at court!"

"Ah-h!" said Mrs Sparsit, with another melancholy shake.

"I only hope, ma'am," pursued Bitzer, "that his friend and relation may not supply him with the means of carrying on. Otherwise, ma'am, we know out of whose pocket that money comes."

"Ah-h!" sighed Mrs Sparsit again, with another melancholy shake.

"He is to be pitied, ma'am. The last party I have alluded to, is to be pitied, ma'am," said Bitzer.

"Yes, Bitzer," said Mrs Sparsit. "I have always pitied the delusion, always."

"As to an individual, ma'am," said Bitzer, dropping his voice and drawing nearer, "he is as improvident as any of the people in this town."

"They would do well," returned Mrs Sparsit, "to take example by you, Bitzer."

"Thank you, ma'am. But, since you do refer to me, now look at me, ma'am. I have put by a little, ma'am, already. That gratuity which I receive at Christmas, ma'am: I never touch it. I don't even go the length of my wages, though they're not high, ma'am. Why can't they do as I have done, ma'am? What one person can do, another can do."

This, again, was among the fictions of Coketown. Any capitalist there, who had made sixty thousand pounds out of sixpence, always professed to wonder why the sixty thousand nearest Hands didn't each make sixty thousand pounds out of sixpence, and more or less reproached them every one for not accomplishing the little feat.

"As to their wanting recreations, ma'am," said Bitzer, "it's stuff and nonsense. I don't want recreations. I never did, and I never shall; I don't like 'em. As to their combining together; there are many of them, I have no doubt, that by watching and informing upon one another could earn a trifle now and then, whether in money or good will, and improve their livelihood. Then, why don't they improve it, ma'am! It's the first consideration of a rational creature, and it's what they pretend to want."

"Pretend indeed!" said Mrs Sparsit.

"I am sure we are constantly hearing, ma'am, till it becomes quite nauseous, concerning their wives and families," said Bitzer. "Why look at me, ma'am! I don't want a wife and family. Why should they?"

"Because they are improvident," said Mrs Sparsit.

"Yes, ma'am," returned Bitzer, "that's where it is. If they were more provident and less perverse, ma'am, what would they do? They would say, 'While my hat covers my family,' or 'while my bonnet covers my family,' – as the case might be, ma'am – 'I have only one to feed, and that's the person I most like to feed.'"

"To be sure," assented Mrs Sparsit, eating muffin.

"Thank you, ma'am," said Bitzer, knuckling his forehead again, in return for the favour of Mrs Sparsit's improving conversation. "Would you wish a little more hot water, ma'am, or is there anything else I could fetch you?"

"Nothing just now, Bitzer."

"Thank you, ma'am. I shouldn't wish to disturb you at your meals, ma'am, particularly tea, knowing your partiality for it," said Bitzer, craning a little to look over into the street from where he stood, "but there's a gentleman been looking up here for a minute or so, ma'am, and he has come across as if he was going to knock. That is his knock, ma'am, no doubt."

He stepped to the window and looking out, and drawing in his head again, confirmed himself with, "Yes, ma'am. Would you wish the gentleman to be shown in, ma'am?"

"I don't know who it can be," said Mrs Sparsit, wiping her mouth and arranging her mittens.

"A stranger, ma'am, evidently."

"What a stranger can want at the Bank at this time of the evening, unless he comes upon some business for which he is too late, I don't know," said Mrs Sparsit, "but I hold a charge in this establishment from Mr Bounderby, and I will never shrink from it. If to see him is any part of the duty I have accepted, I will see him. Use your own discretion, Bitzer."

Here the visitor, unaware of Mrs Sparsit's magnanimous words, repeated his knock so loudly that the light porter hastened down to open the door. Mrs Sparsit took the precaution of hiding her table in a cupboard, and then decamped upstairs, that she might appear, if needful, with the greater dignity.

"If you please, ma'am, the gentleman would wish to see you," said Bitzer, with his eye at Mrs Sparsit's keyhole. So, Mrs Sparsit, who had improved the interval by touching up her cap, took her classical features downstairs again, and entered the board-room in the manner of a Roman matron going outside the city walls to treat with an invading general.

The visitor having strolled to the window, and being then engaged in looking carelessly out, was as unmoved by this impressive entry as man could possibly be. He stood whistling to himself, his hat still on, with a certain air of exhaustion upon him, in part arising from excessive summer, and in part from excessive gentility. For it was obvious that he was a thorough gentleman, made to the model of the time; weary of everything, and putting no more faith in anything than Lucifer.

"I believe, sir," quoth Mrs Sparsit, "you wished to see me."

"I beg your pardon," he said, turning and removing his hat.

"Humph!" thought Mrs Sparsit, as she made a stately bend. "Five-and-thirty, good-looking, good figure, good teeth, good voice, good breeding, well-dressed, dark hair, bold eyes." All which Mrs Sparsit observed in her womanly way, merely in dipping down and coming up again.

"Please to be seated, sir," said Mrs Sparsit.

"Thank you. Allow me." He placed a chair for her, but remained himself carelessly lounging against the table. "I left my servant at the railway looking after the luggage – very heavy train and vast quantity of it in the van – and strolled on, looking about me. Exceedingly odd place. Will you allow me to ask you if it's always as black as this?"

"In general much blacker," returned Mrs Sparsit.

"Is it possible! Excuse me, you are not a native, I think?"

"No, sir," returned Mrs Sparsit. "It was once my good or ill fortune, as it may be – before I was widowed – to move in a very different sphere. My husband was a Powler."

"Beg your pardon, really!" said the stranger. "Was – ?"

Mrs Sparsit repeated, "A Powler."

"Powler Family," said the stranger, after reflecting a few moments. Mrs Sparsit signified assent. The stranger seemed a little more fatigued than before.

"You must be very much bored here?" was the inference he drew.

"I am the servant of circumstances, sir," said Mrs Sparsit, "and I have long adapted myself to the governing power of my life."

"Very philosophical," returned the stranger, "and very exemplary and laudable, and – " It seemed to be scarcely worth his while to finish the sentence, so he played with his watch-chain wearily.

"May I be permitted to ask, sir," said Mrs Sparsit, "to what I am indebted for the favour of – "

"Assuredly," said the stranger. "Much obliged to you for reminding me. I am the bearer of a letter of introduction to Mr Bounderby the banker. Walking through this extraordinary black town, while they were getting dinner ready at the hotel, I asked a fellow whom I met; one of the working people; who appeared to have been taking a shower-bath of something fluffy, which I assume to be the raw material, – "

Mrs Sparsit inclined her head.

" – raw material, – where Mr Bounderby, the banker, might reside. Upon which, hearing the word Banker, he directed me to the Bank. – Fact being, I presume, that Mr Bounderby the Banker, does not reside in the edifice in which I have the honour of offering this explanation?"

"No, sir," returned Mrs Sparsit, "he does not."

"Thank you. I had no intention of delivering my letter at the present moment, nor have I. But strolling on to the Bank to kill time, and having the good fortune to observe at the window," towards which he languidly waved his hand, then slightly bowed, "a lady of a very superior and agreeable appearance, I considered that I could not do better than take the liberty of asking that lady where Mr Bounderby the Banker does live. Which I accordingly venture, with all suitable apologies, to do."

The inattention and indolence of his manner were sufficiently relieved, to Mrs Sparsit's thinking, by a certain gallantry at ease, which offered her homage too. Here he was, for instance, all but sitting on the table, and yet lazily bending over her, as if he acknowledged an attraction in her that made her charming.

"Banks, I know, are always suspicious, and officially must be," said the stranger, whose lightness and smoothness of speech were pleasant likewise. "Therefore I may observe that my letter – here it is – is from the member for this place – Gradgrind – whom I have had the pleasure of knowing in London."

Mrs Sparsit recognised the hand, and by way of confirmation gave Mr Bounderby's address, with all necessary directions.

"Thousand thanks," said the stranger. "Of course you know the Banker well?"

"Yes, sir," rejoined Mrs Sparsit. "In my dependent relation towards him, I have known him ten years."

"Quite an eternity! I think he married Gradgrind's daughter?"

"Yes," said Mrs Sparsit, her mouth tightening, "he had that – honour."

"The lady is quite a philosopher, I am told?"

"Indeed, sir," said Mrs Sparsit. "Is she?"

"Excuse my impertinent curiosity," pursued the stranger, "but you know the family, and know the world. I am about to know the family, and may have much to do with them. Is the lady so very alarming? Her father gives her such a hard-headed reputation, that I have a burning desire to know. Is she absolutely unapproachable? Repellently and stunningly clever? I see, by your meaning smile, you think not. You have poured balm into my anxious soul. As to age, now. Forty! Five-and-thirty?"

Mrs Sparsit laughed outright. "A chit," said she. "Not twenty when she was married."

"I give you my honour, Mrs Powler," returned the stranger, standing, "that I never was so astonished in my life!"

It really did seem to impress him. He looked at his informant for full a quarter of a minute, and appeared to have the surprise in his mind all the time. "I assure you, Mrs Powler," he then said, much exhausted, "that the father's manner prepared me for a grim and stony maturity. I am obliged to you for correcting so absurd a mistake. Pray excuse my intrusion. Many thanks. Good day!"

He bowed himself out; and Mrs Sparsit, hiding in the window curtain, saw him strolling down the shady side of the street.

"What do you think of the gentleman, Bitzer?" she asked the light porter, when he came to take away.

"Spends a deal of money on his dress, ma'am."

"It must be admitted," said Mrs Sparsit, "that it's very tasteful."

"Yes, ma'am," returned Bitzer, "if that's worth the money."

"Besides which, ma'am," resumed Bitzer, while he was polishing the table, "he looks to me as if he gamed."

"It's immoral to game," said Mrs Sparsit.

"It's ridiculous, ma'am," said Bitzer, "because the chances are against the players."

Whether it was that the heat prevented Mrs Sparsit from working, or whether it was that her hand was out, she did no work that night. She sat at the window, when the sun began to sink behind the smoke, turning it burning red. She was still there when the colour faded from it, when darkness seemed to rise slowly out of the ground, and creep upward. Without a candle in the room, Mrs Sparsit sat at the window. Not until the light porter announced that her nocturnal sweetbread was ready, did Mrs Sparsit arouse herself from her reverie, and move upstairs.

"O, you Fool!" said Mrs Sparsit, when she was alone at her supper. Whom she meant, she did not say, but she could scarcely have meant the sweetbread.

CHAPTER 2

The Gradgrind party wanted assistance in cutting the throats of the Graces. They went about recruiting, and where could they enlist recruits more hopefully, than among the fine gentlemen who, having found out everything to be worth nothing, were equally ready for anything?

Moreover, the healthy spirits who had mounted to this sublime height were attractive to many of the Gradgrind school. They liked fine gentlemen, they pretended that they did not, but they did. They became exhausted in imitation of them and they yaw-yawed in their speech like them. They served out, with an enervated air, the little mouldy rations of political economy, on which they regaled their disciples. There never before was seen on earth such a wonderful hybrid race as was thus produced.

Among the fine gentlemen not regularly belonging to the Gradgrind school, there was one of a good family and appearance. This gentleman had a younger brother of still better appearance than himself, who had tried life as a Cornet of Dragoons, and found it a bore; and had afterwards tried it in the train of an English minister abroad, and found that a bore. He had then strolled to Jerusalem, and got bored there; and had then gone yachting about the world, and got bored everywhere. To whom this honourable and jocular member fraternally said one day, "Jem, there's a good opening among the hard Fact fellows, and they want men. I wonder you don't go in for statistics."

Jem, rather taken by the novelty of the idea, and very hard up for a change, was as ready to "go in" for statistics as for anything else. So, he went in. He coached himself up with a blue book or two; and his brother put it about among the hard Fact fellows, and said, "If you want to bring in, for any place, a handsome dog who can make you a devilish good speech, look after my brother Jem, for he's your man." After a few dashes in the public meeting way, Mr Gradgrind and a council of political sages approved of Jem, and it was resolved to send him down to Coketown, to become known there and in the neighbourhood. Hence the letter Jem had last night shown to Mrs Sparsit, which Mr Bounderby now held in his hand; superscribed, "Josiah Bounderby, Esquire, Banker, Coketown. Specially to introduce James Harthouse, Esquire. Thomas Gradgrind."

Within an hour of the receipt of this dispatch and Mr James Harthouse's card, Mr Bounderby put on his hat and went down to the Hotel. There he found Mr James Harthouse looking out of window, in a state of mind so disconsolate, that he was already half disposed to "go in" for something else.

"My name, sir," said his visitor, "is Josiah Bounderby, of Coketown."

Mr James Harthouse was very happy indeed (though he scarcely looked so) to have a pleasure he had long expected.

"Coketown, sir," said Bounderby, obstinately taking a chair, "is not the kind of place you have been accustomed to. Therefore, if you will allow me – or whether you will or not, for I am a plain man – I'll tell you something about it before we go any further."

Mr Harthouse would be charmed.

"Don't be too sure of that," said Bounderby. "I don't promise it. First of all, you see our smoke. That's meat and drink to us. Now, you have heard a lot of talk about the work in our mills, no doubt. You have? Very good. I'll state the fact of it to you. It's the pleasantest work there is, and it's the lightest work there is, and it's the best paid work there is. More than that, we couldn't improve the mills themselves, unless we laid down Turkey carpets on the floors. Which we're not a-going to do."

"Mr Bounderby, perfectly right."

"Lastly," said Bounderby, "as to our Hands. There's not a Hand in this town, sir, man, woman, or child, but has one ultimate object in life – to be fed on turtle soup and venison with a gold spoon. Now, they're not a-going – none of 'em – ever to be fed on turtle soup and venison with a gold spoon. And now you know the place."

Mr Harthouse professed himself in the highest degree instructed, by this condensed epitome of the whole Coketown question.

"Why, you see," replied Mr Bounderby, "it suits my disposition to have a full understanding with a man, particularly with a public man, when I make his acquaintance. I have only one thing more to say to you, Mr Harthouse, before assuring you of the pleasure with which I shall respond, to the utmost of my poor ability, to my friend Tom Gradgrind's letter of introduction. You are a man of family. Don't deceive yourself into thinking that I am a man of family. I am a bit of dirty riff-raff, and a genuine scrap of tag, rag, and bobtail."

If anything could have exalted Jem's interest in Mr Bounderby, it would have been this very circumstance. Or, so he told him.

"So now," said Bounderby, "we may shake hands on equal terms. Although I know what I am, and the exact depth of the gutter I have lifted myself out of, better than any man does, I am as proud as you are. Having now asserted my independence in a proper manner, I may come to how do you find yourself, and I hope you're pretty well."

The better, Mr Harthouse gave him to understand as they shook hands, for the salubrious air of Coketown. Mr Bounderby received the answer with favour.

"Perhaps you know," said he, "or perhaps you don't, I married Tom Gradgrind's daughter. If you have nothing better to do than to walk up-town with me, I shall be glad to introduce you to Tom Gradgrind's daughter."

"Mr Bounderby," said Jem, "you anticipate my dearest wishes."

Mr Bounderby led the new acquaintance who so strongly contrasted with him, to the private red brick dwelling, with the black outside shutters, the green inside blinds, and the black street-door up the two white steps. In the drawing room of which mansion, there presently entered to them the most remarkable girl Mr James Harthouse had ever seen. She was so constrained, and yet so careless; so reserved, and yet so watchful; so cold and proud, and yet so sensitively ashamed of her husband's braggart humility – from which she shrunk as if every example of it were a cut or a blow; that it was quite a new sensation to observe her. In face she was no less remarkable than in manner. Her features were handsome, but their natural play was so locked up, that it seemed impossible to guess at their genuine expression. Utterly indifferent, perfectly self-reliant, never at a loss, and yet never at her ease, with her figure in company with them there, and her mind apparently quite alone – it was of no use "going in" yet awhile to comprehend this girl, for she baffled all penetration.

From the mistress of the house, the visitor glanced to the house itself. There was no mute sign of a woman in the room. The room stared at its present occupants, unsoftened and unrelieved by the least trace of any womanly occupation.

"This, sir," said Bounderby, "is my wife, Mrs Bounderby, Tom Gradgrind's eldest daughter. Loo, Mr James Harthouse. Mr Harthouse has joined your father's muster-roll. If he is not Torn Gradgrind's colleague before long, I believe we shall at least hear of him in connection with one of our neighbouring towns. You observe, Mr Harthouse, that my wife is my junior. I don't know what she saw in me to marry me, but she saw something in me, I suppose, or she wouldn't have married me. She has lots of expensive knowledge, sir, political and otherwise. If you want to cram for anything, I should be troubled to recommend you to a better adviser than Loo Bounderby."

To a more agreeable adviser, or one from whom he would be more likely to learn, Mr Harthouse could never be recommended.

"Come!" said his host. "If you're in the complimentary line, you'll get on here, for you'll meet with no competition. I have never been in the way of learning compliments myself, and I don't profess to understand the art of paying 'em. In fact, despise 'em. But, your bringing-up was different from mine. You're a gentleman, and I don't pretend to be one. I am Josiah Bounderby of Coketown, and that's enough for me. However, though I am not influenced by manners and station, Loo Bounderby may be. She hadn't my advantages – disadvantages you would call 'em, but I call 'em advantages – so you'll not waste your power, I dare say."

"Mr Bounderby," said Jem, turning with a smile to Louisa, "is a noble animal in a comparatively natural state, quite free from the harness in which a conventional hack like myself works."

"You respect Mr Bounderby very much," she quietly returned. "It is natural that you should."

He was thrown, for a gentleman who had seen so much of the world, and thought, "Now, how am I to take this?"

"You are going to devote yourself, as I gather from what Mr Bounderby has said, to the service of your country. You have made up your mind," said Louisa, still standing before him where she had first stopped – still self-possessed, but contrarily obviously very ill at ease – "to show the nation the way out of all its difficulties."

"Mrs Bounderby," he returned, laughing, "upon my honour, no. I will make no such pretence to you. I have seen a little, here and there, up and down; I have found it all to be very worthless, as everybody has, and as some confess they have, and some do not; and I am going in for your respected father's opinions – really because I have no choice of opinions, and may as well back them as anything else."

"Have you none of your own?" asked Louisa.

"I have not so much as the slightest predilection left. I assure you I attach not the least importance to any opinions. The result of the varieties of boredom I have undergone is a conviction that any set of ideas will do just as much good as any other set, and just as much harm as any other set. There's an English family with a charming Italian motto. What will be will be. It's the only truth going!"

This vicious assumption of honesty in dishonesty – a vice so dangerous, so deadly, and so common – seemed, he felt, to impress her slightly in his favour. He followed up the advantage, by saying in his pleasantest manner – a manner to which she might attach as much or as little meaning as she pleased: "The side that can prove anything in a line of units, tens, hundreds, and thousands, Mrs Bounderby, seems to me to afford the most fun, and to give a man the best chance. I am quite as much attached to it as if I believed it. I am quite ready to go in for it, to the same extent as if I believed it. And what more could I possibly do, if I did believe it!"

"You are a singular politician," said Louisa.

"Pardon me; I have not even that merit. We are the largest party in the state, I assure you, Mrs Bounderby, if we fell out of our adopted ranks and were reviewed together."

Mr Bounderby, who had been in danger of bursting in silence, interposed here with a project for postponing the family dinner till half-past six, and taking Mr James Harthouse in the meantime on a round of visits to the voting and interesting notabilities of Coketown and its vicinity. The round of visits was made and Mr James Harthouse, with a discreet use of his blue coaching, came off triumphantly, though with a considerable accession of boredom.

In the evening, he found the dinner table laid for four, but only three sat. It was an appropriate occasion for Mr Bounderby to entertain his guest over the soup and fish, with the calculation that he (Bounderby) had eaten in his youth at least three horses under the guise of polonies and saveloys. Jem received this information with "charming!" every now and then; and it probably would have decided him to "go in" for Jerusalem again tomorrow morning, had he been less curious respecting Louisa.

"Is there nothing," he thought, glancing at her as she sat at the head of the table, where her youthful figure, small and slight, but very graceful, looked as pretty as it looked misplaced, "is there nothing that will move that face?"

Yes! By Jupiter, there was something, and here it was, in an unexpected shape. Tom appeared. She changed as the door opened, and broke into a beaming smile.

A beautiful smile. Mr James Harthouse might not have thought so much of it, but that he had wondered so long at her expressionless face. She put out her hand – a pretty little soft hand, and her fingers closed upon her brother's, as if she would have carried them to her lips.

"Ay, ay?" thought the visitor. "This whelp is the only creature she cares for. So, so!"

The whelp was presented, and took his chair. The appellation was not flattering, but not unmerited.

"When I was your age, young Tom," said Bounderby, "I was punctual, or I got no dinner!"

"When you were my age," returned Tom, "you hadn't a wrong balance to get right, and hadn't to dress afterwards."

"Never mind that now," said Bounderby.

"Well, then," grumbled Tom. "Don't begin with me."

"Mrs Bounderby," said Harthouse, perfectly hearing this understrain as it went on; "your brother's face is quite familiar to me. Can I have seen him abroad, or maybe at some public school?"

"No," she returned, quite interested, "he hasn't been abroad yet, and was educated here, at home. Tom, love, I am telling Mr Harthouse that he never saw you abroad."

"No such luck, sir," said Tom.

There was little enough in him to brighten her face, for he was sullen and ungracious, even to her. So much the greater must have been the solitude of her heart, and her need of some one on whom to bestow it. "So much the more is this whelp the only creature she has ever cared for," thought Mr James Harthouse, turning it over and over. "So much the more."

Both in his sister's presence, and after she had left the room, the whelp took no pains to hide his contempt for Mr Bounderby, whether by making wry faces, or shutting one eye. Without responding to these telegraphic communications, Mr Harthouse encouraged him much in the course of the evening, and showed an unusual liking for him. At last, when he rose to return to his hotel, and was a little doubtful whether he knew the way by night, the whelp immediately proffered his services as guide, and turned out with him to escort him thither.

CHAPTER 3

It was remarkable that a young gentleman who had been brought up under one continuous system of unnatural restraint, should be a hypocrite; but it was certainly the case with Tom. It was strange that a young gentleman who had never been left to his own guidance for five consecutive minutes, should be incapable at last of governing himself; but so it was with Tom. It was altogether unaccountable that a young gentleman, whose imagination had been strangled in his cradle, should be still inconvenienced by its ghost in the form of grovelling sensualities; such a monster, beyond all doubt, was Tom.

"Do you smoke?" asked Mr James Harthouse, when they came to the hotel, and he asked Tom up. Tom could do no less than go up. What with a cooling drink adapted to the weather and what with a rarer tobacco than was to be bought in those parts, Tom was soon in a highly free and easy state at his end of the sofa, and more than ever disposed to admire his new friend at the other end.

Tom blew his smoke aside, after he had been smoking a little while, and took an observation of his friend. "He don't seem to care about his dress," thought Tom, "and yet how capitally he does it. What an easy swell he is!"

Mr James Harthouse, happening to catch Tom's eye, remarked that he drank nothing, and filled his glass.

"Thank'ee," said Tom. "Well, Mr Harthouse, I hope you have had a good dose of old Bounderby tonight." He said this with one eye shut again, and looking over his glass knowingly.

"A very good fellow indeed!" returned Mr James Harthouse.

"You think so, don't you?" said Tom. And shut his eye again.

Mr James Harthouse smiled and moved to the chimney piece. He stood before the empty fire-grate as he smoked, and looking down at Tom, he observed: "What a comical brother-in-law you are!"

"What a comical brother-in-law old Bounderby is, I think you mean," said Tom.

"You are a piece of caustic, Tom," retorted Mr James Harthouse.

There was something so very agreeable in being so intimate with such a waistcoat; in being called Tom, in such an intimate way, by such a voice, that Tom was uncommonly pleased with himself.

"Oh! I don't care for old Bounderby," said he, "if you mean that. I have always called him that when I have talked about him, and I have always thought of him in the same way. I am not going to begin to be polite now, about old Bounderby. It would be rather late in the day."

"Don't mind me," returned James, "but take care when his wife is by, you know."

"His wife?" said Tom. "My sister Loo? O yes!" And he laughed, and took a little more of the cooling drink.

James Harthouse continued to lounge in the same place and attitude, smoking his cigar in his own easy way, and looking pleasantly at the whelp, as if he knew himself to be a kind of agreeable demon. He just had to hover over him, and Tom must give up his whole soul if required. It certainly did seem that the whelp yielded to this influence. He looked at his companion admiringly, looked at him boldly, and put up one leg on the sofa.

"My sister Loo?" said Tom. "She never cared for old Bounderby."

"That's the past tense, Tom," returned Mr James Harthouse. "We are in the present tense, now."

"Verb neuter, not to care. Indicative mood, present tense. First person singular, I do not care; second person singular, thou dost not care; third person singular, she does not care," returned Tom.

"Good! Very quaint!" said his friend. "Though you don't mean it."

"But I do," cried Tom. "Upon my honour! Why, you won't tell me, Mr Harthouse, that you really think my sister Loo does care for old Bounderby."

"My dear fellow," returned the other, "what can I believe, when I find two married people living in harmony and happiness?"

By now Tom had both his legs on the sofa. If his second leg had not been already there when he was called a dear fellow, he would have put it up at that great stage of the conversation. He then stretched himself out, and with the back of his head on the end of the sofa, turned his common face, and not too sober eyes, towards the face looking down upon him so carelessly yet so potently.

"You know our governor, Mr Harthouse," said Tom, "and therefore you needn't be surprised that Loo married old Bounderby. She never had a lover, and the governor proposed old Bounderby, and she took him."

"Very dutiful in your interesting sister," said Mr James Harthouse.

"Yes, but it would not have come off as easily," returned the whelp, "if it hadn't been for me."

The tempter merely lifted his eyebrows; but the whelp was obliged to go on.

"I persuaded her," he said, with an edifying air of superiority. "I was stuck into old Bounderby's bank (where I never wanted to be), and I knew I should get into scrapes there, if she put old Bounderby's pipe out; so I told her my wishes, and she came into them. She would do anything for me. It was very game of her, wasn't it?"

"It was charming, Tom!"

"Not that it was quite so important to her as it was to me," continued Tom coolly. "My liberty and comfort, and perhaps my getting on, depended on it. She had no other lover, and staying at home was like staying in jail – especially when I was gone. It wasn't as if she gave up another lover for old Bounderby – but still it was a good thing in her."

"Perfectly delightful. And she gets on so placidly."

"Oh," returned Tom, with contemptuous patronage, "she's a regular girl. A girl can get on anywhere. She has settled down to the life, and she don't mind. It does just as well as another. Besides, Loo is not a common sort of girl. She can shut herself up within herself, and think – as I have often known her sit and watch the fire – for an hour at a stretch."

"Has resources of her own?" said Harthouse, smoking quietly.

"Not so much of that as you may suppose," returned Tom. "Our governor had her crammed with all sorts of dry bones and sawdust. It's his system."

"Formed his daughter on his own model?" suggested Harthouse.

"His daughter? And everybody else. Why, he formed me that way!" said Tom.

"Impossible!"

"He did, though," said Tom, shaking his head. "Mr Harthouse, when I first left home and went to old Bounderby's, I was as flat as a warming-pan, and knew no more about life than any oyster."

"Come, Tom! I can hardly believe that."

"Upon my soul!" said the whelp. "I am serious!" He smoked with great dignity for a little while, and then added, in a highly complacent tone, "Oh! I have picked up a little since. I don't deny that. But I have done it myself, no thanks to the governor."

"And your intelligent sister?"

"My intelligent sister is about where she was. She used to complain to me that she had nothing that girls usually fall back upon. I don't see how she is to have got over that since. But she don't mind," he added, puffing at his cigar again. "Girls can always get on, somehow."

"Calling at the Bank, for Mr Bounderby's address, I found an ancient lady there, who seems to entertain great admiration for your sister," observed Mr James Harthouse, throwing away the stub of the cigar.

"Mother Sparsit!" said Tom. "You have seen her already?"

His friend nodded. Tom took his cigar out of his mouth and tapped his nose several times with his finger.

"Mother Sparsit's feeling for Loo is more than admiration, I should think," said Tom. "Say affection and devotion. Mother Sparsit never set her cap at Bounderby when he was a bachelor."

These were the last words spoken by the whelp, before a giddy drowsiness came upon him, followed by complete oblivion. He was roused from the latter state by an uneasy dream of being stirred up with a boot, and also of a voice saying: "Come, it's late. Be off!"

"Well!" he said, scrambling from the sofa. "I must take my leave of you though. Yours is very good tobacco, but it's too mild."

"Yes, it's too mild," returned his entertainer.

"It's – it's ridiculously mild," said Tom. "Where's the door! Good-night!"

He had another odd dream of being taken by a waiter through a mist, which, after giving him some trouble and difficulty, resolved itself into the main street, in which he stood alone. He then walked home pretty easily, though not yet free from an impression of the presence and influence of his new friend – as if he were lounging somewhere in the air, in the same negligent attitude, regarding him with the same look.

The whelp went home, and went to bed. If he had had any sense of what he had done that night, and had been less of a whelp and more of a brother, he might have turned away from the road and gone down to the ill-smelling river that was dyed black, to go to bed in it for good and all, curtaining his head for ever with its filthy waters.

CHAPTER 4

"Oh my friends, the down-trodden workers of Coketown! Oh, my friends and fellow-countrymen, the slaves of an iron-handed and grinding despotism! Oh, my friends and fellow-sufferers, and fellow-workmen, and fellow-men! I tell you that the hour is come, when we must rally as One united power, and crumble into dust the oppressors that too long have battened upon the sweat of our brows, upon the labour of our hands, and upon the holy and eternal privileges of Brotherhood!"

"Good!" "Hear, hear, hear!" "Hurrah!" and other cries, arose in many voices from various parts of the densely crowded Hall, in which the orator, perched on a stage, delivered this. He was as hoarse as he was hot. Roaring at the top of his voice under a flaring gas-light, clenching his fists and pounding with his arms, had taken so much out of him, that he stopped, and called for a glass of water.

As he stood there, trying to quench his fiery face with his drink of water, the comparison between the orator and the crowd of attentive faces turned towards him, was extremely to his disadvantage. Judging him by Nature's evidence, he was above the mass in very little but the stage on which he stood. In many great respects he was essentially below them. He was not so honest, he was not so manly, he was not so good-humoured. He substituted cunning for their simplicity, and passion for their safe solid sense. An ill-made, high-shouldered man, with lowering brows, and his features crushed into an habitually sour expression, he contrasted most unfavourably, even in his mongrel dress, with the great body of his hearers in their plain working clothes. It was particularly strange to see this crowd, whose honesty in the main no competent observer free from bias could doubt, so agitated by such a leader.

Good! Hear, hear! Hurrah! The eagerness both of attention and intention, exhibited in all the faces, made them a most impressive sight. There were none of the many shades of indifference to be seen in all other assemblies. Every man felt his condition to be, worse than it might be; every man considered it incumbent on him to join the rest, towards the making of it better; every man felt his only hope to be in his allying himself to the comrades by whom he was surrounded; and that in this belief, right or wrong (unhappily wrong then), the whole of that crowd were gravely, deeply, faithfully in earnest. Nor could a spectator fail to know in his own breast, that these men, through their very delusions, showed great qualities, susceptible of being turned to the happiest and best account; and that to pretend that they went astray wholly without cause, and of their own irrational wills, was to pretend that there could be smoke without fire, death without birth, harvest without seed, anything or everything produced from nothing.

The orator having refreshed himself, wiped his forehead and concentrated all his revived forces in a sneer of great disdain and bitterness.

"But, oh my friends and brothers! Oh men and Englishmen, the down-trodden workers of Coketown! What shall we say of that man – that working-man, that I should find it necessary so to libel the glorious name – who, well acquainted with the grievances and wrongs of you, the injured pith and marrow of this land, and having heard you, with a noble and majestic unanimity that will make Tyrants tremble, resolve to subscribe to the funds of the United Aggregate Tribunal, and to abide by the injunctions issued by that body for your benefit, whatever they may be – what, I ask you, will you say of that working-man? I must acknowledge him as such, who, at such a time, deserts his post, and sells his flag; who, at such a time, turns a traitor and a craven and a recreant, who, at such a time, is not ashamed to make to you the dastardly and humiliating avowal that he will hold himself aloof, and will not be one of those associated in the gallant stand for Freedom and for Right."

The assembly was divided at this point. There were some groans and hisses, but the general sense of honour was much too strong for the condemnation of a man as yet unheard. "Be sure you're right, Slackbridge!" "Put him up!" "Let's hear him!" Such things were said on many sides.

Finally, one strong voice called out, "Is the man heer? If the man's heer, Slackbridge, let's hear the man himseln, 'stead o' yo." This was received with a round of applause.

Slackbridge looked about him with a withering smile. Holding out his right hand at arm's length to still the thundering sea, he waited for silence.

"Oh, my friends and fellow-men!" said Slackbridge then, shaking his head with violent scorn, "I do not wonder that you, the prostrate sons of labour, are incredulous of the existence of such a man. But he who sold his birthright for a mess of pottage existed, and Judas Iscariot existed, and this man exists!"

Here, a brief press and confusion near the stage, ended in the man himself standing at the orator's side before the concourse. He was pale but he stood quiet, with his left hand at his chin, waiting to be heard. There was a chairman to regulate the proceedings, and this functionary now took the case into his own hands.

"My friends," said he, "by virtue o' my office as your president, I askes o' our friend Slackbridge, who may be a little over hetter in this business, to take his seat, whiles this man Stephen Blackpool is heern. You all know

91

this man Stephen Blackpool. You know him awlung o' his misfort'ns, and his good name."

With that, the chairman shook his hand, and sat down again. Slackbridge likewise sat down, wiping his hot forehead.

"My friends," Stephen began, in the midst of a dead calm. "I ha' hed what's been spok'n o' me, and 'tis lickly that I shan't mend it. But I'd liefer you'd hearn the truth concernin myseln, fro my lips than fro any other man's, though I never cud'n speak afore so many, wi'out bein muddled."

Slackbridge shook his head in his bitterness.

"I'm th' one single Hand in Bounderby's mill, o' a' the men theer, as don't coom in wi' th' proposed reg'lations. I canna' coom in wi' 'em. My friends, I doubt their doin' yo any good. Licker they'll do yo hurt."

Slackbridge laughed and folded his arms.

"But 't an't sommuch for that as I stands out. If that were aw, I'd coom in wi' th' rest. But I ha' my reasons – mine, yo see – for being hindered; not on'y now, but awlus – awlus – life long!"

Slackbridge jumped up and stood beside him, gnashing and tearing. "Oh, my friends, what but this did I tell you? Oh, my fellow-countrymen, what warning but this did I give you? And how shows this recreant conduct in a man on whom unequal laws are known to have fallen heavy? Oh, you Englishmen, I ask you how does this subornation show in one of yourselves, who is thus consenting to his own undoing and to yours, and to your children's and your children's children's?"

There was some applause, and some crying of Shame upon the man; but the greater part of the audience was quiet. They looked at Stephen's worn face, rendered more pathetic by the homely emotions it evinced; and, in the kindness of their nature, they were more sorry than indignant.

"'Tis this Delegate's trade t' speak," said Stephen, "an' he's paid for 't, an he knows his work. Let him keep to 't. Let him give no heed to what I ha had'n to bear. That's not for him. It's not for nobbody but me."

There was a dignity in these words, that made the hearers yet more quiet and attentive. The same strong voice called out, "Slackbridge, let the man be heern, and howd thee tongue!" Then the place was wonderfully still.

"My brothers," said Stephen, whose low voice was distinctly heard, "and my fellow-workmen, for that yo are to me, though not, as I knows on, to this delegate here, I ha but a word to sen, and I could sen nommore if I was to speak till Strike o' day. I know weel, aw what's afore me. I know weel that yo aw resolve to ha nommore ado wi' a man who is not wi' yo in this matter. I know weel that if I was a lyin parisht i' th' road, yo'd feel it right to pass me by, as a forrenner and stranger. What I ha getn, I mun mak th' best on."

"Stephen Blackpool," said the chairman, rising, "think on 't agen. Think on't once agen, lad, afore thour't shunned by aw owd friends."

There was a universal murmur to the same effect, though no man articulated a word. Every eye was fixed on Stephen's face. To repent of his determination, would be to take a load from all their minds. He looked around him, and knew that it was so. Not a grain of anger with them was in his heart. He knew them, far below their surface weaknesses and misconceptions, as no one but their fellow-labourer could.

"I ha thowt on't, above a bit, sir. I simply canna coom in. I mun go th' way as lays afore me. I mun tak my leave o' aw heer."

He made a sort of reverence to them by holding up his arms, and stood for the moment in that attitude, not speaking until they slowly dropped at his sides.

"Many's the pleasant word as soom heer has spok'n wi' me; many's the face I see heer, as I first seen when I were yoong and lighter heart'n than now. I ha' never had no fratch afore, sin ever I were born, wi' any o' my like. God knows I ha' none now that's o' my makin'. Yo'll ca' me traitor and that – yo I mean t' say," he addressed Slackbridge, "but 'tis easier to ca' than mak' out. So let be."

He had moved away a pace or two to come down from the platform, when he remembered something he had not said, and returned again.

"Haply," he said, turning his furrowed face slowly about, that he might as it were individually address the whole audience, those both near and distant; "haply, when this question has been tak'n up and discoosed, there'll be a threat to turn out if I'm let to work among yo. I hope I shall die ere ever such a time cooms, and I shall work solitary among yo unless it cooms – truly, I mun do't, my friends; not to brave yo, but to live. I ha nobbut work to live by; and wheerever can I go, I who ha worked sin I were no height at aw, in Coketown heer? I mak' no complaints o' bein turned to the wa', o' bein outcasten and overlooken fro this time forrard, but I hope I shall be let to work. If there is any right for me at aw, my friends, I think 'tis that."

Not a word was spoken. Not a sound was audible in the building, but the slight rustle of men moving a little apart, all along the centre of the room, to open a means of passing out, to the man with whom they had all bound themselves to renounce companionship. Looking at no one, and going his way with a lowly steadiness upon him that asserted nothing and sought nothing, Old Stephen, with all his troubles on his head, left the scene.

Then Slackbridge, who had kept his oratorical arm extended during the going out, as if he were repressing with infinite solicitude and by a wonderful moral power the vehement passions of the multitude, applied himself to raising their spirits. Three cheers for the United Aggregate Tribunal!

Slackbridge acted as fugleman, and gave the time. The multitude of doubtful faces (a little conscience-stricken) brightened at the sound, and took it up. Private feeling must yield to the common cause. Hurrah! The roof vibrated with the cheering.

So Stephen Blackpool fell into the loneliest of lives, the life of solitude among a familiar crowd. The stranger who looks into ten thousand faces for some answering look and never finds it, is far happier compared to him who passes ten averted faces daily, that were once friends. Such experience was to be Stephen's now, in every waking moment of his life; at his work, on his way to it and from it, at his door, at his window, everywhere. By general consent, they even avoided that side of the street on which he habitually walked.

He had been for many years, a quiet silent man, associating but little with other men, and used to his own thoughts for company. He had never known before the strong desire for the frequent recognition of a nod, a look, a word; or the immense amount of relief that had been poured into it by drops through such small means. It was even harder than he could have believed possible, to separate in his own conscience his abandonment by all his fellows from a baseless sense of shame and disgrace.

The first four days of his endurance were days so long and heavy, that he began to be appalled by the prospect before him. Not only did he see no Rachael all the time but he avoided every chance of seeing her. He knew that the prohibition did not yet extend to the working women, but he found that some of those he knew were changed to him, and he feared to try others, dreading that Rachael might be singled out if she were seen in his company. So, he had been quite alone during the four days, and had spoken to no one. But this night, as he was leaving his work, a young man of a very light complexion accosted him in the street.

"Your name's Blackpool, ain't it?" said the young man.

Stephen coloured to find himself with his hat in his hand, in his gratitude for being spoken to. He fiddled with the lining, saying, "Yes."

"You are the Hand they have sent to Coventry, I mean?" said Bitzer, the very light young man in question.

Stephen answered "Yes," again.

"Mr Bounderby wants to speak to you. You know his house, don't you?"

Stephen said "Yes," again.

"Then go straight there, will you?" said Bitzer. "You're expected, so just tell the servant it's you. I belong to the Bank; so, if you go up without me (I was sent to fetch you), you'll save me a walk."

Stephen, who had been bound in the contrary direction, turned and betook himself to the red brick castle of the giant Bounderby.

CHAPTER 5

"Well Stephen," said Bounderby, in his windy manner, "what's this I hear? What have these pests of the earth been doing to you? Come in, and speak up."

He was taken to the drawing room. A tea table was set out and Mr Bounderby's young wife, her brother, and a gentleman from London, were present. To whom Stephen made his obeisance, closing the door and standing near it, with his hat in his hand.

"This is the man I was telling you about, Harthouse," said Mr Bounderby. The gentleman he addressed, who was talking to Mrs Bounderby on the sofa, got up, saying in an indolent way, "Oh really?" and dawdled to the hearth-rug where Mr Bounderby stood.

"Now," said Bounderby, "speak up!"

After the four days he had had, these words fell rudely on Stephen's ear. Besides being a rough handling of his wounded mind, it seemed to assume that he really was the self-interested deserter he had been called.

"What were it, sir," said Stephen, "as yo were pleased to want wi' me?"

"Why, I have told you," returned Bounderby. "Speak up like a man, and tell us about yourself and this Combination."

"Wi' yor pardon, sir," said Stephen Blackpool, "I ha' nowt to sen about it."

Mr Bounderby, who was always more or less like a Wind, finding something in his way here, began to blow at it directly.

"Now, look here, Harthouse," said he, "here's a specimen of 'em. When this man was here once before, I warned him against the mischievous strangers who are always about – and who ought to be hanged wherever they are found – and I told him that he was going in the wrong direction. Now, would you believe it, that although they have put this mark upon him, he is such a slave to them still, that he's afraid to open his lips about them?"

"I sed as I had nowt to sen, sir; not as I was fearfo' o' openin' my lips."

"You said! Ah! More than that, I know what you mean, you see. Not always the same thing, by the Lord Harry! You had better tell us at once, that that fellow Slackbridge is not in the town, stirring up the people to mutiny, and that he is not a regular qualified leader of the people, in other words a confounded scoundrel. You had better tell us so at once; you can't deceive me. Why don't you tell us?"

"I'm as sooary as yo, sir, when the people's leaders is bad," said Stephen, shaking his head. "They take such as offers. Haply 'tis na' the sma'est o' their misfortuns when they can get no better."

The wind began to get boisterous.

"Now, you'll think this pretty well, Harthouse," said Mr Bounderby. "You'll say, upon my soul this is a tidy specimen of what my friends have to deal with – but this is nothing, sir! You shall hear me ask this man a question. Pray, Mr Blackpool" – wind springing up very fast – "may I take the liberty of asking you how it happens that you refused to be in this Combination?"

"How't happens?"

"Ah!" said Mr Bounderby, with his thumbs in the arms of his coat, and jerking his head and shutting his eyes in confidence with the opposite wall, "how it happens."

"I'd leefer not coom to't, sir; but sin you put th' question – an not want'n t' be ill-manner'n – I'll answer. I ha passed a promess."

"Not to me, you know," said Bounderby. (Gusty weather with deceitful calms. One now prevailing.)

"O no, sir. Not to yo."

"As for me, any consideration for me has had just nothing at all to do with it," said Bounderby, still in confidence with the wall. "If only Josiah Bounderby of Coketown had been in question, you would have joined and made no bones about it?"

"Why yes, sir. 'Tis true."

"Though he knows," said Mr Bounderby, now blowing a gale, "that they are a set of rascals and rebels whom transportation is too good for! Now, Mr Harthouse, you have been knocking about in the world some time. Did you ever meet with anything like that man out of this blessed country?" And Mr Bounderby pointed him out for inspection, with an angry finger.

"Nay, ma'am," said Stephen Blackpool, staunchly protesting against the words that had been used, and instinctively addressing himself to Louisa, after glancing at her face. "Not rebels, nor yet rascals. Nowt o' th' kind, ma'am. They've not doon me a kindness, ma'am, as I know and feel. But there's not a dozen men amoong 'em, ma'am – a dozen? Not six – but what believes as he has doon his duty by the rest and by himseln. God forbid as I, that ha known, and had'n experience o' these men aw my life – I, that ha ett'n an droonken wi' 'em, an seet'n wi' 'em, and toil'n wi' 'em, and lov'n 'em, should fail fur to stan by 'em wi' the truth, let 'em ha doon to me what they may!"

He spoke with the rugged earnestness of his place and character – deepened perhaps by a proud consciousness that he was faithful to his class under all their mistrust; but he fully remembered where he was, and did not raise his voice.

"No, ma'am, no. They're true to one another, faithfo' to one another, fectionate to one another, e'en to death. Be poor amoong 'em, be sick amoong 'em, grieve amoong 'em for any o' th' many causes that carries grief to the poor man's door, and they'll be tender wi' yo, gentle wi' yo, comfortable wi' yo, Chrisen wi' yo. Be sure o' that, ma'am. They'd be riven to bits, ere ever they'd be different."

"In short," said Mr Bounderby, "it's because they are so full of virtues that they have turned you adrift. Go through with it while you are about it. Out with it."

"How 'tis, ma'am," resumed Stephen, appearing still to find his natural refuge in Louisa's face, "that what is best in us fok, seems to turn us the most to trouble an misfort'n an mistake, I dunno. But 'tis so. I know 'tis, as I know the heavens is over me ahint the smoke. We're patient too, an wants in general to do right. An' I canna think the fawt is aw wi' us."

"Now, my friend," said Mr Bounderby, "if you will favour me with your attention for half a minute, I should like to have a word or two with you. You said just now, that you had nothing to tell us about this business. You are quite sure of that before we continue."

"Sir, I am sure on 't."

"Here's a gentleman from London," Mr Bounderby made a back-handed point at Mr James Harthouse with his thumb, "a Parliament gentleman. I should like him to hear a short bit of dialogue between you and me, instead of taking the substance of it – for I know precious well, beforehand, what it will be; nobody knows better than I do! – instead of receiving it on trust from my mouth."

Stephen bent his head to the gentleman from London, and showed a rather more troubled mind than usual. He turned his eyes involuntarily to his former refuge, but at a look from that quarter (expressive though instantaneous) he settled them on Mr Bounderby's face.

"Now, what do you complain of?" asked Mr Bounderby.

"I ha' not coom here, sir," Stephen reminded him, "to complain. I coom for that I were sent for."

"What," repeated Mr Bounderby, folding his arms, "do you people, in a general way, complain of?"

Stephen looked at him with some little irresolution for a moment, and then seemed to make up his mind.

"Sir, I were never good at showin o 't, though I ha had'n my share in feeling o 't. 'Deed we are in a muddle, sir. Look round town – so rich as 'tis – and see the numbers o' people as has been broughten into bein heer, fur to weave, an to card, an to piece out a livin', aw the same one way, somehows, twixt their cradles and their graves. Look how we live, and wheer we live, an in what numbers, an by what chances, an wi' what sameness; and look how the mills is awlus a goin, and how they never works us no nigher to any dis'ant object – ceptin awlus, Death. Look how you considers of us, and writes of us, and talks of us, and goes up wi' yor deputations to Secretaries o' State 'bout us, and how yo are awlus right, and how we are awlus wrong, and never had'n no reason in us sin ever we were born. Look how this ha growen an growen, sir, bigger an' bigger, broader an broader, harder an harder, fro year to year, fro generation unto generation. Who can look on 't, sir, and fairly tell a man 'tis not a muddle?"

"Of course," said Mr Bounderby. "Now perhaps you'll let the gentleman know, how you would set this – muddle – to rights."

"I donno, sir. I canna be expecten to 't. 'Tis not me as should be looken to for that, sir. 'Tis them as is put ower me, and ower aw the rest of us. What do they tak upon themseln, sir, if not to do't?"

"I'll tell you something towards it, at any rate," returned Mr Bounderby. "We will make an example of half a dozen Slackbridges. We'll indict the blackguards for felony, and get 'em shipped off to penal settlements."

Stephen gravely shook his head.

"Don't tell me we won't, man," said Mr Bounderby, by this time blowing a hurricane, "because we will, I tell you!"

"Sir," returned Stephen, with the quiet confidence of absolute certainty, "if yo was t' tak a hundred Slackbridges – aw as there is, and aw the number ten times towd – an' was t' sew 'em up in separate sacks, an sink 'em in the deepest oceans, yo'd leave the muddle just wheer 'tis. Mischeevous strangers!" said Stephen, with an anxious smile; "when ha we not heern, I am sure, sin ever we can call to mind, o' th' mischeevous strangers! 'Tis not by them the trouble's made, sir. 'Tis not wi' them 't commences. I ha no favour for 'em – I ha no reason to favour 'em – but 'tis hopeless and useless to dream o' takin them fro their trade, 'stead o' takin their trade fro them! Aw that's now about me in this room were heer afore I coom, an will be heer when I am gone. Put that clock aboard a ship an pack it off to Norfolk Island, an the time will go on just the same. So 'tis wi' Slackbridge every bit."

Reverting for a moment to his former refuge, he observed a cautionary movement of her eyes towards the door. Stepping back, he put his hand upon the lock. But he had not spoken out of his own will and desire; and he felt it in his heart a noble return for his late injurious treatment to be faithful to the last to those who had repudiated him. He stayed to finish what was in his mind.

"Sir, I canna, wi' my little learning an my common way, tell the genelman what will better aw this – though some working-men o' this town could, above my powers – but I can tell him what I know will never do 't. The strong hand will never do 't. Vict'ry and triumph will never do 't. Agreeing fur to mak one side unnat'rally awlus and forever right, and toother side unnat'rally awlus and forever wrong, will never, never do 't. Nor yet lettin alone will never do 't. Let thousands upon thousands alone, aw leading the like lives and aw faw'en into the like muddle, and they will be as one, and yo will be as anoother, wi' a black unpassable world betwixt yo, just as long or short a time as sitch-like misery can last. Not drawin nigh to fok, wi' kindness and patience an cheery ways, that so draws nigh to one another in their many troubles, and so cherishes one another in their distresses wi' what they need themseln – like, I humbly believe, as no people the genelman ha seen in aw his travels can beat – will never do 't till th' Sun turns t' ice. Most o' aw, rating 'em as so much Power, and reg'latin 'em as if they was figures in a soom, or machines: wi'out loves and likens, wi'out memories and inclinations, wi'out souls to weary and souls to hope – when aw goes quiet, draggin on wi' 'em as if they'd nowt o' th' kind, and when aw goes unquiet, reproachin 'em for their want o' sitch humanly feelins in their dealins wi' yo – this will never do 't, sir, till God's work is unmade."

Stephen stood with the open door in his hand, waiting to know if anything more were expected of him.

"Just stop a moment," said Mr Bounderby, excessively red in the face. "I told you, the last time you were here with a grievance, that you had better turn about and come out of that. And I also told you, if you remember, that I was up to the gold spoon lookout."

"I were not up to 't myseln, sir; I do assure yo."

"Now it's clear to me," said Mr Bounderby, "that you are one of those chaps who have always got a grievance. And you go about, sowing it and raising crops. That's the business of your life, my friend."

Stephen shook his head, mutely protesting that indeed he had other business to do for his life.

"You are such a waspish, ill-conditioned chap, you see," said Mr Bounderby, "that even your own Union, the men who know you best, will have nothing to do with you. I never thought those fellows could be right in anything; but I tell you what! I so far go along with them for a novelty, that I'll have nothing to do with you either."

Stephen raised his eyes quickly to his face.

"You can finish off what you're at," said Mr Bounderby, with a meaning nod, "and then go elsewhere."

"Sir, yo know weel," said Stephen expressively, "that if I canna get work wi' yo, I canna get it elsewheer."

The reply was, "What I know, I know; and what you know, you know. I have no more to say about it."

Stephen glanced at Louisa again, but her eyes were raised to his no more; therefore, with a sigh, and saying, barely above his breath, "Heaven help us aw in this world!" he departed.

CHAPTER 6

It was growing dark when Stephen came out of Mr Bounderby's house. He did not look about him when he closed the door, but plodded straight along the street. Nothing was further from his thoughts than the curious old woman he had encountered on his previous visit to the same house, when he heard a step behind him that he knew, and turning, saw her in Rachael's company.

He saw Rachael first, as he had heard her only.

"Ah, Rachael, my dear! Missus, thou wi' her!"

"Well, and now you are surprised to be sure, and with reason I must say," the old woman returned. "Here I am again, you see."

"But how wi' Rachael?" said Stephen, falling into their step, walking between them, and looking from the one to the other.

"Why, I come to be with this good lass pretty much as I came to be with you," said the old woman, cheerfully, taking the reply upon herself. "My visiting time is later this year than usual, for I have been rather troubled with shortness of breath, and so put it off till the weather was fine and warm. For the same reason I divide my journey into two days, and get a bed tonight at the Travellers' Coffee House down by the railroad and go back at six in the morning. Well, but what has this to do with this good lass, says you? I'm going to tell you. I have heard of Mr Bounderby being married. I read it in the paper, where it looked grand – oh, it looked fine!" the old woman dwelt on it with strange enthusiasm. "I want to see his wife. I have never seen her yet. Now, if you'll believe me, she hasn't come out of that house since noon today. So I was waiting about, a little last bit more, when I passed close to this good lass two or three times. Her face being so friendly I spoke to her, and she spoke to me. There!" said the old woman to Stephen, "you can make all the rest out for yourself now!"

Once again, Stephen had to conquer an instinct to dislike this old woman, though her manner was as honest as a manner possibly could be. With a gentleness that was as natural to him as he knew it to be to Rachael, he pursued the subject that interested her in her old age.

"Well, missus," said he, "I ha seen the lady, and she were young and hansom. Wi' fine dark thinkin eyes, and a still way, Rachael, as I ha never seen the like on."

"Young and handsome. Yes!" cried the old woman, quite delighted. "As bonny as a rose! And what a happy wife!"

"Aye, missus, I suppose she be," said Stephen. But with a doubtful glance at Rachael.

"Suppose she be? She must be. She's your master's wife," returned the old woman.

Stephen nodded assent. "Though as to master," said he, glancing again at Rachael, "not master any more. That's aw enden twixt him and me."

"Have you left his work, Stephen?" asked Rachael, anxiously and quickly.

"Why, Rachael," he replied, "whether I ha lef'n his work, or whether his work ha lef'n me, cooms t' th' same. His work and me are parted. 'Tis as weel so – better, I were thinkin when yo coom up wi' me. It would ha brought'n trouble upon trouble if I had stayed theer. Haply 'tis a kindness to many that I go; haply 'tis a kindness to myseln; anyways it mun be done. I mun turn my face fro Coketown fur th' time, and seek a fort'n, dear, by beginnin fresh."

"Where will you go, Stephen?"

"I donno t'night," said he, lifting off his hat, and smoothing his hair.

"But I'm not goin t'night, Rachael, nor yet t'morrow. 'Tan't easy t' know wheer t' turn, but a good heart will coom to me."

Herein, too, the sense of even thinking unselfishly aided him. Before he had so much as closed Mr Bounderby's door, he had reflected that at least his being obliged to go away was good for her, as it would save her from the chance of being brought into question for not withdrawing from him. Though it would cost him a hard pang to leave her, perhaps it was almost a relief to be forced away from the endurance of the last four days, even to unknown difficulties and distresses.

So he said, with truth, "I'm more leetsome, Rachael, under 't, than I could'n ha believed." It was not her part to make his burden heavier. She answered with her comforting smile, and the three walked on together.

"Come to my poor place, missus," said Stephen, "and tak a coop o' tea. Rachael will coom then; and arterwards I'll see thee safe t' thy Travellers' lodgin. 'T may be long, Rachael, ere ever I ha th' chance o' thy coompany agen."

They complied, and the three went on to his lodging. When they turned into the street, Stephen glanced at his window with a dread but it was open, as he had left it, and no one was there. The evil spirit of his life had flitted away again, months ago, and he had heard no more of her since.

He lit a candle, set out his little tea-board, got hot water from below, and brought in small portions of tea and sugar, a loaf, and some butter from the nearest shop. The bread was new and crusty, the butter fresh, and the sugar lump, of course – proving the standard testimony of the Coketown magnates, that these people lived like princes, sir. Rachael made the tea (so large a party necessitated the borrowing of a cup), and the visitor enjoyed it mightily. It was the first glimpse of sociality the host had had for many days. He too, with the world a wide heath before him, enjoyed the meal – again in corroboration of the magnates, as exemplifying the utter want of calculation on the part of these people, sir.

"I ha never thowt yet, missus," said Stephen, "o' askin thy name."

The old lady announced herself as "Mrs Pegler."

"A widder, I think?" said Stephen.

"Oh, many long years!" Mrs Pegler's husband (one of the best on record) was already dead, by Mrs Pegler's calculation, when Stephen was born.

"'Twere a bad job, too, to lose so good a one," said Stephen. "Any children?"

Mrs Pegler's cup rattled against her saucer, indicating some nervousness. "No," she said. "Not now, not now."

"Dead, Stephen," Rachael softly hinted.

"I'm sooary I ha spok'n on 't," said Stephen, "I ought t' hadn in my mind as I might touch a sore place. I blame myseln."

While he excused himself, the old lady's cup rattled more and more. "I had a son," she said, curiously distressed, "and he did well, wonderfully well. But he is not to be spoken of if you please. He is – " Putting down her cup, she moved her hands as if to say, by her action, "dead!" Then she said aloud, "I have lost him."

Stephen had not yet got the better of his having given the old lady pain, when his landlady came stumbling up the narrow stairs, and calling him to the door, whispered in his ear. Mrs Pegler was by no means deaf, for she caught a word as it was uttered.

"Bounderby!" she cried, in a suppressed voice, starting up from the table. "Oh hide me! Don't let me be seen for the world. Don't let him come up till I've got away. Pray, pray!" She trembled, and tried to hide behind Rachael. Rachael tried to reassure her, and she seemed not to know what she was about.

"But hearken, missus, hearken," said Stephen, astonished. "'Tisn't Mr Bounderby; 'tis his wife. Yor not fearfo' o' her. Yo was hey-go-mad about her, but an hour sin."

"But are you sure it's the lady, and not the gentleman?" she asked, still trembling.

"Certain sure!"

"Well then, pray don't speak to me, nor take any notice of me," said the old woman. "Let me stay in this corner."

Stephen nodded, looking to Rachael for an explanation, which she was quite unable to give him. He took the candle, went downstairs, and in a few moments returned, lighting Louisa into the room. She was followed by the whelp.

Rachael stood apart with her shawl and bonnet in her hand, when Stephen, himself profoundly astonished by this visit, put the candle on the table. Then he too stood waiting to be addressed.

For the first time in her life Louisa had come into one of the dwellings of the Coketown Hands. She knew of their existence. She knew what results in work a given number of them would produce in a given space of time. She knew them in crowds passing to and from their nests, like ants or beetles. But she knew from her reading infinitely more of the ways of toiling insects than of these toiling men and women.

She stood for some moments looking round the room. From the few chairs, the few books, the common prints, and the bed, she glanced to the two women, and to Stephen.

"I have come to speak to you, following what passed just now. I should like to help you, if you will let me. Is this your wife?"

Rachael raised her eyes, and they sufficiently answered no, and dropped again.

"I remember," said Louisa, reddening at her mistake. "I recollect, now, to have heard your domestic misfortunes spoken of, though I was not listening to the details at the time. I didn't intend to ask a question that would give pain to any one here. If I should ask any other question that may happen to have that result, give me credit, if you please, for being ignorant of how I should speak to you."

As Stephen had but a little while ago instinctively addressed himself to her, so she now instinctively addressed herself to Rachael. Her manner was short and abrupt, yet faltering and timid.

"He has told you what has passed between himself and my husband? You would be his first resource, I think."

"I have heard the end of it, young lady," said Rachael.

"Did I understand, that, being rejected by one employer, he would probably be rejected by all? I thought he said as much?"

"The chances are very small, young lady – next to nothing – for a man who gets a bad name among them."

"What shall I understand that you mean by a bad name?"

"The name of being troublesome."

"Then, by the prejudices of his own class, and by the prejudices of the other, he is sacrificed alike? Are the two so deeply separated in this town, that there is no place whatever for an honest workman between them?"

Rachael shook her head in silence.

"He fell into suspicion," said Louisa, "with his fellows, because – he had made a promise not to be one of them. I think it must have been to you that he made that promise. Might I ask you why he made it?"

Rachael burst into tears. "I didn't seek it of him, poor lad. I prayed him to avoid trouble for his own good, little thinking he'd come to it through me. But I know he'd die a hundred deaths, ere ever he'd break his word. I know that of him well."

Stephen had remained quietly attentive, in his usual thoughtful attitude, with his hand at his chin. He now spoke in a voice rather less steady than usual.

"No one, excepting myseln, can ever know what honour, an what love, an respect, I bear to Rachael, or wi' what cause. When I passed that promess, I towd her true, she were th' Angel o' my life. 'Twere a solemn promess. 'Tis gone fro' me, for ever."

Louisa turned her head to him, and bent it with a deference that was new in her. She looked from him to Rachael, and her features softened. "What will you do?" she asked him. And her voice had softened too.

"Weel, ma'am," said Stephen, making the best of it, with a smile; "when I ha finished off, I mun quit this part, and try another. Fortnet or misfortnet, a man can but try, there's nowt to be done wi'out tryin' – 'cept laying down and dying."

"How will you travel?"

"Afoot, my kind ledy, afoot."

Louisa coloured, and a purse appeared in her hand. The rustling of a bank note was audible, as she unfolded one and laid it on the table.

"Rachael, will you tell him – for you know how, without offence – that this is freely his, to help him on his way? Will you entreat him to take it?"

"I canna do that, young lady," she answered, turning her head aside. "Bless you for thinking o' the poor lad wi' such tenderness. But he knows his heart, and what is right according to it."

Louisa looked, in part incredulous, in part frightened, in part overcome with quick sympathy, when this man of so much self-command, who had been so plain and steady through the late interview, lost his composure in a moment, and now stood with his hand before his face. She stretched out hers, as if she would have touched him; then checked herself, and remained still.

"Not even Rachael," said Stephen, when he stood again with his face uncovered, "could mak sitch a kind offerin, by any words, kinder. T' show that I'm not a man wi'out reason and gratitude, I'll tak two pound. I'll borrow 't for t' pay 't back. 'Twill be the sweetest work, that puts it in

106

my power t' acknowledge once more my lastin thankfulness for this present action."

She was fain to take up the note again, and to substitute the much smaller sum he had named. He was neither courtly, nor handsome, nor picturesque, in any respect; and yet his manner of accepting it, and of expressing his thanks without more words, had a grace in it that Lord Chesterfield could not have taught his son in a century.

Tom had sat upon the bed, swinging one leg and sucking his walking stick, until this point in the visit. Seeing his sister ready to depart, he got up, rather hurriedly, and put in a word.

"Wait a moment, Loo! Before we go, I should like to speak to him. Something comes to me. If you'll step out on the stairs, Blackpool, I'll mention it."

Stephen followed him out, and Tom closed the room door, and held the lock in his hand.

"I say!" he whispered. "I think I can do you a good turn. Don't ask me what it is, because it may not come to anything. But there's no harm in my trying."

His breath fell like a flame of fire on Stephen's ear, it was so hot.

"That was our light porter at the Bank," said Tom, "who brought you the message tonight. I call him our light porter, because I belong to the Bank too."

Stephen thought, "What a hurry he is in!" He spoke so confusedly.

"Well!" said Tom. "Now look here! When are you off?"

"T' day's Monday," replied Stephen, considering. "Why, sir, Friday or Saturday, nigh 'bout."

"Friday or Saturday," said Tom. "Now look here! I am not sure that I can do you the good turn I want to do you – that's my sister, you know, in your room – but I may be able to, and if I should not be able to, there's no harm done. So I tell you what. You'll know our light porter again?"

"Yes, sure," said Stephen.

"Very well," returned Tom. "When you leave work of a night, between this and your going away, just hang about the Bank an hour or so, will you? Now I shan't put him up to speak to you, unless I find I can do you the service I want to do you. In which case he'll have a note or a message for you, but not otherwise. Now look here! You are sure you understand."

He had wormed a finger, in the darkness, through a buttonhole of

Stephen's coat, and was screwing that corner of the garment tight up round and round, in an extraordinary manner.

"I understand, sir," said Stephen.

"Now look here!" repeated Tom. "Be sure you don't make any mistake then, and don't forget. I shall tell my sister as we go home, what I have in view, and she'll approve, I know. Now look here! You understand all about it? Very well then. Come along, Loo!"

He pushed the door open as he called to her, but did not return into the room, or wait to be lighted down the narrow stairs. He was at the bottom when she began to descend, and was in the street before she could take his arm.

Mrs Pegler remained in her corner until the brother and sister were gone, and until Stephen came back with the candle in his hand. She was in a state of inexpressible admiration of Mrs Bounderby, and wept, "because she was such a pretty dear." Yet Mrs Pegler was so flurried lest the object of her admiration should return by chance, or anybody else should come, that her cheerfulness was ended for that night. It was late too, to people who rose early and worked hard, therefore the party broke up. Stephen and Rachael escorted their mysterious acquaintance to the door of the Travellers' Coffee House, where they parted from her.

They walked back together to the corner of the street where Rachael lived, and as they drew nearer and nearer to it, silence crept upon them. When they came to the dark corner where their infrequent meetings always ended, they stopped, still silent, as if afraid to speak.

"I shall strive t' see thee agen, Rachael, afore I go, but if not – "

"Thou wilt not, Stephen, I know. 'Tis better that we make up our minds to be open wi' one another."

"Thou'rt awlus right. 'Tis bolder and better. I ha been thinkin then, Rachael, that as 'tis but a day or two that remains, 'twere better for thee, my dear, not t' be seen wi' me. 'T might bring thee into trouble, fur no good."

"'Tis not for that, Stephen, that I mind. But thou know'st our old agreement. 'Tis for that."

"Well, well," said he. "'Tis better, anyways."

"Thou'lt write to me, and tell me all that happens, Stephen?"

"Yes. What can I say now, but Heaven be wi' thee, Heaven bless thee, Heaven thank thee and reward thee!"

"May it bless thee, Stephen, too, in all thy wanderings, and send thee peace and rest at last!"

"I towd thee, my dear," said Stephen Blackpool – "that night – that I would never see or think o' anything that angered me, but thou, so much better than me, should'st be beside it. Thou'rt beside it now. Thou mak'st me see it wi' a better eye. Bless thee. Good-night. Good bye!"

It was but a hurried parting in a common street, yet it was a sacred remembrance to these two common people.

Stephen worked the next day, and the next shunned in all his comings and goings as before. At the end of the second day, he saw land, at the end of the third, his loom stood empty.

He had overstayed his hour in the street outside the Bank, on each of the two first evenings. Nothing had happened there, good or bad. That he might not be remiss in his part of the engagement, he resolved to wait full two hours, on this third and last night.

There was the lady who had once kept Mr Bounderby's house, sitting at the first floor window as he had seen her before; and there was the light porter. When he first came out, Stephen thought he might be looking for him, and passed near, but the light porter only cast his winking eyes upon him slightly, and said nothing.

Two hours were a long stretch to lounge about, after a long day's labour. Stephen sat upon the step of a door, leaned against a wall under an archway, strolled up and down, listened for the church clock, stopped and watched children playing in the street. Some purpose or other is so natural to every one, that a mere loiterer always looks and feels remarkable. When the first hour was out, Stephen even began to have an uncomfortable sensation upon him of being for the time the disreputable character.

Then came the lamp-lighter. Eventually Mrs Sparsit closed the first floor window, drew down the blind, and went upstairs. Presently, a light went upstairs after her, passing first the fanlight of the door, and afterwards the two staircase windows, on its way up. By-and-by, one corner of the second floor blind was disturbed, as if Mrs Sparsit's eye were there; also the other corner, as if the light porter's eye were on that side. Still, no communication was made to Stephen. Much relieved when the two hours were at last accomplished, he went away at a quick pace, to make up for so much loitering.

He had only to take leave of his landlady, and lie down on his temporary bed upon the floor; for his bundle was made up for tomorrow. All was arranged for his departure. He meant to be clear of the town very early before the Hands were in the streets.

It was barely daybreak, when, with a parting look round his room, wondering whether he should ever see it again, he went out. The town was as entirely deserted as if the inhabitants had abandoned it. Everything looked wan at that hour. Even the coming sun made but a pale waste in the sky, like a sad sea.

By the place where Rachael lived, though it was not on his way, by the red brick streets, by the great silent factories, by the railway, where the danger-lights were waning in the strengthening day, by scattered red brick villas, by coal-dust paths and many varieties of ugliness – Stephen got to the top of the hill, and looked back.

Day was shining radiantly upon the town then, and the bells were going for the morning work.

So strange turning from the chimneys to the birds. So strange having road-dust on his feet instead of coal-grit. So strange to have lived to his time of life, and yet to be beginning like a boy this summer morning! With these musings in his mind, and his bundle under his arm, Stephen turned along the high road. The trees arched over him, whispering that he left a true and loving heart behind.

CHAPTER 7

Mr James Harthouse, "going in" for his adopted party, soon began to score. With the aid of a tolerable management of the assumed honesty in dishonesty, most effective and most patronised of the polite deadly sins, he speedily came to be considered of much promise. The not being troubled with earnestness was in his favour, enabling him to take to the hard Fact fellows with as good a grace as if he had been born one of the tribe, and to throw all other tribes overboard, as conscious hypocrites.

"Whom none of us believe, my dear Mrs Bounderby, and who do not believe themselves. The only difference between us and the professors of virtue or benevolence, or philanthropy – never mind the name – is, that we know it is all meaningless, and say so; while they know it equally and will never say so."

Why should she be shocked or warned by this reiteration? It was not so unlike her father's principles, and her early training, that it need startle her. Where was the great difference between the two schools, when each chained her down to material realities, and inspired her with no faith in anything else? What was there in her soul for James Harthouse to destroy, which Thomas Gradgrind had nurtured there in its state of innocence!

It was even the worse for her at this point that in her mind – implanted there before her father began to form it – a struggling disposition to believe in a wider and nobler humanity than she had ever heard of, constantly strove with doubts and resentments. With doubts, because the aspiration had been so laid waste in her youth. With resentments, because of the wrong that had been done her, if it were indeed a whisper of the truth. Upon a nature long accustomed to self-suppression, thus torn and divided, the Harthouse philosophy came as a relief and justification. Everything being hollow and worthless, she had missed nothing and sacrificed nothing. What did it matter, she had said to her father, when he proposed her husband. What did it matter, she said still. With a scornful self-reliance, she asked herself, What did anything matter – and went on.

Towards what? Step by step, onward and downward, towards some end, yet so gradually, that she believed herself to remain motionless. As to Mr Harthouse, whither he tended, he neither considered nor cared. He had no particular design or plan before him: no energetic wickedness ruffled his lassitude. He was as much amused and interested, at present, as it became so fine a gentleman to be. Soon after his arrival he wrote to his brother, the honourable member, that the Bounderbys were "great fun", and further, that the female Bounderby, instead of being the Gorgon he had expected, was young, and remarkably pretty. After that, he wrote no more about them, and devoted his leisure chiefly to their house. He was very often in their house and was much encouraged by Mr Bounderby. It was quite Mr Bounderby's gusty way to boast to all in his world that he didn't care about your highly connected people, but that if his wife Tom Gradgrind's daughter did, she was welcome to their company.

Mr James Harthouse began to wonder if the face that changed so beautifully for the whelp would change for him.

He watched and had a good memory, and forgot not a word of the brother's revelations. He interwove them with everything he saw of the sister, and began to understand her. To be sure, the better and profounder part of her character was not within his scope of perception; for in natures, as in seas, depth answers unto depth; but he soon began to read the rest with a student's eye.

Mr Bounderby had taken possession of a house and grounds, about fifteen miles from the town. The bank had foreclosed a mortgage effected on the property. A Coketown magnate, who, in his determination to make a shorter cut than usual to an enormous fortune, over-speculated by about two hundred thousand pounds.

It afforded Mr Bounderby supreme satisfaction to instal himself in this snug little estate, and with demonstrative humility to grow cabbages in the flower-garden.

"Harthouse, you have a couple of horses down here. Bring half a dozen more if you like, and we'll find room for 'em. There's stabling in this place for a dozen horses. You see this place; you know what sort of a place it is; you are aware that there's not a completer place of its size in this kingdom or elsewhere – I don't care where – and here, got into the middle of it, like a maggot into a nut, is Josiah Bounderby. While Nickits (the previous owner) is drivelling at this minute – drivelling, sir! – in a fifth floor, up a narrow dark back street in Antwerp."

It was among the leafy shadows, in the long sultry summer days, that Mr Harthouse began to prove the face that had set him wondering when he first saw it, and to try if it would change for him.

"Mrs Bounderby, it is a most fortunate accident that I find you alone. I have had a particular wish to speak to you for a while."

It was not by any wonderful accident that he found her, as it was the time she was always alone, and the place being her favourite resort near a dark wood, where some felled trees lay. She would sit watching the fallen leaves of last year, as she had watched the falling ashes at home.

He sat down beside her, with a glance at her face.

"Your brother. My young friend Tom – "

Her colour brightened, and she turned to him with a look of interest. "I never in my life," he thought, "saw anything so remarkable and so captivating as the lighting of those features!" His face betrayed his thoughts – perhaps without betraying him.

112

"Pardon me. The expression of your sisterly interest is so beautiful – Tom should be so proud – I know this is inexcusable, but I am so compelled to admire."

"Being so impulsive," she said composedly.

"Mrs Bounderby, you know I make no pretence with you."

"I am waiting," she returned, "for your further reference to my brother."

"You are rigid with me, and I deserve it. I am as worthless a dog as you will find, except that I am not false. But you surprised me from my subject, which was your brother."

"Have you an interest in anything, Mr Harthouse?" she asked, half incredulously and half gratefully.

"If you had asked me when I first came here, I should have said no. But now – at the risk of appearing false, and of justly awakening your incredulity – yes."

She made a slight movement, as if about to speak, and at length she said, "Mr Harthouse, I give you credit for being interested in my brother."

"Thank you. You have done so much for him, you are so fond of him. Your whole life expresses such charming self-forgetfulness on his account – pardon me again – I am running wide of the subject. I am interested in him for his own sake."

She had made the slightest action possible, as if she would have risen in a hurry and gone away. He changed tack, and she stayed.

"Mrs Bounderby," he resumed lightly, yet with a show of effort in assuming it, which was even more expressive than the manner he dismissed. "It is to be expected that a young fellow of your brother's years will be heedless, inconsiderate, and expensive – a little dissipated, in the common phrase. Is he?"

"Yes."

"Allow me to be frank. Do you think he games at all?"

"I think he makes bets." Mr Harthouse waited. A moment later she added, "I know he does."

"Of course he loses?"

"Yes."

"Everybody does lose who bets. May I hint at the probability that you sometimes give him money for these purposes?"

She sat, looking down, but at this question, she looked up a little resentfully.

113

"Forgive my curiosity, my dear Mrs Bounderby. I think Tom may be gradually falling into trouble, and I wish to stretch out a helping hand to him from the depths of my wicked experience. – Shall I say again, for his sake? Is that necessary?"

She seemed to try to answer, but nothing came.

"I will be honest with you," said James Harthouse, again gliding into his more airy manner. "I confide to you my doubt whether he has had many advantages. Whether – forgive my plainness – whether any great amount of confidence is likely to have been established between himself and his father."

"I do not," said Louisa, flushing with her own great remembrance in that wise, "think it likely."

"Or, between himself, and – I am sure you understand my meaning – and his highly esteemed brother-in-law."

She flushed deeper, and was burning red when she replied in a fainter voice, "I do not think that likely, either."

"Mrs Bounderby," said Harthouse, after a short silence, "may there be a better confidence between yourself and me? Tom has borrowed a considerable sum of you?"

"You will understand, Mr Harthouse," she returned, after some indecision. The conversation troubled her, but she still preserved her self-contained manner. "That if I tell you what you press to know, it is not by way of complaint or regret. I would never complain of anything, and I do not in the least regret what I have done."

"So spirited, too!" thought James Harthouse.

"When I married, I found that my brother was even then heavily in debt. Heavily for him, I mean. I willingly sold some trinkets. They were no sacrifice. I attached no value to them."

Either she saw in his face that he knew, or she only feared that he knew, that she spoke of some of her husband's gifts. She stopped, and reddened again. If he had not known it before, he would have known it then.

"Since then, I have given my brother, at various times, what money I could spare, in short, what money I have had. Confiding in you at all, as you profess interest for him, I will not do so by halves. Since you have been visiting here, he wanted in one sum as much as a hundred pounds. I have not been able to give it to him. I have felt uneasy for the consequences of his being so involved, but I have kept these secrets until now, when I trust them to your honour. I have told no-one, because – you anticipated my reason just now." She abruptly broke off.

He was prepared, and he saw and seized an opportunity here of presenting her own image to her, slightly disguised as her brother.

"Mrs Bounderby, though a graceless person, of the world worldly, I feel the utmost interest, I assure you, in what you tell me. I cannot possibly be hard upon your brother. I understand how you regard his errors. With the utmost respect for Mr Gradgrind and Mr Bounderby, I feel he has not been fortunate in his training. Brought up with no knowledge of the society in which he has his part to play, he rushes in from opposite extremes that have long been forced – with the very best intentions we have no doubt – upon him. Mr Bounderby's fine bluff English independence, though a most charming characteristic, does not – as we have agreed – invite confidence. If I might say that it is the least in the world deficient in that delicacy to which a youth mistaken, a character misconceived, and abilities misdirected, would turn for relief and guidance, I should express what it presents to my own view."

As she sat looking straight before her, into the wood beyond, he saw in her face her application of his very distinctly uttered words.

"All allowance," he continued, "must be made. I have one great fault to find with Tom, however, which I cannot forgive."

Louisa turned to him, and asked him what fault was that?

"Perhaps," he returned, "I have said enough. Perhaps it would have been better, on the whole, if no allusion to it had escaped me."

"You alarm me, Mr Harthouse. Pray let me know it."

"To avoid your anxiety – and as this confidence regarding your brother, which I prize above all things, has been established between us – I obey. I cannot forgive him for not being more sensible in every word, look, and act of his life, of the affection and devotion of his best friend; of her unselfishness and her sacrifice. The return he makes her, I find, is a very poor one. What she has done for him demands his constant love and gratitude, not his ill-humour and caprice. Careless fellow as I am, I am not so indifferent, Mrs Bounderby, as to be unaware of this vice in your brother, or inclined to consider it a venial offence."

The wood floated before her, for her eyes were filled with tears. They rose from a deep well, long concealed, and her heart was filled with acute pain that found no relief in them.

"In a word, it is to correct your brother in this, Mrs Bounderby, that I must aspire. My better knowledge of his circumstances, and my advice in extricating them – rather valuable, I hope, as coming from a scape-grace on a much larger scale – will give me some influence over him, and all I gain I shall certainly use towards this end. I have said more than enough. I seem to be protesting that I am a sort of good fellow, when, upon my honour, I have not the least intention of saying that, and openly announce that I am nothing of the sort. Yonder, among the trees," he added, having lifted up his eyes and looked about, for he had watched her closely until now, "is your brother himself. As he seems to be loitering in this direction, it may be as well, perhaps, to walk towards him, and meet him. He has been very silent and doleful of late. Perhaps, his brotherly conscience is touched – if there are such things as consciences."

He assisted her to rise, and she took his arm, and they advanced to meet the whelp. He was idly beating the branches as he lounged along. He was startled when they came upon him.

"Halloa!" he stammered; "I didn't know you were here."

"Whose name, Tom," said Mr Harthouse, putting his hand upon his shoulder and turning him, so that they all three walked towards the house together, "have you been carving on the trees?"

"Whose name?" returned Tom. "Oh! You mean what girl's name? Any fair creature with a slashing fortune at her own disposal who would take a fancy to me. Or she may be as ugly as she was rich, with no fear of losing me. I'd carve her name as often as she liked."

"I am afraid you are mercenary, Tom."

"Mercenary," repeated Tom. "Who is not mercenary? Ask my sister."

"Have you proved it to be a failing of mine, Tom?" said Louisa, showing no other sense of his discontent and ill-nature.

"You know whether the cap fits you, Loo," returned her brother sulkily. "If it does, you can wear it."

"Tom is misanthropical to-day, as all bored people are occasionally," said Mr Harthouse. "Don't believe him, Mrs Bounderby. He knows better. I shall disclose some of his opinions of you, privately expressed to me, unless he relents a little."

"At all events, Mr Harthouse," said Tom, softening in his admiration of his patron, but shaking his head sullenly too, "you can't tell her that I ever praised her for being mercenary. I may have praised her for being the

116

contrary, and I should do it again, if I had as good reason. However, never mind this now; it's not very interesting to you and I am sick of the subject."

They walked on to the house, where Louisa quitted her visitor's arm and went in. He stood looking after her, as she ascended the steps, and passed into the shadow of the door; then put his hand upon her brother's shoulder again, and invited him with a confidential nod to a walk in the garden.

"Tom, my fine fellow, I want to have a word with you."

They had stopped by the roses. Tom sat down on a terrace-parapet, plucking buds and picking them to pieces while his powerful Familiar stood over him, with a foot upon the parapet, and his figure easily resting on the arm supported by that knee. They were just visible from her window. Perhaps she saw them.

"Tom, what's the matter?"

"Oh! Mr Harthouse," said Tom with a groan, "I am hard up, and bothered out of my life."

"My good fellow, so am I."

"You!" returned Tom. "You are the picture of independence. Mr Harthouse, I am in a horrible mess. You have no idea what a state I have got myself into – what a state my sister might have got me out of, if she would only have done it."

He took to tearing the rose buds with a hand that trembled like an infirm old man's. After one exceedingly observant look at him, his companion relapsed into his lightest air.

"Tom, you are inconsiderate: you expect too much of your sister. You have had money of her, you dog, you know you have."

"Well, Mr Harthouse, I know I have. How else was I to get it? Old Bounderby's always boasting that at my age he lived upon twopence a month, or something like that. Here's my father drawing what he calls a line, and tying me down to it from a baby. Here's my mother who never has anything of her own, except her complaints. Where am I to look for money, if not to my sister?"

He was almost crying, and scattered the buds about by dozens. Mr Harthouse took him persuasively by the coat.

"But, my dear Tom, if your sister has not got it – "

"Not got it, Mr Harthouse? I don't say she has got it. I may have

117

wanted more than she was likely to have got. But then she ought to get it. She could get it. I know I have already told you, she didn't marry old Bounderby for her own sake, or for his, but for mine. Then why doesn't she get what I want, out of him, for my sake? She doesn't have to say why she needs it; she is sharp enough; she could coax it out of him, if she chose. Then why doesn't she choose, when I tell her the consequence? But no. There she sits in his company like a stone, instead of making herself agreeable and getting it easily. I don't know what you may call this, but I call it unnatural conduct."

There was an ornamental pond immediately below the parapet, on the other side, into which Mr James Harthouse had a very strong inclination to pitch Mr Thomas Gradgrind junior. But he preserved his easy attitude, and nothing more solid went over the stone balustrades than the accumulated rosebuds now floating about.

"My dear Tom," said Harthouse, "let me try to be your banker."

"For God's sake," replied Tom, suddenly, "don't talk about bankers!" His face visibly whitened.

Mr Harthouse, as a thoroughly well-bred man, accustomed to the best society, raised his eyelids a little more, as if they were lifted by a feeble touch of wonder.

"What is the present need, Tom? Three figures? Out with them. Say what they are."

"Mr Harthouse," returned Tom, now actually crying. "It's too late, the money is of no use to me now. I should have had it before to be of use. But I am much obliged to you; you're a true friend."

A true friend! "Whelp, whelp!" thought Mr Harthouse, lazily, "what an Ass you are!"

"And I take your offer as a great kindness, Mr Harthouse," said Tom, grasping his hand.

"Well," returned the other, "it may be of more use by-and-by. And my good fellow, tell me the problems as they occur, and I may show you better ways out than you can find for yourself."

"Thank you," said Tom, shaking his head. "I wish I had known you sooner, Mr Harthouse."

"Now, you see, Tom," said Mr Harthouse in conclusion, himself tossing over a rose or two, "every man is selfish in everything he does, and I am exactly like the rest of my fellow-creatures. I am desperately intent on your softening towards your sister – which you ought to do; and on your being a more loving and agreeable sort of brother – which you ought to be."

"I will be, Mr Harthouse."

"No time like the present, Tom. Begin at once."

"Certainly I will. And my sister Loo shall say so."

"Having made which bargain, Tom," said Harthouse, clapping him on the shoulder again, with an air which left him free to infer – as he did, poor fool – that this condition was imposed upon him in mere careless good-nature to lessen his sense of obligation, "we will tear ourselves asunder until dinner-time."

Tom appeared for dinner before Mr Bounderby, and though his mind seemed heavy enough, his body was on the alert. "I didn't mean to be cross, Loo," he said, giving her his hand, and kissing her. "I know you are fond of me, and you know I am fond of you."

After this, there was a smile upon Louisa's face that day, for some one else. Alas, for some one else!

"So much the less is the whelp the only creature that she cares for," thought James Harthouse, reversing the reflection of his first day's knowledge of her pretty face. "So much the less."

CHAPTER 8

The next morning was too bright for sleep, and James Harthouse rose early, and sat in the pleasant bay window of his dressing-room, smoking the rare tobacco that had had so wholesome an influence on his young friend. Reposing in the sunlight, he reckoned up his advantages as an idle winner might count his gains.

He had established a confidence with her, from which her husband was excluded – a confidence that absolutely turned upon her indifference towards her husband, and the absence of any congeniality between them. He had artfully, but plainly assured her, that he knew her heart in its last most delicate recesses. He had come near to her through its tenderest sentiment and had associated himself with that feeling. The barrier behind which she lived had melted away. All very odd, and very satisfactory!

And yet he had not, even now, any earnest wickedness of purpose in him.

So, James Harthouse reclined in the window, indolently smoking, and reckoning up the steps he had taken on the road he happened to be travelling. The end was before him, pretty plainly, but he troubled himself with no calculations about it. What will be will be.

He had rather a long ride to take that day – for there was a public occasion "to do" at some distance – so he dressed early, and went down to breakfast. He was anxious to see if she had relapsed since the previous evening. No. He resumed where he had left off. There was a look of interest for him again.

He got through the day and came riding back at six o'clock. There was a sweep of some half mile between the lodge and the house, and he was riding along at a foot pace over the smooth gravel, when Mr Bounderby burst out of the shrubbery, with such violence as to make his horse shy across the road.

"Harthouse!" cried Mr Bounderby. "Have you heard?"

"Heard what?" said Harthouse, soothing his horse, and inwardly favouring Mr Bounderby with no good wishes.

"Then you haven't heard!"

"I have heard you, and so has this brute. I have heard nothing else."

Mr Bounderby, red and hot, planted himself in the centre of the path before the horse's head, to explode his bombshell with more effect.

"The Bank's robbed!"

"You don't mean it!"

"Robbed last night, sir. Robbed in an extraordinary manner. Robbed with a false key."

"Of much?"

Mr Bounderby, in his desire to make the most of it, really seemed mortified by being obliged to reply, "Why, no. Not of very much. But it might have been."

"Of how much?"

"Oh! A sum – of not more than a hundred and fifty pound," said Bounderby, with impatience. "But it's not the sum. It's the fact of the Bank being robbed, that's the important circumstance. I am surprised you don't see it."

"My dear Bounderby," said James, dismounting, and giving his bridle to his servant, "I do see it; and am as overcome as you can possibly desire me to be. Nevertheless, I may be allowed, I hope, to congratulate you – which I do with all my soul, I assure you – on your not having sustained a greater loss."

"Thank'ee," replied Bounderby, ungraciously. "But I tell you what. It might have been twenty thousand pound."

"I suppose it might."

"Suppose it might! By the Lord, you may suppose so. By George!" said Mr Bounderby, with sundry menacing shakes of his head. "It might have been twice twenty. There's no knowing what it would have been, but for the fellows' being disturbed."

Louisa had come up now, with Mrs Sparsit, and Bitzer.

"Here's Tom Gradgrind's daughter. She knows pretty well what it might have been, if you don't," blustered Bounderby. "Dropped, sir, as if she was shot when I told her! Never knew her do such a thing before."

She still looked faint and pale. James Harthouse begged her to take his arm, and as they moved on very slowly, asked her how the robbery had been committed.

"Why, I am going to tell you," said Bounderby, irritably giving his arm to Mrs Sparsit. "If you hadn't been so mighty particular about the sum, I should have begun to tell you before. You know this lady (for she is a lady), Mrs Sparsit?"

"I have already had the honour – "

"Very well. And this young man, Bitzer, you saw him too on the same occasion?" Mr Harthouse inclined his head in assent, and Bitzer knuckled his forehead.

"Very well. They live at the Bank. Yesterday afternoon, at the close of business hours, everything was put away as usual. In the iron room that this young fellow sleeps outside of, there was never mind how much. In the little safe in young Tom's closet, the safe used for petty purposes, there was a hundred and fifty odd pound. Everything was left, all right. Sometime in the night, while this young fellow snored – some fellows, somehow, whether previously concealed in the house or not remains to be seen, got to young Tom's safe, forced it, and abstracted the contents. Being then disturbed, they made off; letting themselves out at the main door, and double-locking it again (it was double-locked, and the key under Mrs Sparsit's pillow) with a false key, which was picked up in the street near the Bank, about twelve o'clock today. No alarm takes place, till this chap, Bitzer, turns out this morning, and begins to open and prepare the offices for business. Then, looking at Tom's safe, he sees the door ajar, and finds the lock forced, and the money gone."

"Where is Tom, by-the-by?" asked Harthouse, glancing round.

"He has been helping the police," said Bounderby, "and stays behind at the Bank."

"Is anybody suspected?"

"Suspected? I should think there was somebody suspected. Egod!" said Bounderby, relinquishing Mrs Sparsit's arm to wipe his heated head. "Josiah Bounderby of Coketown is not to be plundered and nobody suspected. No, thank you!"

Might Mr Harthouse inquire Who was suspected?

"Well," said Bounderby, stopping and facing about to confront them all, "I'll tell you. It's not to be mentioned anywhere: in order that the scoundrels concerned (there's a gang of 'em) may be thrown off their guard. So what should you say to – " here he violently exploded, "to a Hand being in it?"

"I hope," said Harthouse, lazily, "not our friend Blackpot?"

"Say Pool instead of Pot, sir," returned Bounderby, "and that's the man."

Louisa faintly uttered some word of incredulity and surprise.

"O yes! I know!" said Bounderby, immediately catching at the sound. "I am used to that. I know all about it. They are the finest people in the world. They have the gift of the gab, they have. They only want to have their rights explained to them. But I tell you what. Show me a dissatisfied Hand, and I'll show you a man that's fit for anything bad."

"But I am acquainted with these chaps," said Bounderby. "I can read 'em off, like books. Mrs Sparsit, ma'am, I appeal to you. What warning did I give that fellow, the first time he set foot in the house, when the express object of his visit was to know how he could knock Religion over, and floor the Established Church? Did I or did I not say, 'you can't hide the truth from me: you are not the kind of fellow I like; you'll come to no good'?"

"Assuredly, you did sir," returned Mrs Sparsit.

"You can recall for yourself, Harthouse, what I said to him when you saw him. I didn't mince the matter with him. Three days after that, he bolted. Went off, nobody knows where: as my mother did in my infancy. What did he do before he went? What do you say to his being seen – night after night – watching the Bank? To its striking Mrs Sparsit – that he could be lurking for no good – To her calling Bitzer's attention to him – And to its appearing on inquiry today – that he was also noticed by the neighbours?"

"Suspicious," said James Harthouse, "certainly."

"I think so, sir," said Bounderby, with a defiant nod. "I think so. But there are more of 'em in it. There's an old woman. An old woman who flies into town on a broomstick every now and then. She watches the place a whole day before this fellow begins, and on the night when you saw him, she steals away with him, and holds a council with him."

There was such a person in the room that night, and she shrunk from observation, thought Louisa.

"This is not all of 'em, even as we already know 'em," said Bounderby, with many nods. "But I have said enough for the present. You'll have the goodness to keep it quiet, and mention it to no one. It may take time, but we shall have 'em."

"Of course, they will be punished with the utmost rigour of the law, as notice-boards observe," replied James Harthouse, "and serve them right. Fellows who go in for Banks must take the consequences. If there were no consequences, we should all go in for Banks." He had gently taken Louisa's parasol from her hand, and had put it up for her; and she walked under its shade, though the sun did not shine there.

"For the present, Loo Bounderby," said her husband, "here's Mrs Sparsit to look after. Her nerves have been acted upon by this business, and she'll stay here a day or two. So make her comfortable."

"Thank you very much, sir," said the discreet lady, "but pray do not let My comfort be a consideration. Anything will do for Me."

Mrs Sparsit was still determined to pity Mr Bounderby. There were occasions when in looking at him she was involuntarily moved to shake her head. After allowing herself to be betrayed into these evidences of emotion, she would force a lambent brightness, and would be fitfully cheerful, and say, "You have still good spirits, sir, I am thankful to find," and would appear to hail it as a blessing that Mr Bounderby bore up as he did.

One idiosyncrasy for which she often apologised, as she found it excessively difficult to conquer, was the curious propensity to call Mrs Bounderby "Miss Gradgrind". She did this some three or four score times in the course of the evening. Indeed, she said, it seemed so natural to say Miss Gradgrind: whereas, to persuade herself that the young lady whom she had had the happiness of knowing from a child could be really and truly Mrs Bounderby, she found almost impossible.

In the drawing-room after dinner, Mr Bounderby tried the case of the robbery, examined the witnesses, made notes of the evidence, found the suspected persons guilty, and sentenced them to the extreme punishment of the law. That done, Bitzer was dismissed to town with instructions for Tom to come home by the mail-train.

When candles were brought, Mrs Sparsit murmured, "Don't be low, sir. Pray let me see you cheerful, sir, as I used to do." Mr Bounderby, upon whom these consolations had begun to produce the effect of making him, in his own way, sentimental, sighed like some large sea-animal.

"I cannot bear to see you so, sir," said Mrs Sparsit. "Try a hand at backgammon, sir, as you used to do when I had the honour of living under your roof."

"I haven't played backgammon, ma'am," said Mr Bounderby, "since that time."

"No, sir," said Mrs Sparsit, soothingly, "I am aware that you have not. I remember that Miss Gradgrind takes no interest in the game. But I shall be happy, sir, if you will condescend."

They played near a window, opening on the garden. It was a fine night, sultry and fragrant. Louisa and Mr Harthouse strolled out into the garden, where their voices could be heard in the stillness, though not what they said. Mrs Sparsit, from her place at the backgammon board, was constantly straining her eyes to pierce the shadows without.

"What's the matter, ma'am?" said Mr Bounderby; "you don't see a Fire, do you?"

"Oh dear no, sir," returned Mrs Sparsit, "I was thinking of the dew."

"What have you got to do with the dew, ma'am?" said Mr Bounderby.

"It's not myself, sir," returned Mrs Sparsit, "I am fearful of Miss Gradgrind's taking cold."

"She never takes cold," said Mr Bounderby.

"Really, sir?" said Mrs Sparsit, with a slight cough.

When the time drew near for retiring, Mr Bounderby took a glass of water. "Oh, sir?" said Mrs Sparsit. "Not your sherry warm, with lemon-peel and nutmeg?"

"Why, I have got out of the habit of taking it now, ma'am," said Mr Bounderby.

"The more's the pity, sir," returned Mrs Sparsit; "you are losing all your good old habits. Cheer up, sir! If Miss Gradgrind will permit me, I will offer to make it for you, as I have often done."

Miss Gradgrind readily permitting Mrs Sparsit to do anything she pleased, that considerate lady made the beverage, and handed it to Mr Bounderby. "It will do you good, sir. It is the sort of thing you want, and ought to take, sir."

And when Mr Bounderby said, "Your health, ma'am!" she answered with great feeling, "Thank you, sir. The same to you, and happiness also." Finally, she wished him good-night, with great pathos; and Mr Bounderby went to bed, with a maudlin persuasion that he had been crossed in something tender, though he could not, for his life, have mentioned what it was.

Long after Louisa had undressed and lain down, she watched and waited for her brother's coming home. That could hardly be, she knew, until an hour past midnight; but in the country silence, time lagged wearily. At last, she heard the bell at the gate.

She waited another quarter of an hour, then arose, put on a loose robe and went out of her room in the dark, and up the staircase to her brother's room. His door being shut, she softly opened it and spoke to him, approaching his bed silently.

She kneeled down beside it, passed her arm over his neck, and drew his face to hers. She knew that he only feigned sleep, but she said nothing.

He started by-and-by as if he were just then awakened, and asked who that was, and what was the matter?

"Tom, have you anything to tell me? If ever you loved me in your life, and have anything concealed from every one besides, tell it to me."

"I don't know what you mean, Loo. You have been dreaming."

"My dear brother:" she laid her head down on his pillow, and her hair flowed over him as if she would hide him from every one but herself: "is there nothing that you have to tell me? You can tell me nothing that will change me. O Tom, tell me the truth!"

"I don't know what you mean, Loo!"

"As you lie here alone, my dear, in the melancholy night, so you must lie somewhere one night, when even I, if I am living then, shall have left you. Tom, tell me the truth now!"

"What is it you want to know?"

"You may be certain;" in the energy of her love she took him to her bosom as if he were a child; "that I will not reproach you. You may be certain that I will be compassionate and true to you. You may be certain that I will save you at whatever cost. O Tom, have you nothing to tell me? Whisper very softly. Say only 'yes,' and I shall understand you!"

She turned her ear to his lips, but he remained doggedly silent.

"Not a word, Tom?"

"How can I say Yes, or No, when I don't know what you mean? Loo, you are a brave, kind girl, worthy I begin to think of a better brother than I am. But I have nothing more to say. Go to bed."

"You are tired," she whispered presently, more in her usual way.

"Yes, I am quite tired out."

"You have been so hurried and disturbed today. Have any fresh discoveries been made?"

"Only those you have heard of, from – him."

"Tom, have you said to any one that we made a visit to those people, and that we saw those three together?"

"No. Didn't you yourself particularly ask me to keep it quiet when you asked me to go there with you?"

"Yes. But I did not know then what was going to happen."

"Nor I neither. How could I?"

He was very quick upon her with this retort.

"Ought I to say, after what has happened," said his sister, now standing by the bed, "that I made that visit? Must I say so?"

"Good Heavens, Loo," returned her brother, "you don't usually ask my advice. Say what you like. If you keep it to yourself, I shall do the same. If you disclose it, there's an end of it."

It was too dark for either to see the other's face; but each seemed very attentive, and to consider before speaking.

"Tom, do you believe the man I gave the money to, is really implicated in this crime?"

"I don't know. I don't see why he shouldn't be."

"He seemed to me an honest man."

126

"Another person may seem to you dishonest, and yet not be so."
There was a pause, for he had hesitated and stopped.

"In short," he resumed, as if he had made up his mind, "if you come to that, perhaps I was so far from being altogether in his favour, that I took him outside the door to tell him quietly, that I thought he might consider himself very well off to get such a windfall as he had got from my sister, and that I hoped he would make good use of it. I say nothing against the man; he may be a very good fellow, for anything I know; I hope he is."

"Was he offended by what you said?"

"No, he took it pretty well; he was civil enough. Where are you, Loo?" He sat up in bed and kissed her. "Good-night, my dear!"

"You have nothing more to tell me?"

"No. What should I have? You wouldn't have me tell you a lie!"

"I wouldn't have you do that tonight, Tom, of all the nights in your life; many and much happier as I hope they will be."

"Thank you, my dear Loo. I am so tired. Go to bed, go to bed."

Kissing her again, he turned round, drew the coverlet over his head, and lay still. She stood for some time at the bedside before she slowly moved away. She stopped at the door, looked back when she had opened it, and asked him if he had called her? But he lay still, and she softly closed the door and returned to her room.

Then the wretched boy looked cautiously up and found her gone, crept out of bed, fastened his door, and threw himself upon his pillow again. Tearing his hair, morosely crying, grudgingly loving her, hatefully but impenitently spurning himself, and no less hatefully and unprofitably, spurning all the good in the world.

CHAPTER 9

Mrs Sparsit, lying by to recover the tone of her nerves in Mr Bounderby's retreat, kept a sharp look-out, night and day.

She was a most wonderful woman for prowling about the house. How she got from storey to storey was a mystery beyond solution. Another noticeable circumstance in Mrs Sparsit was that she was never hurried.

She would shoot with consummate velocity from the roof to the hall, yet would be in full possession of her breath and dignity on the moment of her arrival there. Neither was she ever seen by human vision to go at a great pace.

She took very kindly to Mr Harthouse, and had some pleasant conversation with him soon after her arrival. She made him her stately curtsey in the garden, one morning before breakfast.

"It appears but yesterday, sir," said Mrs Sparsit, "that I had the honour of receiving you at the Bank, when you were so good as to wish to be made acquainted with Mr Bounderby's address."

"An occasion, I am sure, not to be forgotten by myself," said Mr Harthouse, inclining his head to Mrs Sparsit.

"We live in a singular world, sir," said Mrs Sparsit.

"I have had the honour, by a coincidence of which I am proud, to have made a remark, similar in effect, though not so epigrammatically expressed."

"A singular world, I would say, sir," pursued Mrs Sparsit. "I recall, sir, that on that occasion you went so far as to say you were actually apprehensive of Miss Gradgrind."

"Your memory does me more honour than my insignificance deserves."

"You found Miss Gradgrind – I really cannot call her Mrs Bounderby, it's very absurd of me – as youthful as I described her?" asked Mrs Sparsit, sweetly.

"You drew her portrait perfectly," said Mr Harthouse.

"Very engaging, sir," said Mrs Sparsit.

"Highly so."

"It used to be considered," said Mrs Sparsit, "that Miss Gradgrind was wanting in animation, but I confess she appears to me considerably and strikingly improved in that respect. Ay, and indeed here is Mr Bounderby!" cried Mrs Sparsit. "How do you find yourself this morning, sir? Pray let us see you cheerful, sir."

Now, these persistent assuagements of his misery had by this time begun to make Mr Bounderby softer than usual towards Mrs Sparsit, and harder to most other people from his wife downward. Mrs Sparsit then said with forced lightness of heart, "You want your breakfast, sir, but I dare say Miss Gradgrind will soon be here to preside at the table."

To this Mr Bounderby replied, "If I waited to be taken care of by my wife, ma'am, I believe you know I should wait till Doomsday, so please take charge of the teapot." Mrs Sparsit complied, and assumed her old position at table.

This again made the excellent woman vastly sentimental. She was so humble, that when Louisa appeared, she rose, protesting she never could think of sitting in that place under existing circumstances, often as she had had the honour of making Mr Bounderby's breakfast, before Mrs Gradgrind – she begged pardon, she meant to say Miss Bounderby – she really could not get it right yet, though she trusted to become familiar with it by-and-by – had assumed her present position. It was only (she observed) because Miss Gradgrind happened to be a little late, and Mr Bounderby's time was so very precious, and she knew it of old to be so essential that he should breakfast to the moment, that she had taken the liberty of complying with his request.

"There! Stop where you are, ma'am," said Mr Bounderby, "Mrs Bounderby will be very glad to be relieved of the trouble, I believe."

"Don't say that, sir," returned Mrs Sparsit, almost with severity, "because that is very unkind to Mrs Bounderby. And to be unkind is not to be you, sir."

"Set your mind at rest, ma'am. – You can take it very quietly, can't you, Loo?" said Mr Bounderby, in a blustering way.

"Of course. It is of no moment. Why should it be of any importance to me?"

"Why should it be of any importance to anyone, Mrs Sparsit, ma'am?" said Mr Bounderby, swelling with a sense of slight. "You attach too much importance to these things, ma'am. You are old-fashioned, ma'am. You are behind Tom Gradgrind's children's time."

"What gives you offence?" asked Louisa, coldly surprised.

"Offence!" repeated Bounderby. "Do you suppose if there was any offence given me, I shouldn't name it, and request to have it corrected? I am a straightforward man, I believe. I don't go beating about for side-winds."

"I suppose no-one ever would think you too diffident, or too delicate," Louisa answered him composedly. "I have never made that objection to you, either as a child or as a woman. I don't understand what you would have."

"Have?" returned Mr Bounderby. "Nothing. Otherwise, don't you, Loo Bounderby, know thoroughly well that I, Josiah Bounderby of Coketown, would have it?"

She looked at him, as he struck the table and made the tea-cups ring, with a proud colour in her face that was a new change, Mr Harthouse thought. "You are incomprehensible this morning," said Louisa. "Pray take no further trouble to explain yourself. I am not curious to know your meaning. What does it matter?"

Nothing more was said on this theme, and Mr Harthouse was soon idly gay on indifferent subjects. But from this day, the Sparsit action upon Mr Bounderby threw Louisa and James Harthouse more together, and strengthened the dangerous alienation from her husband and confidence against him with another, into which she had fallen by degrees so fine that she could not retrace them if she tried. But whether she ever tried or no, lay hidden in her own closed heart.

Mrs Sparsit assisted Mr Bounderby to his hat after breakfast, and being then alone with him in the hall, she imprinted a chaste kiss upon his hand. "My benefactor!" she murmured and retired. Yet five minutes after he had left the house in the self-same hat, this same lady shook her right-hand mitten at his portrait, made a contemptuous grimace at that work of art, and said "Serve you right, you Noodle, and I am glad of it."

Mr Bounderby had not been long gone, when Bitzer appeared. He had come by train with an express from Stone Lodge. It was a hasty note to inform Louisa that Mrs Gradgrind lay very ill. She had never been well within her daughter's knowledge but she had declined within the last few days, and was now as nearly dead, as her limited capacity to get out of it allowed.

Accompanied by the porter Louisa rumbled to Coketown. She dismissed the messenger to his own devices, and rode away to her old home.

She had seldom been there since her marriage. Her father was usually sifting and sifting at his parliamentary cinder-heap in London, and was still hard at it in the national dust-yard. Sissy she had never softened to again, since the night when the stroller's child had raised her eyes to look at Mr Bounderby's intended wife. She had no inducements to go back, and had rarely gone.

Neither, as she approached her old home now, did any of the best influences of old home descend upon her. The dreams of childhood –

what had she to do with these? Her remembrances of home and childhood were remembrances of the drying up of every spring and fountain in her young heart as it gushed out.

She went, with a heavy, hardened kind of sorrow upon her, into the house and into her mother's room. Since the time of her leaving home, Sissy had lived with the rest of the family on equal terms. Sissy was at her mother's side; while her sister Jane, now ten or twelve years old, was in the room.

There was great trouble before it could be made known to Mrs Gradgrind that her eldest child was there. She reclined, propped up, from mere habit, on a couch. She had positively refused to take to her bed; on the ground that if she did, she would never hear the last of it.

Her feeble voice sounded so far away in her bundle of shawls, and the sound of another voice addressing her seemed to take such a long time in getting down to her ears, that she might have been lying at the bottom of a well. The poor lady was nearer Truth than she ever had been: which had much to do with it.

On being told that Mrs Bounderby was there, she replied, "Well, my dear, and I hope you are going on satisfactorily to yourself. It was all your father's doing. He set his heart upon it."

"I want to hear of you, mother; not of myself."

"You want to hear of me, my dear? That's something new, I am sure, when anybody wants to hear of me. Not at all well, Louisa. Very faint and giddy."

"Are you in pain, dear mother?"

"I think there's a pain somewhere in the room," said Mrs Gradgrind, "but I couldn't positively say that I have got it."

After this strange speech, she lay silent for some time. Louisa, holding her hand, could feel no pulse; but kissing it, could see a slight thin thread of life in fluttering motion.

"You very seldom see your sister," said Mrs Gradgrind. "She grows like you. Do look at her. Sissy, bring her here."

She was brought, and stood with her hand in her sister's. Louisa had observed her with her arm round Sissy's neck, and she felt the difference of this approach.

"Do you see the likeness, Louisa?"

"Yes, mother. I should think her like me. But – "

"Eh! Yes, I always say so," Mrs Gradgrind cried, with unexpected quickness. "And that reminds me. I – I want to speak to you, my dear. Sissy, my good girl, leave us alone a minute."

Louisa had relinquished the hand: had thought that her sister's was a better and brighter face than hers had ever been.

Left alone with her mother, Louisa saw her lying with an awful lull upon her face, like one who was floating away. She put the shadow of a hand to her lips again, and recalled her.

"You were going to speak to me, mother."

"Eh? Yes, to be sure, my dear. You know your father is almost always away now, and therefore I must write to him about it."

"About what, mother? Don't be troubled."

"You must remember, my dear, that whenever I have said anything, on any subject, I have never heard the last of it: and consequently, that I have long left off saying anything."

"I can hear you, mother." But, it was only by dint of bending down to her ear, and at the same time attentively watching the lips as they moved, that she could understand her.

"You learnt a great deal, Louisa, and so did your brother. Ologies of all kinds, from morning to night. If there is any Ology left, of any description, that has not been worn to rags in this house, all I can say is, I hope I shall never hear its name."

"I can hear you, mother, when you have strength to go on." This, to keep her from floating away.

"But there is something – not an Ology at all – that your father has missed, or forgotten, Louisa. I have often sat with Sissy near me, and thought about it. I shall never get its name now. But your father may. It makes me restless. I want to write to him, to find out for God's sake, what it is. Give me a pen, give me a pen."

Even the power of restlessness was gone, except from the poor head, which could just turn from side to side.

She fancied, however, that her request had been complied with, and that the pen she could not have held was in her hand. It matters little what figures of wonderful no-meaning she began to trace upon her wrappers. The hand soon stopped in the midst of them; the light that had always been feeble and dim behind the weak transparency, went out.

132

CHAPTER 10

Mrs Sparsit's nerves being slow to recover, the worthy woman stayed some weeks at Mr Bounderby's retreat, where she resigned herself with noble fortitude to lodging, as one may say, in clover, and feeding on the fat of the land. During this break from the Bank, Mrs Sparsit was a pattern of consistency; continuing to take such pity on Mr Bounderby to his face, and to call his portrait a Noodle, with the greatest acrimony and contempt.

Mr Bounderby, having got it into his explosive composition that Mrs Sparsit was a highly superior woman, and further that Louisa would have objected to her as a frequent visitor, resolved not to lose sight of Mrs Sparsit easily. So when her nerves were strung up to the pitch of again consuming sweetbreads in solitude, he said to her at the dinner-table, on the day before her departure, "I tell you what, ma'am; you shall come down here of a Saturday, while the fine weather lasts, and stay till Monday." To which Mrs Sparsit returned: "To hear is to obey."

Now, Mrs Sparsit was not a poetical woman; but she took an idea in the nature of an allegorical fancy, into her head. She erected in her mind a mighty Staircase, with a dark pit of shame and ruin at the bottom; and down those stairs, from day to day and hour to hour, she saw Louisa coming.

It became the business of Mrs Sparsit's life, to look up at her staircase, and to watch Louisa coming down. Sometimes slowly, sometimes quickly, sometimes several steps at once, sometimes stopping, never turning back. If she had once turned back, it might have been the death of Mrs Sparsit in spleen and grief.

She had been descending steadily, to the day, and on the day, when Mr Bounderby issued the weekly invitation. Mrs Sparsit was in good spirits, and inclined to be conversational.

"And pray, sir," said she, "if I may venture to ask a question – have you received intelligence respecting the robbery?"

"Why, ma'am, no; not yet. Under the circumstances, I didn't expect it yet. Rome wasn't built in a day, ma'am."

"Very true, sir," said Mrs Sparsit, shaking her head.

"Nor yet in a week, ma'am."

"No, indeed, sir," returned Mrs Sparsit, with a gentle melancholy upon her.

"In a similar manner, ma'am," said Bounderby, "I can wait. If Romulus and Remus could wait, so can Josiah Bounderby. They were better off in their youth than I was, however. They had a she-wolf for a nurse; I had only a she-wolf for a grandmother."

"Ah!" Mrs Sparsit sighed and shuddered.

"No, ma'am," continued Bounderby, "I have not heard anything more. It's in hand, though; and young Tom is helping. My order is, Keep it quiet, and let it seem to blow over. Don't give a sign of what you're about; or half a hundred of 'em will combine together to get this fellow who has bolted out of reach for good. Keep it quiet, and the thieves will grow in confidence little by little, and we shall have 'em."

"Very sagacious indeed, sir," said Mrs Sparsit. "The old woman you mentioned, sir – "

"The old woman I mentioned, ma'am," said Bounderby, cutting the matter short, "is not laid hold of; but she will be, if that is any satisfaction to her villainous old mind. In the meantime, ma'am, I am of the opinion, that the less she is talked about, the better."

CHAPTER 11

Mr Gradgrind, appraised of his wife's decease, made an expedition from London, and buried her in a business-like manner. He then returned quickly to the national cinder-heap, and resumed his sifting for the odds and ends he wanted – in fact resumed his parliamentary duties.

In the meantime, Mrs Sparsit kept unwinking watch and ward. She maintained her cat-like observation of Louisa, through her husband, through her brother, through James Harthouse, through the outsides of letters and packets, through everything animate and inanimate that at any time went near the stairs. "Your foot on the last step, my lady," said Mrs Sparsit, apostrophising the descending figure, with the aid of her threatening mitten, "and all your art shall never blind me."

Art or nature though, the original stock of Louisa's character or the graft of circumstances upon it, – her curious reserve did baffle, while it stimulated, one as sagacious as Mrs Sparsit. There were times when Mr

James Harthouse was not sure of her. There were times when he could not read the face he had studied so long; and when this lonely girl was a greater mystery to him, than any woman of the world with a ring of satellites to help her.

It so happened that Mr Bounderby was called away from home by business which required his presence elsewhere, for three or four days. It was on a Friday that he intimated this to Mrs Sparsit at the Bank, adding, "but you'll go down tomorrow, ma'am, all the same. Just as if I was there. It will make no difference to you."

"Pray, sir," returned Mrs Sparsit, reproachfully, "your absence will make a vast difference to me, sir, as I think you very well know."

"Well, ma'am, then you must get on in my absence as well as you can," said Mr Bounderby, not displeased.

"Mr Bounderby," retorted Mrs Sparsit, "I am not sure that it will be quite so agreeable to Miss Gradgrind to receive me, as it ever is to your own munificent hospitality. But you shall say no more, sir. I will go, upon your invitation."

"When I invite you to my house, ma'am," said Bounderby, opening his eyes, "I should hope you want no other invitation."

"No, indeed, sir," returned Mrs Sparsit, "Say no more, sir. I would, sir, I could see you gay again."

"What do you mean, ma'am?" blustered Bounderby.

"Sir," rejoined Mrs Sparsit, "there was wont to be an elasticity in you which I sadly miss. Be buoyant, sir!"

Mr Bounderby could only scratch his head in a feeble and ridiculous manner, and afterwards assert himself at a distance, by being heard to bully the small fry of business all the morning.

"Bitzer," said Mrs Sparsit that afternoon, when her patron was gone on his journey, and the Bank was closing, "present my compliments to young Mr Thomas, and ask him if he would step up and partake of a lamb chop and walnut ketchup, with a glass of India ale?" Young Mr Thomas being usually ready for anything in that way, returned a gracious answer, and followed on its heels. "Mr Thomas," said Mrs Sparsit, "these plain viands being on table, I thought you might be tempted."

"Thank'ee, Mrs Sparsit," said the whelp. And gloomily fell to.

"How is Mr Harthouse, Mr Tom?" asked Mrs Sparsit.

"Oh, he's all right," said Tom.

"Where may he be at present?" Mrs Sparsit asked lightly, after mentally devoting the whelp to the Furies for being so uncommunicative.

"He is shooting in Yorkshire," said Tom. "Sent Loo a basket half as big as a church, yesterday."

"The kind of gentleman, now," said Mrs Sparsit, sweetly, "whom one might wager to be a good shot!"

"Crack," said Tom.

He had long been a down-looking young fellow, but this characteristic had so increased of late, that he never raised his eyes to any face for three seconds together. Mrs Sparsit consequently had ample time to watch his face, if so inclined.

"Mr Harthouse is a great favourite of mine," said Mrs Sparsit, "as indeed he is of most people. May we expect to see him again shortly, Mr Tom?"

"Why, I expect to see him tomorrow," returned the whelp.

"Good news!" cried Mrs Sparsit, blandly.

"I have an appointment to meet him in the evening at the station here," said Tom, "and then to dine with him afterwards, I believe. He is not coming down to the country house for a week or so, being due somewhere else. But I shouldn't wonder if he was to stop here over Sunday, and stray that way."

"Which reminds me!" said Mrs Sparsit. "Would you remember a message to your sister, Mr Tom, if I was to charge you with one?"

"Well? I'll try," returned the reluctant whelp, "if it isn't a long un."

"It is merely my respectful compliments," said Mrs Sparsit, "and I fear I may not trouble her with my society this week."

"Oh! If that's all," observed Tom, "it wouldn't much matter, even if I was to forget it, for Loo's not likely to think of you unless she sees you."

Having paid for his entertainment with this compliment, he relapsed into silence until there was no more India ale left. Then he said, "Well, Mrs Sparsit, I must be off!" and went off.

Next day, Saturday, Mrs Sparsit sat at her window all day long looking at the customers coming in and out, watching the postmen, keeping an eye on the general traffic of the street, but, above all, keeping her attention on her staircase. The evening come, she put on her bonnet and shawl, and went quietly out. She had her reasons for hovering furtively about the station by which a passenger would arrive from Yorkshire, and

136

for preferring to peep out of ladies' waiting-room windows, to appearing in its precincts openly.

Tom loitered about until the expected train came in. It brought no Mr Harthouse. Tom waited until the crowd had dispersed, and the bustle was over; and then referred to a posted list of trains, and took counsel with porters. That done, he strolled away idly, looked up and down the street, showing all the symptoms to be expected in one who had still to wait until the next train should come in, an hour and forty minutes hence.

"This is a device to keep him out of the way," said Mrs Sparsit, starting from the dull office window whence she had watched him last. "Harthouse is with his sister now!"

She shot off with her utmost swiftness to work it out. The station for the country house was at the opposite end of the town but soon she was borne along the arches spanning the land of coalpits.

All the journey, immovable in the air though never left behind; plain to the dark eyes of her mind, Mrs Sparsit saw her staircase, with the figure coming down. Very near the bottom now. Upon the brink of the abyss.

An overcast September evening, just at nightfall, saw Mrs Sparsit glide out of her carriage, pass down the wooden steps of the little station into a stony road and become hidden in a summer-growth of leaves and branches.

She went up to the house, keeping within the shrubbery, and went round it, peeping between the leaves at the lower windows. Most were open, as they usually were in such warm weather, but there were no lights yet, and all was silent. She tried the garden with no better effect. She thought of the wood, and stole towards it, heedless of long grass and briars. Mrs Sparsit softly crushed her way through the thick undergrowth, intent upon her object.

Hark!

Mrs Sparsit stopped and listened.

Low voices close at hand. His voice and hers. The appointment was a device to keep the brother away! There they were yonder, by the felled tree.

Bending low among the dewy grass, Mrs Sparsit advanced closer to them. She drew herself up, and stood behind a tree, so near to them that at a small spring, she could have touched them both. He was there secretly, and had not shown himself at the house. He had come on horseback for his horse was tied to the meadow side of the fence, within a few paces.

"My dearest love," said he, "what could I do? Knowing you were alone, was it possible that I could stay away?"

"You may hang your head, to make yourself the more attractive; I don't know what they see in you when you hold it up," thought Mrs Sparsit, "but you little think, my dearest love, whose eyes are on you!"

That she hung her head, was certain. She urged him to go away, she commanded him to go away; but she never looked at him. And yet she sat as still as ever the amiable woman in ambuscade had seen her sit, at any period in her life. Her hands rested in one another, like the hands of a statue.

"My dear child," said Harthouse – Mrs Sparsit saw with delight that his arm embraced her. "May I not stay with you a while?"

"Not here."

"Where, Louisa?

"Not here."

"But we have so little time, and I have come so far, and am altogether so devoted, and distracted. There never was a slave at once so devoted and ill-used by his mistress. To look for your sunny welcome that has warmed me into life, and to be received in your frozen manner, is heart-rending."

"Must I say again, that I should be left to myself here?"

"But we must meet, my dear Louisa. Where shall we meet?"

They both started. The listener started, guiltily, too; for she thought there was another listener among the trees. It was only rain, beginning to fall fast, in heavy drops.

"Shall I ride up to the house a few minutes hence, innocently supposing that its master is at home and will be charmed to receive me?"

"No!"

"Your cruel commands are implicitly to be obeyed; though I am the most unfortunate fellow in the world, I believe, to have been insensible to all other women, and to have fallen prostrate at last under the foot of the most beautiful, and the most engaging, and the most imperious. My dearest Louisa, I cannot go myself, or let you go, in this hard abuse of your power."

Mrs Sparsit saw him hold her with his encircling arm, and heard him

138

then and there, within her greedy hearing, tell Louisa how he loved her, and how she was the stake for which he ardently desired to play away all that he had in life. The objects he had lately pursued, turned worthless beside her; such success as was almost in his grasp, he flung away from him like the dirt it was, compared with her. Its pursuit, nevertheless, if it kept him near her, or its renunciation if it took him from her, or flight if she shared it, or secrecy if she commanded it, or any fate, all was alike to him, so that she was true to him, – the man who had seen how cast away she was, whom she had inspired at their first meeting with an admiration, an interest, of which he had thought himself incapable, whom she had received into her confidence, who was devoted to her and adored her. All this, and more, in his hurry, and in hers, in the whirl of her own gratified malice, in the dread of being discovered, in the rapidly increasing noise of heavy rain among the leaves, and a thunder-storm rolling up – Mrs Sparsit received into her mind, with such an unavoidable halo of confusion, that when at length he climbed the fence and led his horse away, she was not sure where they were to meet, or when, except that they had said it was to be that night.

But one of them was still in the darkness before her; and while she tracked that one she must be right. "Oh, my dearest love," thought Mrs Sparsit, "you little think how well attended you are!"

Mrs Sparsit saw her leave the wood, and enter the house. What next? It rained now, in a sheet of water. Mrs Sparsit's white stockings were of many colours, green predominating; prickly things were in her shoes; caterpillars slung themselves from various parts of her dress; rills ran from her bonnet. In such condition, Mrs Sparsit stood hidden in the density of the shrubbery, considering what next?

Lo, Louisa coming out of the house! Hastily cloaked and muffled, and stealing away. She elopes! She falls from the lowermost stair, and is swallowed up in the gulf.

Indifferent to the rain, and moving with a quick determined step, she struck into a side-path parallel with the ride. Mrs Sparsit followed in the shadow of the trees, but it was not easy to keep a figure in view going quickly through the darkness.

When she stopped to close the side-gate without noise, Mrs Sparsit stopped. When she went on, Mrs Sparsit went on. She went by the way Mrs Sparsit had come, emerged from the green lane, crossed the stony road, and ascended the wooden steps to the railroad. A train for Coketown would come through presently, Mrs Sparsit knew.

In Mrs Sparsit's limp and streaming state, no extensive precautions were necessary to change her usual appearance, so she stopped by the station wall, and put her shawl on over her bonnet. She then she followed up the railroad steps, and paid her money in the small office. Louisa sat waiting in a corner. Mrs Sparsit sat waiting in another corner. Both listened to the thunder and the rain.

The surge of trembling in the building announced the train. Fire and steam, and smoke, and red light; a hiss, a crash, a bell, and a shriek; Louisa put into one carriage, Mrs Sparsit put into another.

Though her teeth chattered in her head from wet and cold, Mrs Sparsit exulted hugely. The figure had plunged down the precipice, and she felt herself, as it were, attending on the body. Could she, who had been so active in the getting up of the funeral triumph, do less than exult? "She will be at Coketown long before him," thought Mrs Sparsit. "Where will she wait for him? And where will they go together? Patience. We shall see."

The tremendous rain caused great confusion when the train stopped at its destination. Gutters and pipes had burst, drains had overflowed, and streets were under water. As she alighted, Mrs Sparsit turned towards the waiting coaches, which were in great request. "She will get into one," she considered, "and will be away before I can follow in another. At the risk of being run over, I must hear the order given to the coachman."

But, Mrs Sparsit was wrong. Louisa was already gone. The black eyes returned to the railroad-carriage in which she had travelled a moment too late. The door not being opened after several minutes, Mrs Sparsit passed it, saw nothing, looked in, and found it empty. Wet through and through, with her feet squelching and squashing in her shoes whenever she moved, with all her clothes spoiled, with damp impressions of every button, string, and hook-and-eye she wore, printed off upon her highly connected back, Mrs Sparsit could only burst into bitter tears and say, "I have lost her!"

CHAPTER 12

Mr Gradgrind was at home for the vacation.

He sat writing. The noise of the rain did not disturb him much, enough to make him raise his head sometimes, as if he were rather remonstrating with the elements. When it thundered very loudly, he glanced towards Coketown, wondering if some of the tall chimneys might be struck by lightning.

The thunder was rolling into distance, and the rain was pouring down like a deluge, when the door of his room opened. He looked round the lamp upon his table, and saw, with amazement, his eldest daughter.

"Louisa!"

"Father, I want to speak to you."

"What is the matter? How strange you look! Good Heaven," said Mr Gradgrind, wondering more and more, "have you come here in this storm?"

She put her hands to her dress, as if she hardly knew. "Yes." Then she uncovered her head, and letting her cloak and hood fall where they might, stood looking at him: so colourless, so dishevelled, so defiant and despairing, that he was afraid of her.

"What is it? Tell me, Louisa, what is the matter."

She dropped into a chair before him, and put her cold hand on his arm.

"Father, you have trained me from my cradle?"

"Yes, Louisa."

"I curse the hour in which I was born to such a destiny."

He looked at her in doubt and dread, vacantly repeating: "Curse the hour?"

"How could you give me life, and take from me all the inappreciable things that raise it from the state of conscious death? Where are the graces of my soul? Where are the sentiments of my heart? What have you done, O father, with the garden that should have bloomed once, in this great wilderness here!"

She struck herself with both her hands upon her bosom.

"If it had ever been here, its ashes alone would save me from the void in which my whole life sinks. I did not mean to say this; but, father, you remember the last time we conversed in this room?"

He had been so wholly unprepared for what he heard now, that it was with difficulty he answered, "Yes, Louisa."

"What has risen to my lips now, would have risen to my lips then, if you had given me a moment's help. I don't reproach you, father. What you have never nurtured in me, you have never nurtured in yourself. But O! if you had only done so long ago, or if you had only neglected me, what a much better and much happier creature I should have been this day!"

On hearing this, after all his care, he bowed his head upon his hand and groaned aloud.

"Father, if you had known, when we were last together here, what even I feared while I strove against it – as it has been my task from infancy to strive against every natural prompting that has arisen in my heart; if you had known that there lingered in my breast, sensibilities, affections, would you have given me to the husband whom I am now sure that I hate?"

He said, "No. No, my poor child."

"Yet, father, if I had been stone blind; if I had groped my way by my sense of touch, and had been free, while I knew the shapes and surfaces of things, to exercise my fancy somewhat, in regard to them; I should have been a million times wiser, happier, more loving, more contented, more innocent and human in all good respects, than I am with the eyes I have. Now, hear what I have come to say."

He moved to support her with his arm. She stared in his face.

"With a hunger and thirst upon me, father, which have never been for a moment appeased; with an ardent impulse towards some region where rules, and figures, and definitions were not quite absolute; I have grown up, battling every inch of my way."

"I never knew you were unhappy, my child. And you so young, Louisa!" he said with pity.

"And I so young. In this condition, father – for I show you now, without fear or favour, the ordinary deadened state of my mind as I know it – you proposed my husband to me. I took him. I never made a pretence to him or you that I loved him. I knew, and, father, you knew, and he knew, that I never did. I was not wholly indifferent, for I had a hope of being pleasant and useful to Tom. I made that wild escape into something visionary, and have slowly found out how wild it was. But Tom had been the subject of all the little tenderness of my life; perhaps he became so because I knew so well how to pity him. It matters little now, except as it may dispose you to think more leniently of his errors."

As her father held her in his arms, she went on.

"When I was irrevocably married, there rose up into rebellion against the tie, the old strife, made fiercer by all those causes of disparity which arise out of our two individual natures, and which no general laws shall ever rule or state for me, father, until they shall be able to direct the anatomist where to strike his knife into the secrets of my soul."

"Louisa!" he said, and said imploringly; for he well remembered what had passed between them in their former interview.

"I do not reproach you, father. I am here with another object."

"What can I do, child? Ask me what you will."

"I am coming to it. Father, chance then threw into my way a new acquaintance; a man such as I had had no experience of; used to the world; light, polished, easy; making no pretences; avowing the low estimate of everything, that I was half afraid to form in secret; conveying to me almost immediately, though I don't know how or by what degrees, that he understood me, and read my thoughts. I could not find that he was worse than I. There seemed to be a near affinity between us. I only wondered it should be worth his while, who cared for nothing else, to care so much for me."

"For you, Louisa!"

Her father almost loosened his hold, but he felt her strength departing from her, and saw a wild dilating fire in the eyes.

"I say nothing of his plea for claiming my confidence. It matters very little how he gained it. Father, he did gain it. What you know of the story of my marriage, he soon knew, just as well."

Her father's face was ashy white, and he held her in both his arms.

"I have not disgraced you. But if you ask me whether I have loved him, or do love him, I tell you, father, it may be so. I don't know."

She took her hands suddenly from his shoulders, and pressed them both upon her side; while the feelings long suppressed broke loose.

"This night, my husband being away, he has been with me, declaring himself my lover. This minute he expects me, for I could release myself of his presence by no other means. I do not know that I am sorry, I do not know that I am ashamed, I do not know that I am degraded in

143

my own esteem. I do know that your philosophy and your teaching will not save me. Now, father, you have brought me to this. Save me by some other means!"

He tightened his hold in time to prevent her sinking on the floor, but she cried out in a terrible voice, "I shall die if you hold me! Let me fall upon the ground!" And he laid her down there, and saw the pride of his heart and the triumph of his system, lying, an insensible heap, at his feet.

BOOK 3

CHAPTER 1

Louisa awoke to find herself in her old bed at home, and her old room. It seemed, at first, as if all that had happened since the days when these objects were familiar to her were the shadows of a dream; but gradually, as the objects became more real to her sight, the events became more real to her mind.

She could scarcely move her head for pain and heaviness, her eyes were strained and sore, and she was very weak. It was some time before she noticed her little sister in the room. Even when their eyes had met, and her sister had approached the bed, Louisa lay looking at her in silence, and suffering her timidly to hold her passive hand, before she asked:

"When was I brought to this room?"

"Last night, Louisa."

"Who brought me here?"

"Sissy, I believe."

"Why do you believe so?"

"Because I found her here this morning. She didn't come to my bedside to wake me, as she always does; and I went to look for her. She was not in her own room either so I went looking for her all over the house. I found her here taking care of you and cooling your head. Will you see father? Sissy said I was to tell him when you woke."

"What a beaming face you have, Jane!" said Louisa, as her young sister – timidly still – bent down to kiss her.

144

"Have I? I am very glad you think so. I am sure it must be Sissy's doing."

The arm Louisa had begun to twine around her neck, unbent itself. "You can tell father if you will." Then, staying her for a moment, she said, "It was you who made my room so cheerful, and gave it this look of welcome?"

"Oh no, Louisa, it was done before I came. It was – "

Louisa turned upon her pillow, and heard no more. When her sister had gone, she turned her head back again, watching until her father entered.

He had an anxious look upon him, and his hand, usually steady, trembled in hers. He sat down at the side of the bed, tenderly asking how she was, saying she must keep quiet after her exposure to the weather last night. He spoke in a subdued and troubled voice, very different from his usual dictatorial manner; and was often at a loss for words.

"My dear Louisa. My poor daughter." He was so much at a loss that he stopped altogether. He tried again.

"My unfortunate child." It was so difficult, that he tried again.

"I cannot tell you, Louisa, how overwhelmed I have been, and still am, by what broke upon me last night. The ground beneath my feet is no longer solid. The only support on which I leaned, and the strength of which it seemed, and still does seem, impossible to question, has given way in an instant. I am stunned by these discoveries."

She could give him no comfort. She had suffered the wreck of her whole life upon the rock.

"I will not say, Louisa, that if you had by any happy chance undeceived me some time ago, it would have been better for us both; better for your peace, and better for mine. For I realise that it may not have been my way to invite any confidence of that kind. I had proved my – my system to myself, and I have rigidly administered it. I must bear the responsibility of its failures. I only entreat you to believe, my favourite child, that I have meant to do right."

He said it earnestly, and to do him justice he had. He had meant to do great things. But within the limits of his short tether he had tumbled about, annihilating the flowers of existence with great singleness of purpose.

"I know you mean well, father. I know I have been your favourite child. I know you have intended to make me happy. I have never blamed you, and I never shall."

145

He took her outstretched hand, and retained it in his.

"My dear, I have spent all night at my table, over what has so painfully passed between us. When I consider that what has been known to me for hours, has been concealed by you for years; when I consider under what immediate pressure it has been forced from you at last; I come to the conclusion that I cannot but mistrust myself."

He might have added more, when he saw the face now looking at him. He did add it in effect, perhaps, as he softly moved her scattered hair from her forehead with his hand. Such little actions, slight in another man, were very noticeable in him; and his daughter received them as if they had been words of contrition.

"But," said Mr Gradgrind, slowly, and with hesitation, as well as with a wretched sense of happiness, "if I see reason to mistrust myself for the past, Louisa, I should also mistrust myself for the present and the future. To speak unreservedly to you, wondering how to help you, and to set you right, my child."

She had turned upon her pillow, and lay with her face upon her arm, so that he could not see it.

"Some persons hold," he pursued, still hesitating, "that there is a wisdom of the Head, and that there is a wisdom of the Heart. I have not supposed so; but, as I have said, I mistrust myself now. I thought the Head to be all-sufficient. It may not be all-sufficient; how can I venture this morning to say it is! If that other kind of wisdom should be what I have neglected, and should be the instinct that is wanted, Louisa – "

He suggested it very doubtfully, as if he were half unwilling to admit it even now. She made him no answer, lying before him on her bed, still half dressed, much as he had seen her lying on the floor of his room last night.

"Louisa," and his hand rested on her hair again, "I have been absent from here, my dear, a good deal of late; and though your sister's training has been pursued according to – the system," he appeared to come to that word with great reluctance always, "it has necessarily been modified by daily associations begun, in her case, at an early age. I ask you – ignorantly and humbly, my daughter – for the better, do you think?"

"Father," she replied, without stirring, "if any harmony has been awakened in her young breast that was mute in mine until it turned to discord, let her thank Heaven for it, and go upon her happier way, taking it as her greatest blessing that she has avoided my way."

"O my child, my child!" he said, in a forlorn manner, "I am an unhappy man to see you thus! And you do not reproach me, while I so bitterly reproach myself!" He bent his head, and spoke low to her. "Louisa, I have a misgiving that some change may have been slowly working about me in this house, by mere love and gratitude: that what the Head had left undone and could not do, the Heart may have been doing silently. Can it be so?"

She made him no reply.

"I am not too proud to believe it, Louisa. How could I be arrogant, and you before me! Can it be so, my dear?" He looked upon her once more, and without another word went out of the room. He had not been long gone, when she heard a light tread near the door, and knew that some one stood beside her.

She did not raise her head. A dull anger that she should be seen in her distress, and that the involuntary look she had so resented should come to this, smouldered within her like an unwholesome fire. So in her bosom even now the strongest qualities she possessed, long turned upon themselves, became a heap of obduracy, that rose against a friend.

It was well that soft touch came upon her neck, and that she understood herself to be supposed to have fallen asleep. The sympathetic hand did not claim her resentment. Let it lie there, let it lie.

It lay there, warming into life a crowd of gentler thoughts; and she rested. As she softened with the quiet, and the consciousness of being watched, some tears came to her eyes. The face touched hers, and she knew that there were tears upon it too, and she the cause of them.

As Louisa pretended to rouse herself, and sat up, Sissy retired, so that she stood placidly near the bedside.

"I hope I have not disturbed you. I have come to ask if you would let me stay with you?"

"Why should you stay with me? My sister will miss you. You are everything to her."

"Am I?" returned Sissy, shaking her head. "I would be something to you, if I might."

"What?" said Louisa, almost sternly.

"Whatever you want most. At least, I would like to try to be as near it as I can. Will you let me?"

"My father sent you to ask me."

"No indeed," replied Sissy. "He told me that I might come in now, but he sent me away from the room this morning – or at least – " She hesitated and stopped.

"At least, what?" said Louisa, with her searching eyes upon her.

"I thought it best myself that I should be sent away, for I felt very uncertain whether you would like to find me here."

"Have I always hated you so much?"

"I hope not, for I have always loved you, and have always wished that you should know it. But you changed to me a little, shortly before you left home. But then you knew so much, and I knew so little, and it was natural as you were among other friends. I had nothing to complain of, and was not at all hurt."

Her colour rose as she said it hurriedly. Louisa understood the loving pretence, and her heart smote her.

"May I try?" said Sissy, emboldened to raise her hand to the neck that was insensibly drooping towards her.

Louisa, taking down the hand that would have embraced her in another moment, held it in one of hers, and answered:

"First, Sissy, do you know what I am? I am so proud and so hardened, so confused and troubled, so resentful and unjust to every one and to myself, that everything is stormy, dark, and wicked to me. Does not that repel you?"

"No!"

"I am so unhappy, and all that should have made me otherwise is so laid waste, that if I had been bereft of sense to this hour, and instead of being as learned as you think me, had to begin to acquire the simplest truths, I could not want a guide to peace, contentment, honour, all the good of which I am quite devoid, more abjectly than I do. Does not that repel you?"

"No!"

In the innocence of her brave affection, and the brimming up of her old devoted spirit, the once deserted girl shone like a beautiful light upon the darkness of the other.

Louisa fell upon her knees, and clung to this stroller's child.

"Forgive me, help me! Have compassion on my great need, and let me lay this head of mine upon a loving heart!"

"O lay it here, my dear!" cried Sissy.

CHAPTER 2

Mr James Harthouse passed a whole night and a day in a state of agitation. He several times spoke with an emphasis, similar to the vulgar manner. He went in and went out in an unaccountable way, like a man without an object. He rode like a highwayman. In a word, he was so horribly bored by existing circumstances, that he forgot to go in for boredom in the manner prescribed by the authorities.

After putting his horse at Coketown through the storm, as if it were a leap, he waited up all night. From time to time he rang for the porter, accusing him of withholding letters or messages that could not fail to have been entrusted to him. Day came, and neither message nor letter coming with it, so he went down to the country-house. There, the report was, Mr Bounderby away, and Mrs Bounderby in town. Left for town suddenly last evening. Not even known to be gone until receipt of message, saying that her return was not to be expected for the present.

So he followed her to town. He went to the house. Mrs Bounderby not there. He looked in at the Bank. Mr Bounderby away and Mrs Sparsit away. Mrs Sparsit away? Who could have been reduced to sudden extremity for the company of that griffin!

"Well! I don't know," said Tom, who had his own reasons for being uneasy about it. "She was off somewhere at daybreak this morning. She's always full of mystery; I hate her. And that white chap, he's always got his blinking eyes upon a fellow."

"Where were you last night, Tom?"

"Where was I last night!" said Tom. "Come! I like that. I was waiting for you, Mr Harthouse! Where were you, you mean."

"I was prevented from coming – detained."

"Detained!" murmured Tom. "Two of us were detained. I was detained looking for you. I was obliged to sleep in town after all."

"Where?"

"In my own bed at Bounderby's."

"Did you see your sister?"

"How the deuce," returned Tom, staring, "could I see my sister when she was fifteen miles off?"

What could all this mean? Harthouse made only one thing clear. It was, that whether she was in town or out of town, whether he had been premature with her who was so hard to comprehend, or she had lost courage, or they were discovered, or some mischance had occurred, he must remain to confront his fortune, whatever it was. The hotel where he was known to live when condemned to that region of blackness, was the stake to which he was tied. As to all the rest – What will be, will be.

"So, whatever I'm waiting for – I'll dine," said Mr James Harthouse.

Therefore he rang the bell, and tossing himself negligently on a sofa, ordered "Some dinner at six – with a beefsteak in it," and got through the intervening time as well as he could. That was not particularly well; for he remained in the greatest perplexity, and, as the hours went on, and no kind of explanation offered itself, his perplexity augmented at compound interest.

It was impossible, even before dinner, to avoid often walking about in the pattern of the carpet, looking out of the window, listening at the door for footsteps, and occasionally becoming rather hot when any steps approached that room. But, after dinner, when the day turned to twilight, and the twilight turned to night, and still no communication was made to him, it began to be as he expressed it, "like slow torture." However, still true to his conviction that indifference was the genuine high-breeding (the only conviction he had), he seized this crisis as the opportunity for ordering candles and a newspaper.

He had been trying in vain, for half an hour, to read this newspaper, when the waiter appeared and said, at once mysteriously and apologetically: "Beg your pardon, sir. You are wanted, sir, if you please."

Mr Harthouse asked the waiter in return, what the Devil he meant by "wanted"?

"Beg your pardon, sir. Young lady outside, sir, wishes to see you."

"Outside? Where?"

"Outside this door, sir."

Mr Harthouse hurried into the gallery. A young woman whom he had never seen stood there. Plainly dressed, very quiet, very pretty. As he conducted her into the room and placed a chair for her, he observed, by the light of the candles, that she was even prettier than he had at first believed. Her face was innocent and youthful. She was not afraid of him, or in any way disconcerted. She seemed entirely preoccupied with the occasion of her visit.

"I speak to Mr Harthouse?" she said, when they were alone.

"To Mr Harthouse." He added in his mind, "And you speak to him with the most confiding eyes I ever saw, and the most earnest voice (though so quiet) I ever heard."

"If I do not understand – and I do not, sir," – said Sissy, "what your honour as a gentleman binds you to, in other matters," the blood really rose in his face as she began with these words: "I am sure I may rely upon it to keep my visit secret, and to keep secret what I am going to say. I will rely upon it, if you will tell me I may so far trust – "

"You may, I assure you."

"I am young and alone, as you see. In coming to you, sir, I have no advice or encouragement beyond my own hope."

He thought, "But that is very strong," as he followed the momentary upward glance of her eyes. He thought besides, "This is a very odd beginning. I don't see where we are going."

"I think," said Sissy, "you have already guessed whom I left just now!"

"I have been in the greatest concern and uneasiness during the last four-and-twenty hours (which have appeared as many years)," he returned, "on a lady's account. I believe that you come from her."

"I left her within an hour."

"At – !"

"At her father's."

Mr Harthouse's face lengthened in spite of his coolness, and his perplexity increased. "Then I certainly," he thought, "do not see where we are going."

"She hurried there last night. She arrived there in great agitation, and was insensible all through the night. I live at her father's, and was with her. You may be sure, sir, you will never see her again as long as you live."

Mr Harthouse drew a long breath; and found himself, truthfully, at a total loss for words. The child-like ingenuousness with which his visitor spoke, her modest fearlessness, her truthfulness which put all artifice aside, her entire forgetfulness of herself as she held to her subject; all this, together with her reliance on his easily given promise – which in itself shamed him – rendered him speechless.

At last he said: "Such a startling announcement is really disconcerting. May I inquire, if you were given this task by the lady of whom we speak?"

"I have no charge from her."

"The drowning man catches at the straw. But can I cling to the belief that there is yet hope that I am not condemned to perpetual exile from that lady's presence."

"There is not the least hope. The first object of my coming here, sir, is to make you believe that there is no more hope of your ever speaking with her again, than there would be if she had died when she returned last night."

"Believe that? But if I can't – or if I should be obstinate – and won't – "

"There is no hope."

James Harthouse looked at her with an incredulous smile upon his lips; but her mind looked beyond him, and the smile was useless.

He bit his lip, and considered a moment.

"Well! If it should unhappily appear," he said, "after due pains and duty on my part, that I am brought to a position so desolate as this banishment, I shall not become the lady's persecutor. But you said you had no commission from her?"

"I have only the commission of my love for her, and her love for me. I have no other trust, than that I have been with her since she came home, and that she has given me her confidence. I have no further trust, than that I know something of her character and her marriage. O Mr Harthouse, I think you had that trust too!"

He was touched in the cavity where his heart should have been by the fervour of this reproach.

"I am not a moral sort of fellow," he said, "and I never make any pretensions to the character of a moral sort of fellow. At the same time, in bringing any distress upon the lady or in unfortunately compromising her in any way, or in committing myself by any expression of sentiments towards her, not perfectly reconcilable with – in fact with – the domestic hearth; or in taking any advantage of her father's being a machine, or of her brother's being a whelp, or of her husband's being a bear; I beg to assure you that I have had no evil intentions, but have glided on from one step to another, that I had not the slightest idea the catalogue was half so long until I began to turn it over. Whereas I find," said Mr James Harthouse, in conclusion, "that it is really in several volumes."

Though he said all this in his frivolous way, the way seemed, for once, a conscious polishing of but an ugly surface. He was silent for a moment;

and then proceeded with a more self-possessed air, though with traces of vexation and disappointment that would not be polished out.

"After what you have just told me, in a manner I find impossible to doubt – I know of hardly any other source from which I could have accepted it so readily – I feel bound to say to you, in whom the confidence you have mentioned has been reposed, that I cannot refuse to contemplate the possibility (however unexpected) of my seeing the lady no more. I am solely to blame for the thing having come to this – and – and, I cannot say," he added, "that I can ever hope to become a moral sort of fellow, or that I have any belief in any moral sort of fellow whatever."

Sissy's face showed that her appeal to him was not finished.

"You spoke," he resumed, as she raised her eyes to him again, "of your first object. I may assume that there is a second?"

"Yes."

"Will you oblige me by confiding it?"

"Mr Harthouse," returned Sissy, with a blending of gentleness and steadiness that quite defeated him, "the only reparation that remains with you, is to leave here immediately and finally. I am quite sure that it is the only compensation you have left it in your power to make. I do not say that it is much, or that it is enough; but it is something, and it is necessary. Therefore, I ask you to depart from this place tonight, never to return to it."

If she had asserted any influence over him beyond her plain faith in the truth and right of what she said, or shown, or felt, the lightest trace of any sensitiveness to his ridicule or his astonishment, he would have carried it against her at this point. But he could as easily have changed a clear sky by looking at it, as affect her.

"But do you know," he asked, quite at a loss, "what you ask? You are probably unaware that I am here on a public kind of business, which I have gone in for, and sworn by, and am supposed to be devoted to in quite a desperate manner? I assure you it's the fact."

It had no effect on Sissy, fact or no fact.

"Besides which," said Mr Harthouse, taking a turn or two across the room, "it's so alarmingly absurd. It would make a man so ridiculous, after going in for these fellows, to back out in such an incomprehensible way."

"I am quite sure," repeated Sissy, "that it is the only reparation in your power, sir. I am quite sure, or I would not have come here."

He glanced at her face, and walked about again. "Upon my soul, I don't know what to say."

It fell to his lot, now, to stipulate for secrecy.

"If I were to do such a very ridiculous thing," he said, stopping again presently, "it could only be in the utmost confidence."

"I will trust to you, sir," returned Sissy, "and you will trust to me."

His leaning against the chimney-piece reminded him of the night with the whelp. But this time he felt as if he were the whelp. He could make no way at all.

"I suppose a man never was placed in a more ridiculous position," he said, after looking about, and laughing, and frowning, and walking to and fro. "But I see no way out of it. What will be will be. This will be, I suppose. I must take off myself, I imagine – in short, I engage to do it."

Sissy rose. She was not surprised by the result, but she was happy in it, and her face beamed brightly.

"You will permit me to say," continued Mr James Harthouse, "that I doubt if any one else could have had the same success. I regard myself as being vanquished at all points. Will you allow me the privilege of remembering my enemy's name?"

"My name?" said the girl.

"The only name I could possibly care to know, tonight."

"Sissy Jupe."

"Pardon my curiosity at parting. Related to the family?"

"I am only a poor girl," returned Sissy. "I was separated from my father – he was only a stroller – and taken pity on by Mr Gradgrind. I have lived in the house ever since."

She was gone.

"It wanted this to complete the defeat," said Mr James Harthouse, sinking, with a resigned air, on the sofa. "The defeat may now be considered perfectly accomplished. Only a poor girl – only a stroller – only James Harthouse made nothing of – only James Harthouse a Great Pyramid of failure."

The Great Pyramid put it into his head to go up the Nile. He took a pen upon the instant, and wrote the following note (in appropriate hieroglyphics) to his brother:

154

Dear Jack,
– All up at Coketown. Bored out of the place, and going in for camels.
Affectionately,
JEM.

He rang the bell. "Send my fellow here."

"Gone to bed, sir."

"Tell him to get up, and pack up."

He wrote two more notes. One to Mr Bounderby, announcing his retirement from that part of the country, and showing where he would be found for the next fortnight. The other, similar in effect, to Mr Gradgrind. Almost as soon as the ink was dry upon their superscriptions, he had left the tall chimneys of Coketown behind, and was in a railway carriage, tearing and glaring over the country.

The moral sort of fellows might suppose that Mr James Harthouse derived some comfortable reflections from this prompt retreat, as one of his few actions that made any amends for anything. But it was not so, at all. A secret sense of having failed and been ridiculous – a dread of what other fellows who went in for similar sorts of things, would say at his expense if they knew it – so oppressed him, that what was about the very best passage in his life was the very one he could not own up to and the only one that made him ashamed of himself.

CHAPTER 3

The indefatigable Mrs Sparsit, with a violent cold upon her, her voice reduced to a whisper, gave chase to her patron until she found him in the metropolis. There, she majestically swept in upon him at his hotel in St James's Street, exploded the combustibles with which she was charged, and blew up. She then fainted away on Mr Bounderby's coat-collar.

Mr Bounderby's first procedure was to shake Mrs Sparsit off, and leave her to progress as she might through various stages of suffering on the floor. He next administered potent restoratives, such as screwing the patient's thumbs, smiting her hands, abundantly watering her face, and inserting salt in her mouth. When these attentions had recovered her (which they speedily did), he hustled her into a fast train without offering any other refreshment, and carried her back to Coketown more dead than alive.

Regarded as a classical ruin, Mrs Sparsit was an interesting spectacle on her arrival at her journey's end. Utterly heedless of the wear and tear of her clothes and constitution, and adamant to her pathetic sneezes, Mr Bounderby immediately crammed her into a coach, and bore her off to Stone Lodge.

"Now, Tom Gradgrind," said Bounderby, bursting into his father-in-law's room late at night; "here's a lady – you know Mrs Sparsit – who has something to tell you that will strike you dumb."

"You have missed my letter!" exclaimed Mr Gradgrind, surprised by the apparition.

"Missed your letter, sir!" bawled Bounderby. "This is no time for letters. No man shall talk to Josiah Bounderby of Coketown about letters, with his mind in the state it's in now."

"Bounderby," said Mr Gradgrind, in a tone of temperate remonstrance, "I speak of a very special letter I have written to you, in reference to Louisa."

"Tom Gradgrind," replied Bounderby, knocking the flat of his hand several times with great vehemence on the table, "I speak of a very special messenger that has come to me, in reference to Louisa. Mrs Sparsit, ma'am, stand forward!"

That unfortunate lady hereupon tried to speak, with no voice and an inflamed throat. Mr Bounderby, unable to bear it, seized her by the arm and shook her.

"If you can't get it out, ma'am," said Bounderby, "leave me to do it. Tom Gradgrind, Mrs Sparsit recently, by accident, overheard a conversation between your daughter and your precious gentleman friend, Mr James Harthouse."

"Indeed!" said Mr Gradgrind.

"Ah! Indeed!" cried Bounderby. "And in that conversation – "

"It is not necessary to repeat it, Bounderby. I know what passed."

"You do? Perhaps," said Bounderby, staring at his so quiet father-in-law, "you know where your daughter is at the moment!"

"She is here."

"Here?"

"My dear Bounderby, Louisa is here. The moment she could get away

156

from the person of whom you speak, and whom I deeply regret having introduced to you, Louisa hurried here, for protection. She hurried by the train to town, she ran from town to this house, through a raging storm, and presented herself before me in a state of distraction. Of course, she has remained here ever since. So, for your own sake and hers, do be more quiet."

Mr Bounderby silently gazed about him, and then, abruptly turned upon Mrs Sparsit, saying to that wretched woman:

"Now, ma'am! We shall be happy to hear any apology you may think proper to offer, for going about the country, with no other luggage than a Cock-and-a-Bull, ma'am!"

Mrs Sparsit burst into tears.

"Well, Madam, we'll pack you home to the Bank where you can put your feet into the hottest water you can bear, and take a glass of scalding rum and butter after you get into bed." Mr Bounderby extended his right hand to the weeping lady, and escorted her to the carriage. He soon returned alone.

"Now, as you showed me in your face, Tom Gradgrind, that you wanted to speak to me," he resumed, "here I am. But, I am not in a very agreeable state. You have your opinion, I dare say; and I have mine, I know."

"My dear Bounderby," Mr Gradgrind began.

"Now, you'll excuse me," said Bounderby, "but I don't want to be dear. When I begin to be dear to a man, I generally find that his intention is to come over me."

"Bounderby," said Mr Gradgrind, "we can all make mistakes – "

"I thought you couldn't make 'em," interrupted Bounderby.

"Perhaps I thought so. But, I say we can all make mistakes, and I doubt whether I have understood Louisa. I doubt whether I have been quite right in the manner of her education."

"There I agree with you," returned Bounderby. "You have found it out at last, have you? Education! I'll tell you what education is – To be tumbled out of doors and put upon the shortest allowance of everything except blows. That's what I call education."

"I think your good sense will perceive," Mr Gradgrind remonstrated in all humility, "that whatever the merits of such an education, it would be difficult to apply to girls."

157

"I don't see it at all, sir," returned the obstinate Bounderby.

"Well," sighed Mr Gradgrind, "we will not enter into the question. I assure you I have no desire to be controversial. I seek to repair what is amiss, if possible, and I hope you will assist, Bounderby, for I have been very much distressed."

"I don't understand you, yet," said Bounderby, with determined obstinacy, "so I won't make any promises."

"In the course of a few hours, my dear Bounderby," Mr Gradgrind proceeded, in the same depressed manner, "I have become better informed as to Louisa's character, than in previous years. The process has been painful. I think there are – Bounderby, you will be surprised to hear me say this – there are qualities in Louisa, which – which have been harshly neglected, and – and a little perverted. And – and I would suggest to you, that – that you leave her to her better nature for a while – and to encourage it to develop itself by tenderness and consideration. Louisa," said Mr Gradgrind, shading his face with his hand, "has always been my favourite child."

The blustrous Bounderby crimsoned and said: "You'd like to keep her here for a time?"

"I – I had intended to recommend, my dear Bounderby, that Louisa remains here on a visit, attended by Sissy (I mean of course Cecilia Jupe), who understands her, and in whom she trusts."

"I gather from all this, Tom Gradgrind," said Bounderby, hands in pockets, "that you think that there's what people call some incompatibility between Loo Bounderby and myself."

"I fear there is at present a general incompatibility between Louisa, and – and almost all the relations in which I have placed her," was her father's sorrowful reply.

"Now, look you here, Tom Gradgrind," said Bounderby the flushed, confronting him with his legs wide apart, his hands deeper in his pockets. "You have said your say; I am going to say mine. I am Josiah Bounderby of Coketown. I know the bricks of this town, and I know the works of this town, and I know the Hands of this town. When a man tells me anything about imaginative qualities, I always tell that man, whoever he is, that I know what he means. He means turtle-soup and venison, with a gold spoon, and that he wants to be set up with a coach and six. That's what your daughter wants. So, I recommend you provide it for her. Because, Tom Gradgrind, she will never have it from me."

"Bounderby," said Mr Gradgrind, "I hoped you would have taken a different tone."

"Just wait a bit," retorted Bounderby; "you have said your say, I believe. So hear me out, if you please. Now, there's an incompatibility of some sort or another, I am given to understand by you, between your daughter and me. There unquestionably is an incompatibility of the first magnitude – that is – your daughter don't properly know her husband's merits, and is not impressed with such a sense as would become her, by George! of the honour of his alliance. That's plain speaking, I hope."

"Bounderby," urged Mr Gradgrind, "this is unreasonable."

"Is it?" said Bounderby. "I am glad to hear you say so. Because when Tom Gradgrind tells me that what I say is unreasonable, I am convinced at once it must be devilish sensible. With your permission I'll continue. You know my origin and you know that for a good many years I didn't want a shoeing-horn as I didn't have shoes. Yet you may believe or not, that there are ladies – belonging to families – Families! – who worship the ground I walk on."

He discharged this like a Rocket, at his father-in-law's head.

"Whereas your daughter," he continued, "is far from being a born lady. Not that I care a pinch of candle-snuff about such things for you are very well aware I don't. But that is the fact, and you, Tom Gradgrind, can't change it. Why do I say this?"

"Not, I fear," said Mr Gradgrind, in a low voice, "to spare me."

"Hear me out," said Bounderby, "and refrain from cutting in till your turn comes round. I say this, because highly connected females have been astonished to see the way in which your daughter has conducted herself, and to witness her insensibility. They wonder how I suffered it. And I wonder myself now, and I won't suffer it."

"Bounderby," returned Mr Gradgrind, rising, "the less we say tonight the better, I think."

"On the contrary, Tom Gradgrind, the more we say tonight, the better, I think. I come to a question that may shorten the business. What do you mean by the proposal you made just now?"

"What do I mean, Bounderby?"

"By your visiting proposition," said Bounderby.

"I mean that I hope you may allow Louisa a period of repose and reflection here, which may tend to a gradual alteration for the better in many respects."

"To a softening of your ideas of incompatibility?" said Bounderby.

"If you put it in those terms."

"What made you think of this?" said Bounderby.

"I have already said, Louisa has not been understood. Is it asking too much, Bounderby, that you, so far her elder, should aid in trying to set her right? You have accepted a great charge of her; for better for worse, for – "

"Come!" said Bounderby with a start, "I know what I took her for, as well as you do. So never you mind – that's my look-out."

"I was merely going to say, Bounderby, that we may all be more or less in the wrong, even you; and that some yielding on your part, remembering the trust you have accepted, may not only be an act of true kindness, but perhaps a debt incurred towards Louisa."

"I think differently," blustered Bounderby. "I am going to finish this business according to my own opinions. As to your daughter, whom I made Loo Bounderby, and might have done better by leaving Loo Gradgrind, if she don't come home tomorrow, by twelve o'clock at noon, I shall understand that she prefers to stay away, and I shall send her wearing apparel and so forth over here, and you'll take charge of her for the future. What I shall say to people is that I am Josiah Bounderby, and I had my bringing up; she's the daughter of Tom Gradgrind, and she had her bringing up; and the two horses wouldn't pull together. I am pretty well known as an uncommon man, I believe; and most people will understand that it must be a woman rather out of the common, also, who, in the long run, would come up to my mark."

"Let me seriously entreat you to reconsider this, Bounderby," urged Mr Gradgrind.

"I always come to a decision at once," said Bounderby, tossing his hat on. "I should be surprised at Tom Gradgrind's addressing such a remark to Josiah Bounderby of Coketown, knowing what he knows of him, if I could be surprised by anything Tom Gradgrind did, after his making himself a party to sentimental humbug. I have given you my decision, and I have no more to say. Good-night!"

So Mr Bounderby went home to his town house to bed. At five minutes past twelve o'clock next day, he directed Mrs Bounderby's property to be carefully packed up and sent to Tom Gradgrind's. He advertised his country retreat for sale by private contract, and resumed a bachelor life.

CHAPTER 4

The robbery at the Bank had not languished before, and did not cease to occupy a front place in the attention of the principal of that establishment now. He liked to show how little his domestic affairs abated his business ardour. Consequently, in the first few weeks of his resumed bachelorhood, he every day made such a rout in renewing his investigations into the robbery, that the officers who had it in hand almost wished it had never been committed.

They were at fault too, and off the scent. No implicated man or woman took untimely courage, or made a self-betraying step. More remarkable yet, Stephen Blackpool could not be heard of, and the mysterious old woman remained a mystery.

Things having come to this pass, and showing no latent signs of stirring beyond it, Bounderby resolved to hazard a bold burst. He drew up a placard, offering Twenty Pounds reward for the apprehension of Stephen Blackpool, suspected of complicity in the robbery of Coketown Bank on such a night; he described the said Stephen Blackpool by dress, complexion, estimated height, and manner, as minutely as he could. He recited how he had left the town, and in what direction he was last seen going. He had the whole printed in great black letters on a staring broadsheet, and he caused the walls to be posted with it in the dead of night, so that it should strike upon the sight of the whole population at one blow.

The factory-bells rang their loudest that morning to disperse the groups of workers who stood in the tardy daybreak, collected round the placards, devouring them with eager eyes. Not the least eager of the eyes assembled, were the eyes of those who could not read. These people listened to the friendly voice that read aloud – there was always some such ready to help them. Many ears and eyes were busy with a vision of these placards, among turning spindles, rattling looms, and whirling wheels, for hours afterwards; and when the Hands cleared out again into the streets, there were still as many readers as before.

Slackbridge, the delegate, had to address his audience too that night and had obtained a clean bill from the printer, bringing it in his pocket. Oh, my friends and fellow countrymen, the down-trodden operatives of

Coketown, oh, my fellow brothers and fellow workmen and fellow citizens, what a to-do was there, when Slackbridge unfolded what he called "that damning document," and held it up to the gaze of the working-man community! "Oh, my fellow-men, behold of what a traitor is appropriately capable! Oh my prostrate friends, with the galling yoke of tyrants on your necks – oh, my brothers, and shall I as a man not add, my sisters too, what do you say, now, of Stephen Blackpool, with a slight stoop in his shoulders and about five foot seven in height, as set forth in this degrading and disgusting document, this abominable advertisement. With what majesty of denouncement will you crush the viper, who would bring this stain and shame upon the God-like race that happily has cast him out for ever! You remember how he stood here before you on this platform, how, face-to-face and foot-to-foot, I pursued him through all his intricate windings. You remember how he sneaked and slunk, and sidled, and splitted of straws, until, with not an inch of ground to which to cling, I hurled him out from amongst us – an object for the undying finger of scorn to point at! And now, my friends – my labouring friends, for I rejoice and triumph in that stigma – and now, I say, my friends, what appellation has that dastard craven taken to himself? What? A thief! A plunderer! A proscribed fugitive, with a price upon his head! Therefore, my band of brothers in a sacred bond, to which your children and your children's children yet unborn have set their infant hands and seals, I propose to you on the part of the United Aggregate Tribunal, ever watchful for your welfare, ever zealous for your benefit, that this meeting does Resolve: That Stephen Blackpool, weaver, referred to in this placard, having been already solemnly disowned by the community of Coketown Hands, the same are free from the shame of his misdeeds, and cannot as a class be reproached with his dishonest actions!"

A few stern voices called out "No!" and a score or two hailed, with assenting cries of "Hear, hear!" the caution from one man, "Slackbridge, y' or over hetter in't; y'or a goen too fast!" But these were pigmies against an army; the general assemblage subscribed to the gospel according to Slackbridge, and gave three cheers for him, as he sat demonstratively panting at them.

These men and women were still in the streets, going home, when Sissy, who had been called away from Louisa some minutes before, returned.

162

"Who is it?" asked Louisa.

"It is Mr Bounderby," said Sissy, timid of the name, "and your brother Mr Tom, and a young woman who says her name is Rachael, and that you know her."

"What do they want, Sissy dear?"

"They want to see you. Rachael has been crying, and seems angry."

"Father," said Louisa, for he was present, "I cannot refuse to see them, for a reason that will explain itself."

Sissy went away to bring them. She reappeared directly. Tom was last and remained near the door.

"Mrs Bounderby," said her husband, entering with a cool nod, "I don't disturb you, I hope. This is an unseasonable hour, but this young woman has been saying things that make my visit necessary. Tom Gradgrind, as your son, young Tom, refuses for some reason or other to say anything at all about those statements, I am obliged to confront her with your daughter."

"You have seen me once before, young lady," said Rachael, standing in front of Louisa.

Tom coughed.

"You have seen me, young lady," repeated Rachael, as she did not answer, "once before."

Tom coughed again.

"I have."

Rachael looked proudly towards Mr Bounderby, and said, "Will you make it known, young lady, where, and who was there?"

"I went to Stephen Blackpool's house on the night he was discharged from work, and I saw you there. He was there too and also an old woman who did not speak, and whom I could scarcely see in a dark corner. My brother was with me."

"Why couldn't you say so, young Tom?" demanded Bounderby.

"I promised my sister I wouldn't." Which Louisa hastily confirmed. "And besides," said the whelp bitterly, "she tells her own story so precious well – and so full – that what business had I to take it out of her mouth!"

"Say, young lady, if you please," pursued Rachael, "why, in an evil hour, you ever came to Stephen's that night."

"I felt compassion for him," said Louisa, her colour deepening, "and

I wished to know what he was going to do, and wished to offer him assistance."

"Much flattered and obliged," said Bounderby.

"Did you offer him," asked Rachael, "a bank-note?"

"Yes, but he refused it, and would only take two pounds in gold."

Rachael cast her eyes towards Mr Bounderby again.

"Oh, certainly!" said Bounderby. "Well, I'm bound to say your ridiculous and improbable account has been confirmed."

"Young lady," said Rachael, "Stephen Blackpool is now named as a thief in public print all over this town, and where else! There's been a meeting tonight where he's been spoken of in the same shameful way. Stephen! The honestest lad, the truest lad, the best!" Her indignation failed her, and she broke off sobbing.

"I am very, very sorry," said Louisa.

"Oh, young lady, young lady," returned Rachael, "I hope you may be, but I don't know! I can't say what you may ha' done. I am not sure why you came that night. I can't tell but what you may ha' come wi' some aim of your own, not mindin to what trouble you brought such as the poor lad. I said then, Bless you for coming; and I said it of my heart, you seemed to take so pitifully to him; but I don't know now, I don't know!"

Louisa could not reproach her for her unjust suspicions; she was so faithful to her idea of the man, and so afflicted.

"And when I think," said Rachael through her sobs, "that the poor lad was so grateful, thinkin you so good to him – when I mind that he put his hand over his hard-worken face to hide the tears that you brought up there – Oh, I hope you may be sorry, and ha' no bad cause to be it; but I don't know!"

"You're a pretty article," growled the whelp, moving uneasily in his dark corner, "to come here with these precious imputations! You ought to be bundled out for not knowing how to behave yourself."

She said nothing in reply; and her low weeping was the only sound that was heard, until Mr Bounderby spoke.

"Come!" said he, "you know what you have engaged to do. You had better give your mind to that; not this."

"'Deed, I am loath," returned Rachael, drying her eyes, "that any here should see me like this; but I won't be seen so again. Young lady, when I had read what's put in print of Stephen – that has just as much truth in it as if it had been about you – I went straight to the Bank to say I knew where Stephen was, and to give sure and certain promise that he should be here in two days. I couldn't meet wi' Mr Bounderby then, and your brother sent me away, and I tried to find you, but you was not to be found, and I went back to work. Soon as I come out of the Mill tonight, I hastened to hear what was said of Stephen – for I know wi' pride he will come back! And then I went again to Mr Bounderby, and I told him every word I knew and he believed no word and brought me here."

"So far, that's true enough," assented Mr Bounderby, with his hands in his pockets. "But I have known you people before today, and I know you never die for want of talking. Now, I recommend you do something."

"I have written to Stephen as I have written to him once before sin' he went away," said Rachael; "and he'll be here in two days."

"Then, I'll tell you something. You are not aware perhaps," retorted Mr Bounderby, "that you yourself have been considered not quite free from suspicion on account of being judged by the company you keep. The post-office hasn't been forgotten either. And no letter to Stephen Blackpool has ever got into it. Therefore, what has become of yours, I leave you to guess. Perhaps you're mistaken, and never wrote any."

"He hadn't been gone from here, young lady," said Rachael, turning appealingly to Louisa, "as much as a week, when he sent me the only letter I have had, saying he was forced to seek work in another name."

"Oh, by George!" cried Bounderby, shaking his head, with a whistle, "he changes his name, does he! That's rather unlucky, too, for such an immaculate chap. It's considered a little suspicious in Courts of Justice, I believe, when an Innocent happens to have many names."

"What," said Rachael, with the tears in her eyes again, "in the name of Mercy, was the poor lad to do! The masters against him on one hand, the men against him on the other, he only wantin to work hard in peace, and do what he felt right. Can a man have no soul of his own, no mind of his own? Must he go wrong all through wi' this side, or wi' that, or else be hunted like a hare?"

"Indeed, I pity him from my heart," returned Louisa. "I hope that he will clear himself."

"You need have no fear of that, young lady. He is sure!"

"All the surer, I suppose," said Mr Bounderby, "for your refusing to tell where he is? Eh?"

"He shall not, through any act of mine, be brought back. He shall come back of his own accord to clear himself, and put all those that have injured his good character, and he not here for its defence, to shame. I have told him what has been done against him," said Rachael, throwing off all distrust as a rock throws off the sea, "and he will be here, at furthest, in two days."

"But," added Mr Bounderby, "if he can be laid hold of sooner, he shall have an earlier opportunity of clearing himself. As to you, I have nothing against you. You came and told me the truth, and I gave you the chance to prove it, and there's an end of it. I wish you good-night all! I must be off to look a little further into this."

Tom came out of his corner when Mr Bounderby moved and went away with him. The only parting salutation of which he delivered himself was a sulky "Good-night, father!" With a brief speech, and a scowl at his sister, he left the house.

Louisa mildly said: "Rachael, you will not distrust me one day, when you know me better."

"It goes against me," Rachael answered, in a gentler manner, "to mistrust any one; but when I am so mistrusted, I cannot keep such things quite out of my mind. I ask your pardon for having done you an injury. I don't think what I said now. Yet I might come to think it again, wi' the poor lad so wronged."

"Did you tell him in your letter," inquired Sissy, "that suspicion seemed to have fallen upon him, because he had been seen about the Bank at night? He would then know what he would have to explain on coming back, and would be ready."

"Yes, dear," she returned; "but I can't guess what can have taken him there. It was never on his way. His way was the same as mine, and not near it."

Sissy had already been at her side asking her where she lived, and whether she might come tomorrow night, to inquire if there were news of him.

"I doubt," said Rachael, "if he can be here till next day."

"Then I will come next night too," said Sissy.

When Rachael, agreeing, was gone, Mr Gradgrind lifted up his head, and said to his daughter:

"Louisa, my dear, I have never, that I know of, seen this man. Do you believe him to be implicated?"

"I think I may have believed it, father, though with great difficulty. I do not believe it now."

"That is to say, you once persuaded yourself to believe it, from knowing him to be suspected. His appearance and manner; are they so honest?"

"Very honest."

"And her confidence is not shaken! I ask myself," said Mr Gradgrind, musing, "does the real culprit know of these accusations? Where is he? Who is he?"

His hair had latterly begun to change its colour. As he leaned upon his hand again, looking grey and old, Louisa, with a face of fear and pity, hurried over to him. Her eyes met Sissy's at that moment. Sissy flushed, and Louisa put her finger on her lip.

Next night, when Sissy returned home and told Louisa that Stephen was not come, she told it in a whisper. Next night again, she came home with the same account, and added that he had not been heard of. From the moment of that interchange of looks, they never uttered his name, or any reference to him, aloud; nor ever pursued the subject of the robbery, when Mr Gradgrind spoke of it.

The two appointed days ran out, three days and nights passed, and Stephen Blackpool was still unheard of. On the fourth day, Rachael, with unabated confidence, but feeling her letter to have miscarried, went up to the Bank, and showed her letter from him with his address, at a working colony, some sixty miles away. Messengers were sent to that place, and the whole town looked for Stephen to be brought in next day.

During this whole time the whelp followed Mr Bounderby as his shadow, assisting in all the proceedings. He was greatly excited, bit his nails down to the quick, and spoke in a hard rattling voice. At the hour when the suspected man was looked for, the whelp was at the station, offering to wager that he had made off and that he would not appear.

The whelp was right. The messengers returned alone. Rachael's letter had been delivered. Stephen Blackpool had decamped in that same hour and no soul knew more of him. Opinion was divided over whether Rachael had written believing that he really would come back, or had warned him to fly.

Six days, seven days, into another week. The wretched whelp began to grow defiant. "Was the suspected fellow the thief? A pretty question! If not, where was he, and why did he not return?"

CHAPTER 5

Days and nights passed. No Stephen Blackpool. Where was the man, and why did he not come back?

Every night, Sissy sat with Rachael at her lodging. All day, Rachael toiled as such people must toil. Day and night passed again. The monotony was unbroken. Even Stephen Blackpool's disappearance was falling into the general way, and becoming as monotonous a wonder as any piece of machinery in Coketown.

"I doubt," said Rachael, "if there is twenty left in all this place, who have any trust in the poor dear lad now."

She said this to Sissy, as they sat in her lodging, lighted only by the lamp at the street corner.

"If I didn't have you to speak to," pursued Rachael, "times are, when I think my mind would not have kept right. But I get hope and strength through you, and you believe that though appearances may rise against him, he will be proved clear?"

"I do believe so," returned Sissy, "with my whole heart. I feel so certain, Rachael, that your confidence cannot be wrong, that I have no more doubt of him than if I had known him through as many years of trial as you have."

"And I, my dear," said Rachel, with a tremble in her voice, "have known him through them all, to be, in his own quiet way, so faithful to everything honest and good, that if he was never to be heard of again, and I was to live to a hundred, I could say with my last breath, God knows my heart. I have never once doubted Stephen Blackpool!"

"We all believe, up at the Lodge, Rachael, that he will be freed from suspicion, sooner or later."

"The better I know it to be so believed there, my dear," said Rachael, "and the kinder I feel it that you come away from there, purposely to comfort me, and keep me company, and be seen wi' me when I am not yet free from all suspicion myself, the more grieved I am that I should ever have spoken those mistrusting words to the young lady. And yet – "

"You don't mistrust her now, Rachael?"

"Now that we have been more together, no. But I can't at all times keep out of my mind – "

Her voice sunk so low that Sissy, sitting by her side, was obliged to listen with attention.

"I can't at all times keep out of my mind, mistrustings of someone. I can't think who 'tis, I can't think how or why it may be done, but I mistrust that some one has put Stephen out of the way. I mistrust that someone – to prevent him declaring his innocence – has stopped him, and put him out of the way."

"That is a dreadful thought," said Sissy, turning pale.

"It is a dreadful thought to think he may be murdered."

Sissy shuddered, and turned paler yet.

"When it makes its way into my mind, dear," said Rachael, "and it does sometimes, however tired I am, I want to walk fast, miles and miles. I must get the better of this before bedtime. I'll walk home wi' you."

"He might fall ill upon the journey back," offered Sissy, "and in such a case, there are many places where he might stop."

"But he is in none of them. He has been sought for in all, and he's not there."

"True," was Sissy's reluctant admission.

"He'd walk the journey in two days. If he was footsore and couldn't walk, I sent him in the letter, the money to ride, lest he should have none of his own to spare."

"Let us hope that tomorrow will bring something better, Rachael. Come into the air!"

Her gentle hand adjusted Rachael's shawl upon her shining black hair, and they went out. The night being fine, little knots of Hands were here and there lingering; but it was supper-time and there were few people in the streets.

"You're not so hurried now, Rachael, and your hand is cooler."

"I get better, dear, if I can only walk, and breathe a little fresh. Times when I can't, I turn weak and confused."

"But you must not begin to fail, Rachael, for you may be wanted at any time to stand by Stephen. Tomorrow is Saturday. If there is no news, let us walk in the country Sunday morning, to strengthen you for another week. Will you go?"

"Yes, dear."

They were by this time in the street where Mr Bounderby's house stood. Some train had newly arrived, which had put a number of vehicles in motion. Several coaches were rattling before them and behind them as they approached Mr Bounderby's. One drew up as they were in the act of passing the house. They looked round involuntarily. The bright gas-light over Mr Bounderby's steps showed them Mrs Sparsit in the coach, in an ecstasy of excitement, struggling to open the door; Mrs Sparsit seeing them at the same moment, called to them to stop.

"It's a coincidence," exclaimed Mrs Sparsit, as she was released by the coachman. "It's a Providence! Come out, ma'am!" then said Mrs Sparsit, to some one inside, "or we'll have you dragged out!"

At this, no other than the mysterious old woman descended.

"Leave her alone, everybody!" cried Mrs Sparsit, with great energy. "Let nobody touch her. She belongs to me. Come in, ma'am, or we'll have you dragged in!"

Moments later some five-and-twenty neighbours, witnessing the spectacle of one old lady holding another by the throat, closed in after Sissy and Rachael, as they closed in after Mrs Sparsit and her prize. The whole body made a disorderly entrance into Mr Bounderby's dining room, where the people behind lost not a moment's time in mounting on the chairs, to get the better of the people in front.

"Fetch Mr Bounderby!" cried Mrs Sparsit. "Rachael, young woman; you know who this is?"

"It's Mrs Pegler," said Rachael.

"I should think it is!" cried Mrs Sparsit, exulting. "Fetch Mr Bounderby. Stand away, everybody!" Here old Mrs Pegler, muffling herself up, and shrinking from sight, whispered a word of entreaty. "Don't tell me," said Mrs Sparsit, aloud. "I have told you twenty times, coming along, that I will not leave you till I have handed you over to him myself."

Mr Bounderby now appeared, accompanied by Mr Gradgrind and the whelp, with whom he had been holding conference upstairs. Mr Bounderby looked astonished at the sight of this uninvited party in his dining room.

"Why, what's the matter now!" said he. "Mrs Sparsit, ma'am?"

"Sir," explained that worthy woman, "I trust it is my good fortune to produce a person you have much desired to find. Connecting together such imperfect clues to the part of the country in which that person might reside, as have been afforded by the young woman, Rachael, fortunately now present to identify, I have had the happiness to succeed, and to bring that person with me. It has not been, sir, without some trouble that I have managed this; but trouble in your service is to me a pleasure."

Here Mrs Sparsit ceased, for Mr Bounderby's visage exhibited an extraordinary combination of colours and expressions of discomfiture, as old Mrs Pegler was disclosed to his view.

"Why, what do you mean by this?" was his highly unexpected demand. "What do you mean by this, Mrs Sparsit?"

"Sir!" exclaimed Mrs Sparsit, faintly.

"Mind your own business, ma'am?" roared Bounderby. "How dare you go and poke your officious nose into my family affairs?"

This allusion to her favourite feature overpowered Mrs Sparsit. She sat down stiffly in a chair, as if she were frozen, and with a fixed stare at Mr Bounderby, slowly grated her mittens against one another, as if they were frozen too.

"My dear Josiah!" cried Mrs Pegler, trembling. "My darling boy. It's not my fault, Josiah. I told this lady over and over, that she was doing what would not be agreeable to you, but she would do it."

"What did you let her bring you for?" asked Bounderby.

"My own boy! She threatened me that if I resisted, I should be brought by constables, and it was better to come quietly than make a stir in such a – " Mrs Pegler glanced timidly but proudly round – "such a fine house as this. Indeed, it is not my fault! My dear, noble, boy! I have always lived quiet, and secret, Josiah, my dear. I have never broken the condition once. I have never said I was your mother. I have admired you at a distance; and if I have come to town occasionally, to take a proud peep at you, I have done it secretly, my love, and gone away again."

Mr Bounderby, hands in his pockets, walked up and down the length of the long dining table, while the spectators greedily took in every syllable of Mrs Pegler's appeal, becoming more and more round-eyed. Mr Bounderby still walked up and down when Mrs Pegler had done.

Mr Gradgrind turned to the old lady: "I am surprised, ma'am," he observed with severity, "that in your old age you have the face to claim Mr Bounderby for your son, after your unnatural and inhuman treatment of him."

"Me unnatural!" cried poor old Mrs Pegler. "Me inhuman! To my dear boy?"

"Dear!" repeated Mr Gradgrind. "Yes – dear in his self-made prosperity, madam, I dare say. Not very dear, however, when you deserted him in his infancy, and left him to the brutality of a drunken grandmother."

"I deserted my Josiah!" cried Mrs Pegler, clasping her hands. "May the Lord forgive you, sir, for your wicked words against the memory of my poor mother, who died in my arms before Josiah was born."

She was so very earnest, that Mr Gradgrind, shocked by the possibility which dawned upon him, said in a gentler tone:

"Do you deny, then, madam, that you left your son to – to be brought up in the gutter?"

"Josiah in the gutter!" exclaimed Mrs Pegler. "No such thing, sir. Never! My dear boy knows, and will tell you, that though he come of humble parents, they loved him as dear as the best could, and never thought it hardship on themselves to pinch a bit that he might write and cipher beautiful. I've his books at home to show it! And my dear boy knows, and will give you to know, sir, that after his beloved father died, when he was eight years old, his mother, too, could pinch a bit, as it was her duty, pleasure and pride to do it, to help him out in life, and put him 'prentice. And a steady lad he was, and a kind master he had to lend him a hand, and well he worked his own way forward to be rich and thriving. And I'll give you to know, sir – for this my dear boy won't – that though his mother kept but a little village shop, he never forgot her. He pensioned me on thirty pound a year – more than I want – only making the condition that I was to stay where I was, and make no boasts about him, nor trouble him. And I never have, except with looking at him once a year, unbeknown to him. And it's right," said poor old Mrs Pegler, "that I should stay put. I have no doubt that if I was here I should do many unbefitting things. I am well contented, and I can keep my pride in my Josiah to myself, and I can love for love's own sake! And I am ashamed of you, sir," said Mrs Pegler, lastly, "for your slanders and suspicions. And I never stood here before, nor never wanted to stand here when my dear son said no. And I shouldn't be here now, if it hadn't been for being brought here. And for shame upon you, Oh, for shame, to accuse me of being a bad mother to my son, with my son standing here to tell you so different!"

The bystanders, on and off the dining-room chairs, raised a murmur of sympathy with Mrs Pegler, and Mr Gradgrind felt himself innocently placed in a very distressing predicament. Mr Bounderby, who had never ceased walking up and down, growing redder and redder, stopped short.

"I don't exactly know," he said, "how I come to be favoured with the attendance of the present company, but I don't inquire. Perhaps they'll be so good as to disperse. I'm not bound to deliver a lecture on my family affairs. Those expecting any explanation will be disappointed – particularly Tom Gradgrind. In reference to the Bank robbery, there has been a mistake made concerning my mother. If there hadn't been over-officiousness it wouldn't have been made. Good evening!"

Mr Bounderby held the door open for the company to depart, with a blustering sheepishness upon him. Detected as the Bully of humility, who had built his windy reputation upon lies, putting the honest truth as far away from him as if he had gone the other way and given himself a pedigree, he cut a most ridiculous figure. He knew the people filing past him would carry what had passed to the whole town. Even unlucky Mrs Sparsit, fallen from her pinnacle of exultation to the Slough of Despond, was not in so bad a plight as that remarkable and self-made Humbug, Josiah Bounderby of Coketown.

Rachael and Sissy left Mrs Pegler to occupy a bed at her son's for that night, and walked together to the gate of Stone Lodge. Mr Gradgrind joined them before they had gone very far, and spoke of Stephen Blackpool. He felt this signal failure of the suspicions against Mrs Pegler was likely to work well.

As to the whelp – throughout this scene as before, he stayed close to Bounderby. As long as Bounderby made no discovery without his knowledge, he felt safe. He never visited his sister, and had only seen her once since she went home.

One fearful thought still occurred to his sister, to which she never gave utterance concerning her brother. The same dark possibility had presented itself in the same shapeless guise, this very day, to Sissy, when Rachael spoke of someone who confounded by Stephen's return, may have put him out of the way. Louisa had never spoken of her suspicions of her brother and the robbery. She and Sissy had not raised the subject, save in that one exchange of looks when her father rested his grey head on his hand; but it was understood between them, and they both knew it. This other awful fear hovered about each of them like a ghostly shadow.

And still the whelp continued. If Stephen Blackpool was not the thief, let him show himself. Why didn't he?

Another night. Another day and night. No Stephen Blackpool. Where was the man, and why did he not come back?

CHAPTER 6

Sissy and Rachael met one bright Sunday in autumn to walk in the country.

It was customary for those who now and then thirsted for pure air, to get a few miles away by train, and then begin their walk, or their lounge in the fields. Sissy and Rachael took this route, and were put down at a station about midway between the town and Mr Bounderby's retreat.

Though the green landscape was blotted here and there with heaps of coal, it was green elsewhere, and there were trees to see, and there were larks singing, and there were pleasant scents in the air, and all was overarched by a bright blue sky. In the distance one way, Coketown showed as a black mist; in another distance hills began to rise; in a third, there was a faint change in the light of the horizon where it shone upon the far-off sea. Under their feet, the grass was fresh; hedgerows were luxuriant; everything was at peace. Engines at pits' mouths, and lean old horses that had worn the circle of their daily labour into the ground, were alike quiet.

They walked on across the fields and down the shady lanes, following paths and tracks, however slight. Mounds where the grass was rank and high, and where brambles, dock-weed, and such-like vegetation, were confusedly heaped together, they always avoided, for such areas often hid old pits.

The sun was high when they sat to rest. They had seen no one, near or distant, for a long time.

"It is so still here, Rachael, and the way is so untrodden, that I think we must be the first here all summer."

As Sissy said it, she glanced at rotten fragments of fence upon the ground. She got up to look. "And yet – this has not been broken very long. The wood is quite fresh. Here are footsteps too. – O Rachael!"

She ran back. Rachael had already started up.

"What is the matter?"

"I don't know. There is a hat lying in the grass."

They went forward together. Rachael took it up, shaking from head to foot. She broke into sobs: Stephen Blackpool was written in his own hand on the inside.

174

"O the poor lad! He has been made away with. He is lying murdered here!"

"Is there – has the hat any blood upon it?" Sissy faltered.

They were afraid to look, but finally examined it. There was no mark of violence, inside or out. It had been there some days, for rain and dew had stained it, and the mark of its shape was on the grass. They looked fearfully about them, without moving, but could see nothing more. "Rachael," Sissy whispered, "I will go on a little by myself."

She had unclasped her hand, and was about to step forward, when Rachael caught her in both arms with a scream. Before them, at their very feet, was the brink of a black ragged chasm hidden by the thick grass. They sprang back, and fell upon their knees, each hiding her face upon the other's neck.

"O, my good Lord! He's down there!" At first this, and her terrific screams, were all that could be got from Rachael. It was impossible to hush her; and it was deadly necessary to hold her, or she would have flung herself down the shaft.

"Rachael, dear Rachael, for the love of Heaven, not these dreadful cries! Think of Stephen, think of Stephen!"

By an earnest repetition of this entreaty, Sissy at last brought her to be silent, and to look at her with a tearless face of stone.

"Rachael, Stephen may be living. You wouldn't leave him lying at the bottom of this dreadful place, if you could help him?"

"No, no, no!"

"Don't move, for his sake! Let me go and listen."

She crept towards the pit on her hands and knees, and called as loud as she could. She listened, but no sound replied. She called twenty, thirty times. She took a little clod of earth from the broken ground where he had stumbled, and threw it in. She could not hear it fall.

The wide prospect, so beautiful but a few minutes ago, almost made her despair, as she rose and saw no help. "Rachael, we must lose not a moment. We must go in different directions, seeking aid. You shall go back the way we came, and I will go on. Tell anyone you see what has happened. Think of Stephen, think of Stephen!"

Looking at Rachael's face she knew she could trust her. And after standing for a moment to see her running, wringing her hands as she ran, she turned to her own search. She stopped at the hedge to tie her shawl

175

there as a guide to the place, then threw her bonnet aside, and ran as she had never run before.

She ran from field to field, and place to place, as she had never run before. At last she came to a shed by an engine-house, where two men lay sleeping in the shade.

First to wake them, and next to tell them, wild and breathless as she was, what brought her there. But no sooner understood than their spirits were on fire like hers. One was in a drunken slumber, but on his comrade's shouting to him that a man had fallen down the Old Hell Shaft, he started out to a pool of dirty water, put his head in it, and came back sober.

With these two men she ran a further half mile, and then another, while they ran elsewhere. A horse was found and a man to ride to the railroad, with a message to Louisa. By now a whole village was up: and windlasses, ropes, poles, candles, lanterns, all things necessary were being brought together, to be carried to the Old Hell Shaft.

It seemed hours since she had left the lost man lying in the grave where he had been buried alive. She could not bear to remain away any longer – it was like deserting him. She hurried back, along with half a dozen labourers. When they came to the Old Hell Shaft, they found it as lonely as she had left it. The men called and listened as she had done, examining the edge of the chasm, and settled how it had happened. They then waited for the tools they needed.

Every sound made Sissy tremble, for she thought it was a cry at the bottom of the pit. But no sound arose to the surface, and they sat upon the grass, waiting. After a while, straggling people who had heard of the accident began to come up; then the implements began to arrive. In the midst of this, Rachael returned. With her party there was a surgeon, who brought some wine and medicines. But, the expectation that Stephen would be found alive was very slight indeed.

There were now enough people to impede the work, so the sobered man put himself at the head, and made a large ring round the Old Hell Shaft, choosing men to keep it. Besides those accepted to work, only Sissy and Rachael were at first permitted within this ring. Later in the day, when the message brought an express from Coketown, Mr Gradgrind and Louisa, Mr Bounderby, and the whelp, were also there.

The sun was four hours lower than when Sissy and Rachael had first sat upon the grass, before a means of enabling two men to descend securely was rigged. It was five o'clock in the afternoon, before a candle was sent down to try the air, while three or four rough faces stood crowded close together, attentively watching it. The candle was brought up again, feebly burning, and then some water was cast in. Then the bucket was hooked on; and the sobered man and another got in with lights, giving the word "Lower away!"

As the rope went out, tight and strained, and the windlass creaked, the one or two hundred men and women looking on held their breath. The signal was given and the windlass stopped, with abundant rope to spare. Five long minutes passed, when the windlass was reversed and worked again. Practised eyes knew that it did not go heavily and only one was returning.

The rope came in tight and strained; ring after ring was coiled upon the barrel of the windlass. All eyes were fastened on the pit. The sobered man was brought up and leaped out briskly on the grass. There was a universal cry of "Alive or dead?" and then a deep hush.

When he said "Alive!" a great shout arose and many eyes had tears in them.

"But he's hurt very bad," he added, as soon as he could make himself heard again. "Where's doctor? He's hurt so very bad, sir, that we donno how to get him up."

They all consulted together, looking anxiously at the surgeon, as he asked some questions. He shook his head at the replies. The sun was setting now; and the red light touched every face there.

The consultation ended in the men returning to the windlass, and the pitman going down again, carrying the wine and other small matters with him. Then the other man came up. In the meantime, some men brought a hurdle, on which others made a thick bed of spare clothes covered with loose straw. The doctor contrived some bandages and slings from shawls and handkerchiefs. They were hung upon an arm of the pitman who had last come up, with instructions how to use them.

It appeared from the little this man said to those about him, which was quickly repeated, that the lost man had fallen upon a mass of crumbled rubbish and earth. He lay upon his back with one arm doubled under him, and had hardly stirred since he fell, except to move his free hand to a side pocket, in which he knew he had some bread and meat. He had also

177

scooped up a little water now and then. He had left his work, on being written to, and had walked the whole journey. He was on his way to Mr Bounderby's country house after dark, when he fell. He was crossing that dangerous area because he was innocent of what he was accused, and had to come the quickest way to deliver himself up. The Old Hell Shaft, the pitman said, was worthy of its bad name; for though Stephen could speak now, he believed it would soon be found to have mangled the life out of him.

When all was ready, this man, still taking his last hurried charges from the surgeon as the windlass lowered him, disappeared into the pit. The rope went out as before, the signal was made as before, and the windlass stopped. No man removed his hand from it now. Every one waited with his grasp set, and his body bent, ready to reverse and wind in. At length the signal was given.

For, now, the rope came in, tightened and strained to its utmost as it appeared, and the men turned heavily, and the windlass complained. One could hardly look at the rope, and think of its giving way. But, ring after ring was coiled upon the barrel of the windlass, and the connecting chains appeared. Finally the bucket was there, with the two men holding on, tenderly supporting between them, slung and tied within, the figure of a poor, crushed, human creature.

A low murmur of pity went round the throng, and the women wept aloud, as the body was moved very slowly and laid upon the bed of straw. At first, none but the surgeon went close. He did what he could to make him comfortable, but the best that he could do was to cover him. That gently done, he called to Rachael and Sissy. The pale, worn, patient face was seen looking up at the sky, with the broken right hand lying bare on the outside of the covering garments, as if waiting to be taken by another hand.

They gave him drink, moistened his face with water, and administered some drops of cordial and wine. Though he lay quite motionless looking up at the sky, he smiled and said, "Rachael."

She stooped down on the grass at his side, and bent over him until her eyes were between his and the sky, for he could not turn them to look at her.

"Rachael, my dear."

She took his hand. He smiled again and said, "Don't let 't go."

178

"Thou'rt in great pain, my own dear Stephen?"

"I ha' been, but not now. I ha' been – dreadful, and dree, and long, my dear – but 'tis ower now. Ah, Rachael, aw a muddle! Fro' first to last, a muddle!"

The spectre of his old look seemed to pass as he said the word.

"I ha' fell into th' pit, my dear, as have cost wi'in the knowledge o' old fok now livin, hundreds and hundreds o' men's lives – fathers, sons, brothers, dear to thousands an thousands, an keeping 'em fro' want and hunger. I ha' fell into a pit that ha' been wi' th' Fire-damp crueller than battle. I ha' read on 't in the public petition, as onny one may read, fro' the men that works in pits, in which they ha' pray'n and pray'n the lawmakers for Christ's sake not to let their work be murder to 'em, but to spare 'em for th' wives and children that they loves as well as gentlefok loves theirs. When it were in work, it killed wi'out need; when 'tis let alone, it kills wi'out need. See how we die an no need, one way an another – in a muddle – every day!"

He faintly said it, without any anger against any one. Merely as the truth.

"Thy little sister, Rachael, thou hast not forgot her. Thou'rt not like to forget her now, and me so nigh her. Thou know'st – poor, patient, suff'rin, dear – how thou didst work for her, seet'n all day long in her little chair at thy winder, and how she died, young and misshapen. A muddle! Aw a muddle!"

Louisa approached but he could not see her, lying with his face turned up to the night sky.

"If aw th' things that tooches us, my dear, was not so muddled, I should'n had'n need to coom heer. If we was not in a muddle among ourseln, I should'n ha' been, by my own fellow weavers and workin' brothers, so mistook. If Mr Bounderby had ever know'd me right – if he'd ever know'd me at aw – he would'n ha' took'n offence wi' me. He would'n ha' suspect'n me. But look up yonder, Rachael! Look aboove!"

Following his eyes, she saw that he was gazing at a star.

"It ha' shined upon me," he said reverently, "in my pain and trouble down below. It ha' shined into my mind. I ha' look'n at 't and thowt o' thee, Rachael, till the muddle in my mind have cleared awa. If soom ha' been wantin' in unnerstan'in me better, I, too, ha' been wantin' in unnerstan'in them better. When I got thy letter, I easily believen that what the yoong ledy sen and done to me, and what her brother sen and done to me, was one, and that there were a wicked plot betwixt 'em. When I fell, I were in anger wi' her, an hurryin' on t' be as onjust t' her as oothers was t' me. But in our judgments, like as in our doins, we mun bear and forbear. In my pain an trouble, lookin up yonder, – wi' it shinin' on me – I ha' seen more clear, and ha' made it my dyin prayer that aw th' world may on'y coom toogether more, an get a better unnerstan'in o' one another, than when I were in't my own weak seln."

Louisa hearing what he said, bent over him on the opposite side to Rachael, so that he could see her.

"You ha' heard?" he said, after a few moment's silence. "I ha' not forgot you, ledy."

"Yes, Stephen, I have heard you. And your prayer is mine."

"You ha' a father. Will yo' tak' a message to him?"

"He is here," said Louisa, with dread. "Shall I bring him to you?"

"If yo please."

Louisa returned with her father. Standing hand in hand, they both looked down upon the solemn countenance.

"Sir, yo will clear me an mak my name good wi' aw men. This I leave to yo."

Mr Gradgrind was troubled and asked how?

"Sir," was the reply: "yor son will tell yo how. Ask him. I mak no charges: I leave none ahint me: not a single word. I ha' seen an spok'n wi' yor son, one night. I ask no more o' yo than that yo clear me – an I trust to yo to do 't."

The bearers were ready to carry him away, and the surgeon was anxious for his removal. Those with torches or lanterns prepared to go in front of the litter. Before it was raised, and while they were arranging how to go, he said to Rachael, looking upward at the star:

"Often as I coom to myseln, and found it shinin on me down there in my trouble, I thowt it were the star as guided to Our Saviour's home. I awmust think it be the very star!"

They lifted him up, and he was overjoyed to find that they were about to take him in the direction the star seemed to him to lead.

"Rachael, beloved lass! Don't let go my hand. We may walk toogether t'night, my dear!"

"I will hold thy hand, and keep beside thee, Stephen, all the way."

"Bless thee! Will soombody be pleased to coover my face!"

They carried him very gently along the fields, and down the lanes, and over the wide landscape. Rachael held the hand in hers. Very few whispers broke the mournful silence. It was soon a funeral procession. The star had shown him where to find the God of the poor; and through sorrow, and forgiveness, he had gone to his Redeemer's rest.

CHAPTER 7

Mr Bounderby and his shadow had not stood near Louisa, who held her father's arm, but in a retired place by themselves. When Mr Gradgrind was summoned to the couch, Sissy, attentive to all that happened, slipped behind that wicked shadow and whispered in his ear. Without turning his head, he conferred with her a few moments, and vanished.

When the father reached home, he sent a message to Mr Bounderby's, desiring his son to come to him directly. The reply was, that Mr Bounderby having missed him in the crowd, and seeing nothing of him since, had supposed him to be at Stone Lodge.

"I believe, father," said Louisa. "He will not come back to town tonight." Mr Gradgrind turned away, and said no more.

In the morning, he went down to the Bank as soon as it was opened, and seeing his son's place empty, went back along the street to meet Mr Bounderby. To whom he said that, for reasons he would soon explain, but entreated not then to be asked for, he had found it necessary to keep his son at a distance for a while. Also, that he was charged with the duty of vindicating Stephen Blackpool's memory, and declaring the thief. Mr Bounderby stood stock-still in the street after his father-in-law had left him, swelling like an immense soap bubble, without its beauty.

Mr Gradgrind went home, and locked himself in his room all that day. When Sissy and Louisa tapped at his door, he said, without opening it, "Not now, my dears; in the evening." On their return, he said, "I am not able yet – tomorrow." He ate nothing all day, and they heard him walking to and fro late at night.

But, in the morning he appeared at breakfast at the usual hour, and took his usual place at the table. Aged and bent he looked and yet also wiser, and a better man, than in the days when he wanted nothing but Facts. Before he left the room, he told them when to come to him.

"Dear father," said Louisa, when they kept their appointment, "you have three young children left. They will be different, I will be different yet, with Heaven's help."

She gave her hand to Sissy, as if she meant with her help too.

"Your wretched brother," said Mr Gradgrind. "Do you think he had planned this robbery when he went with you to the lodging?"

"I fear so, father. I know he had wanted money very much."

"The poor man was about to leave the town, so it came into his evil brain to cast suspicion on him?"

"I think it must have occurred to him there, father. For, I asked him to go there with me. The visit was not his idea."

"Did he take the poor man aside?"

"He took him out of the room. I asked him afterwards, why he had done so, and he made a plausible excuse. But since last night, father, and when I remember the circumstances, I am afraid I can imagine only too well what passed between them."

"Do your thoughts," said her father, "present your guilty brother in the same dark view as mine."

"I fear, father," hesitated Louisa, "that he suggested to Stephen Blackpool – perhaps in my name, perhaps in his own – to do something, in good faith, that he had never done before. To wait near the Bank those two or three nights before he left the town."

"Too plain!" returned the father.

He shaded his face, remaining silent for some moments. Recovering himself, he said: "So, how is he to be found and saved from justice? In the few hours that I can possibly allow to elapse before I publish the truth, how is he to be found by us, and only by us? Ten thousand pounds could not effect it."

"Sissy has effected it, father."

He raised his eyes to where she stood, like a good fairy in his house, and said in a tone of softened gratitude and grateful kindness, "It is always you, my child!"

"We had our fears," Sissy explained, glancing at Louisa, "before yesterday. And when I saw you close to the litter last night, and heard what passed, I went to him when no one saw. 'Don't look at me,' I said. 'See where your father is. Escape at once, for his sake and your own!' He was shaking before I whispered to him, and he started and said, 'Where can I go? I have very little money, and who will hide me?' I thought of father's old circus. I read of Mr Sleary in a paper only the other day. I told him to hurry there, and tell his name, and ask Mr Sleary to hide him till I came. 'I'll get to him before the morning,' he said. And I saw him shrink away among the people."

"Thank Heaven!" exclaimed his father. "He may be got abroad yet."

The town to which Sissy had directed him was within three hours' journey of Liverpool, whence he could be swiftly dispatched to any part of the world. But, caution was necessary in contacting him. There was a greater danger every moment of his being suspected now, and nobody could be sure what Mr Bounderby might do in a bullying vein of public zeal. It was consented that Sissy and Louisa should go there alone, by a circuitous route. The unhappy father should get there by another and wider route. It was further agreed that communication should be left to Sissy and Louisa to open; and that they should inform the cause of so much misery and disgrace of his father's being at hand and of the purpose for which they had come. When these arrangements had been well considered and were fully understood by all three, it was time to begin to carry them into execution. Early in the afternoon, Mr Gradgrind walked direct from his own house into the country, to be taken up on the line by which he was to travel. That night the remaining two set forth upon their different course, encouraged by not seeing any face they knew.

The two travelled all night, and, early in the morning arrived at the town they sought.

The first thing they saw was the skeleton of Sleary's Circus. The company had departed for another town more than twenty miles off, and had opened there last night. Travelling on the road was very slow. They took a hasty breakfast, but it was noon before they began to find the bills of Sleary's Horse-riding on barns and walls, and one o'clock when they stopped in the market place.

A Grand Morning Performance by the Riders, commencing at that very hour, was in course of announcement by the bellman as they set their feet upon the stones of the street. Sissy recommended they present themselves to pay at the door. Mr Sleary would be sure to know her, and would proceed with discretion.

Therefore, they repaired to the well-remembered booth. The flag with the inscription "Sleary's Horse-riding", was there but Mr Sleary was not. Master Kidderminster, grown too mature to play Cupid any more, presided on this occasion over the exchequer. In his look-out for base coin, Mr Kidderminster never saw anything but money, so Sissy passed him unrecognised, and they went in.

Miss Josephine Sleary was then announced by a new clown and Mr Sleary appeared, leading her in.

Mr Sleary had only made one cut at the Clown with his long whip-lash, and the Clown had only said, "If you do it again, I'll throw the horse at you!" when Sissy was recognised both by father and daughter. But they got through the Act with great self-possession; and Mr Sleary, saving for the first instant, conveyed no more expression into his locomotive eye than into his fixed one. At last, little fair-haired Josephine made her curtsey amid great applause. Sissy was touched on the shoulder, and beckoned out.

She took Louisa with her; and they were received by Mr Sleary in a very little private apartment, with canvas sides, a grass floor, and a wooden ceiling all aslant. "Thethilia," said Mr Sleary, who had brandy and water at hand, "it doth me good to thee you. You wath alwayth a favourite with uth, and you've done uth credit thinth the old timeth I'm thure. You mutht thee our people, my dear, afore we thpeak of bithnith, or they'll break their hearth – ethpethially the women." True to his word he brought in Josephine, and E.W.B. Childers and their son, and in a word, all the company. Amazing creatures they were in Louisa's eyes, so white and pink of complexion, so scant of dress, and so demonstrative of leg; but it was very agreeable to see them crowding about Sissy, and very natural in Sissy to be unable to refrain from tears.

"There! Now Thethilia hath kithd all the children, and hugged all the women, and thaken handth all round with all the men, clear, every one of you, and ring in the band for the thecond part!"

As soon as they were gone, he continued in a low tone. "Now, Thethilia, I don't athk to know any thecreth, but I thuppothe I may conthider thith to be Mith Thquire."

"This is his sister. Yes."

184

"And t'other on'th daughter. That'h what I mean. Hope I thee you well, mith. And I hope the Thquire'th well?"

"My father will be here soon," said Louisa, anxious to bring him to the point. "Is my brother safe?"

"Thafe and thound!" he replied. "I want you jutht to take a peep at the Ring, mith, through here."

They each looked through a chink in the boards.

"That'h Jack the Giant Killer – piethe of comic infant bithnith," said Sleary. "There'th a houthe, for Jack to hide in. There'th my Clown with a thauthepan-lid and a thpit, for Jack'th thervant. There'th little Jack himthelf. There'th two comic black thervanth, twithe ath big ath the houthe, to thtand by it and to bring it in and clear it. Now, do you thee 'em all?"

"Yes," they both said.

"Look at 'em again," said Sleary, "look at 'em well. Now, mith;" he put a form for them to sit on; "I have my opinionth, and the Thquire your father hath hith. I don't want to know what your brother'th been up to; ith better for me not to know. I know the Thquire hath thtood by Thethilia, and I'll thtand by the Thquire. Your brother ith one o' them black thervanth."

Louisa uttered an exclamation, partly of distress, partly of satisfaction.

"Ith a fact," said Sleary, "and even knowin' it, you couldn't put your finger on him. Let the Thquire come. I thall keep your brother here after the performanth. I thant undreth him, nor yet wath hith paint off. Let the Thquire come here after the performanth, or come here yourthelf after the performanth, and you thall find your brother, and have the whole plathe to talk to him in. Never mind the lookth of him, ath long ath he'th well hid."

Louisa, with many thanks and with a lightened load, detained Mr Sleary no longer then. She left her love for her brother, with her eyes full of tears; and she and Sissy went away until later in the afternoon.

Mr Gradgrind arrived within an hour afterwards. As none of the three could be his companion to Liverpool without almost identifying him under any disguise, he prepared a letter to one he could trust, beseeching him to ship the bearer off at any cost, to any distant part of the world to which he could be the most speedily and privately dispatched.

This done, they walked about, waiting for the Circus to be quite

185

vacated. After watching it a long time, they saw Mr Sleary bring out a chair and sit down by the side-door, smoking; as if that were his signal that they might approach.

"Your thervant, Thquire," was his cautious salutation as they passed in. "If you want me you'll find me here. You muthn't mind your thon having a comic livery on."

They all three went in; and Mr Gradgrind sat down forlorn, on the Clown's performing chair in the middle of the ring. On one of the back benches, remote in the subdued light sat the villainous whelp, sulky to the last, whom he had the misery to call his son.

In a preposterous coat, like a beadle's, with exaggerated cuffs and flaps; in an immense waistcoat, knee-breeches, buckled shoes, and a mad cocked hat; with nothing fitting him, and everything of coarse material, full of holes; with seams in his black face, where fear and heat had started through the greasy composition daubed all over it; anything so grimly, detestably, ridiculously shameful as the whelp in his comic livery, Mr Gradgrind never could by any other means have believed in, fact though it was. And one of his model children had come to this!

At first the whelp would draw no nearer. Yielding at length, if any concession so sullenly made can be called yielding, to the entreaties of Sissy – for Louisa he disowned altogether – he came down, bench by bench, until he stood on the verge of the circle, as far as possible, within its limits from his father.

"How was this done?" asked the father.

"How was what done?" moodily answered the son.

"This robbery," said the father, raising his voice upon the word.

"I forced the safe myself overnight, and shut it up ajar before I left. I had had the key that was found, made long before. I dropped it that morning, so it might be supposed to have been used. I didn't take the money all at once. I pretended to put my balance away every night, but I didn't. Now you know all about it."

"If a thunderbolt had fallen on me," said the father, "it would have shocked me less than this!"

"I don't see why," grumbled the son. "So many people are employed in situations of trust; so many people, out of so many, will be dishonest. I have heard you say a hundred times of its being a law. How can I help laws? You have comforted others with such things, father. Comfort yourself!"

The father buried his face in his hands, and the son stood in his disgraceful grotesqueness, biting straw: his hands, with the black partly worn away inside, looking like the hands of a monkey. The evening was fast closing in; and from time to time, he turned the whites of his eyes restlessly and impatiently towards his father.

"You must be got to Liverpool, and sent abroad."

"I suppose I must. I can't be more miserable anywhere," whimpered the whelp, "than I have been here, ever since I can remember. That's one thing."

Mr Gradgrind went to the door, and returned with Sleary, to whom he asked, How to get this deplorable object away?

"Why, I've been thinking of it, Thquire. There'th not muth time to lothe, tho you muth thay yeth or no. Ith over twenty mileth to the rail. There'th a coath in half an hour, that goeth to the rail, "purpothe to cath the mail train. That train will take him right to Liverpool."

"But look at him," groaned Mr Gradgrind. "Will any coach – "

"I don't mean that he thould go like that," said Sleary. "Thay the word, and I'll make a Jothkin of him, out of the wardrobe, in five minutes."

"I don't understand," said Mr Gradgrind.

"A Jothkin – a Carter. Make up your mind quick, Thquire. There'll be beer to feth. Only beer'll clean a comic blackamoor."

Mr Gradgrind rapidly assented; Mr Sleary rapidly turned out from a box, a smock frock, a felt hat, and other essentials. The whelp rapidly changed clothes behind a screen of baize; Mr Sleary rapidly brought beer, and washed him white again.

"Now," said Sleary, "come along to the coath, and jump up behind. Thay farewell to your family, and tharp'th the word." With which he delicately retired.

"Here is your letter," said Mr Gradgrind. "All necessary means will be provided for you. Atone, by repentance and better conduct, for the shocking action you have committed, and the dreadful consequences to which it has led. Give me your hand, my poor boy, and may God forgive you as I do!"

The culprit was moved to a few abject tears by these words. But, when Louisa opened her arms, he repulsed her afresh.

"Not you. I don't have anything to say to you!"

"O Tom, Tom, do we end so, after all my love!"

"After all your love!" he returned, obdurately. "Pretty love! You left old Bounderby to himself, and packed my best friend Mr Harthouse off. You went home just when I was in the greatest danger. Pretty love that! Telling how we went to that place, when you saw the net was gathering round me. Pretty love that! You have regularly given me up. You never cared for me."

"Tharp'th the word!" said Sleary, at the door.

They all confusedly went out: Louisa crying to him that she forgave him, and loved him still. Mr Gradgrind and Sissy, who were both before him while his sister yet clung to his shoulder, stopped and recoiled.

For, there was Bitzer, out of breath, his thin lips parted, his thin nostrils distended, his white eyelashes quivering. There he stood, panting and heaving, as if he had never stopped since the night, now long ago, when he had run them down before.

"I'm sorry to interfere with your plans," said Bitzer, "but I can't allow myself to be done by horse-riders. I must have young Mr Tom; here he is in a smock frock, and I must have him!"

By the collar, too, it seemed. For, so he took possession of him.

CHAPTER 8

They returned to the booth, Sleary shutting the door to keep intruders out. Bitzer, still holding the paralysed culprit by the collar, stood in the Ring, blinking at his old patron through the darkness of the twilight.

"Bitzer," said Mr Gradgrind, broken down, "have you a heart?"

"Circulation, sir," returned Bitzer, smiling at the oddity of the question, "couldn't be carried on without one. No man acquainted with the facts established by Harvey relating to the circulation of blood, can doubt that I have a heart."

"Is it accessible," cried Mr Gradgrind, "to any compassionate influence?"

"It is accessible to Reason, sir," returned the excellent young man. "And to nothing else."

They stood looking at each other; Mr Gradgrind's face as white as the pursuer's.

"What motive can you have for preventing the escape of this wretched youth?" said Mr Gradgrind.

"Sir," returned Bitzer, in a very business-like manner. "I have suspected young Mr Tom of this bank robbery from the first. I had had my eye upon him, for I knew his ways. I have kept my observations to myself, and I have got ample proofs against him besides his own confession, which I was just in time to overhear. I had the pleasure of watching your house yesterday morning, and following you here. I am going to take young Mr Tom back to Coketown, to deliver him to Mr Bounderby. Sir, I have no doubt that Mr Bounderby will then promote me to young Mr Tom's situation. And I wish to have his situation, sir, for it will be a rise to me."

"If this is solely a question of self-interest with you – " Mr Gradgrind began. "What sum of money, will you set against your expected promotion?"

"Thank you, sir," returned Bitzer, "but I will not set any sum against it. I have gone over the calculations in my mind and I find that to compound a felony, even on very high terms, would not be as safe and good for me as my improved prospects in the Bank."

"Bitzer," said Mr Gradgrind, stretching out his hands as though to say, See how miserable I am! "Bitzer, you were many years at my school. If, in remembrance of the pains bestowed upon you there, you can persuade yourself in any degree to disregard your present interest and release my son, I entreat and pray you to give him the benefit of that remembrance."

"I really wonder, sir," rejoined the old pupil, "to find you taking a position so untenable. My schooling was paid for; it was a bargain; and when I came away, the bargain ended."

It was a fundamental principle of the Gradgrind philosophy that everything was to be paid for. Nobody was ever on any account to give anybody anything, or render anybody help without purchase. Gratitude was to be abolished, and the virtues springing from it were not to be.

"I don't deny," added Bitzer, "that my schooling was cheap. But that comes right, sir. I was made in the cheapest market, and have to dispose of myself in the dearest."

He was a little troubled here, by Louisa and Sissy crying.

"Pray don't do that," said he, "it only worries. You seem to think that I have some animosity against young Mr Tom; but I don't. I am only going,

189

on the reasonable grounds I have mentioned, to take him back to Coketown. If he resists, I shall cry Stop Thief! But, he won't resist, you may depend upon it."

Mr Sleary had listened to these doctrines with profound attention, and stepped forward.

"Thquire, you know perfectly well, and your daughter knowth perfectly well that I didn't know what your thon had done, and that I didn't want to know – I thed it wath better not, though I thought it wath thome thkylarking. However, thith young man thayth it'th a robbery of a bank. That'th a theriouth thing; muth too theriouth a thing for me to compound, ath thith young man hath very properly called it. Conthequently, Thquire, you muthn't quarrel with me if I take thith young man'th thide, and thay he'th right and there'th no help for it. But I tell you what I'll do, Thquire; I'll drive your thon and thith young man over to the rail, and prevent expothure here. I can't conthent to do more, but I'll do that."

Fresh lamentations from Louisa, and deeper affliction on Mr Gradgrind's part, followed this desertion of them by their last friend. But, Sissy glanced at him with great attention. As they were all going out again, he favoured her with one slight roll of his movable eye, desiring her to linger behind. As he locked the door, he said excitedly:

"The Thquire thtood by you, Thethilia, and I'll thtand by the Thquire. It'll be a dark night. I've got a horthe that'll do anything but thpeak; I've got a pony that'll go fifteen mile an hour with Childerth driving of him; I've got a dog that'll keep a man to one plathe four-and-twenty hourth. Tell the young Thquire, when he theeth our horthe begin to danthe, not to be afraid of being thpilt, but to look out for a pony-gig coming up. Tell him, when he theeth that gig clothe by, to jump down, and it'll take him off at a rattling pathe. If my dog leth thith young man thtir a peg on foot, I give him leave to go. Tharp'th the word!"

The word was so sharp, that ten minutes later Mr Childers, sauntering about the market place in a pair of slippers, had his cue, and Mr Sleary's gig was ready. It was a fine sight, to behold the learned dog barking round it, and Mr Sleary instructing him, with his one practicable eye, that Bitzer was the object of his particular attentions. Soon after dark they all three got in and started; the learned dog already pinning Bitzer with his eye, and sticking close to the wheel on his side, that he might be ready for him in the event of his showing the slightest disposition to alight.

The other three sat up at the inn all night in great suspense. At eight o'clock in the morning Mr Sleary and the dog reappeared: both in high spirits.

"All right, Thquire!" said Mr Sleary, "your thon may be aboard-a-thip by thith time. Childerth took him off, an hour and a half after we left there latht night. The horthe danthed the polka 'till he wath dead beat – he would have walthed if he hadn't been in harneth – and then I gave him the word and he went to thleep comfortable. When that prethiouth young Rathcal thed he'd go for'ard afoot, the dog hung on to hith neck-hankercher and pulled him down and rolled him over. Tho he come back into the drag, and there he that, 'till I turned the horthe'th head, at half-patht thixth thith morning."

Mr Gradgrind overwhelmed him with thanks, of course; and hinted as delicately as he could, at a handsome remuneration in money.

"I don't want money mythelf, Thquire; but Childerth ith a family man, and if you wath to like to offer him a five-pound note, it mightn't be unactheptable. Likewithe if you wath to thtand a collar for the dog, or a thet of bellth for the horthe, I thould be very glad to take 'em. Brandy and water I alwayth take. A little thpread for the company at about three and thixth a head, not reckoning Luth, would make 'em happy."

All these little tokens of his gratitude, Mr Gradgrind very willingly undertook to render.

"If you'll only give a Horthe-riding, a bethpeak, whenever you can, you'll more than balanthe the account. Now, Thquire, if your daughter will ethcuthe me, I thould like a parting word with you."

Louisa and Sissy withdrew into an adjoining room; Mr Sleary, stirring and drinking his brandy and water as he stood, went on:

"Thquire, you don't need to be told that dogth ith wonderful animalth."

"Their instinct," said Mr Gradgrind, "is surprising."

"Whatever you call it – and I'm bletht if I know what to call it" – said Sleary, "it ith athtonithing. The way in with a dog'll find you – the dithtanthe he'll come!"

"His scent," said Mr Gradgrind, "being so fine."

"I'm bletht if I know what to call it," repeated Sleary, shaking his head,

191

"but I have had dogth find me, Thquire, in a way that made me think whether that dog hadn't gone to another dog, and thed, 'You don't happen to know a perthon of the name of Thleary, do you? Perthon of the name of Thleary, in the Horthe-riding way – thtout man – game eye?' And whether that dog mightn't have thought it over, and thed, 'Thleary, Thleary! O yeth, to be sure! A friend of mine menthioned him to me at one time. I can get you hith addreth directly.'"

Mr Gradgrind seemed to be quite confounded by this speculation.

"Any way," said Sleary, after putting his lips to his brandy and water, "ith fourteen months ago, Thquire, thinthe we wath at Chethter. One morning, there cometh into our Ring by the thtage door, a dog. He had travelled a long way, he wath in very bad condithon, he wath lame, and pretty well blind. He went round our children, one after another, as if he wath a-theeking for a child he know'd. Then he come to me, and throwd hithelf up behind, and thtood on hith two forelegth, weak ath he wath, and then he wagged hith tail and died. Thquire, that dog wath Merrylegth."

"Sissy's father's dog!"

"Thethilia'th father'th old dog. Now, Thquire, I can take my oath, from my knowledge of that dog, that that man wath dead – and buried – afore that dog come back to me. Joth'phine and Childerth and me talked it over a long time, whether I thould write or not. But we agreed, 'No. There'th nothing comfortable to tell; why unthettle her mind, and make her unhappy?'"

"She keeps the bottle that he sent her for, to this hour; and she will believe in his affection to the last moment of her life," said Mr Gradgrind.

"It theemth to prethent two thingth to a perthon, don't it, Thquire?" said Mr Sleary, musing as he looked into his drink: "one, that there ith a love in the world, not all Thelf-intereht after all, but thomething very different; t'other, that it hath a way of ith own of calculating or not calculating, whith thomehow or another ith at leatht ath hard to give a name to, ath the wayth of the dogth ith!"

Mr Gradgrind looked out of window, and made no reply. Mr Sleary emptied his glass and recalled the ladies.

"Thethilia my dear, kith me, and good-bye! Mith Thquire, to thee you treating of her like a thithter, and a thithter that you trutht and honour with all your heart and more, ith a very pretty thight to me. I hope your brother may live to be better detherving of you, and a greater comfort to you.

192

Thquire, thake handth, firtht and latht! Don't be croth with uth poor
vagabondth. People mutht be amuthed. They can't be alwayth a learning,
nor yet they can't be alwayth a working, they an't made for it. You mutht
have uth, Thquire. Do the withe thing and the kind thing too, and make
the betht of uth; not the wurtht!"

CHAPTER 9

It is a dangerous thing to see anything in the sphere of a vain blusterer,
before the vain blusterer sees it himself. Mr Bounderby felt that Mrs
Sparsit had audaciously anticipated him, and presumed to be wiser than
he. Totally indignant for her triumphant discovery of Mrs Pegler, he
turned this presumption, on the part of a woman in her dependent
position, over and over in his mind, until it accumulated with turning like
a great snowball. At last he realised that to discharge this highly
connected female would be to get the utmost amount of crowning glory
out of the connection, and at the same time to punish Mrs Sparsit.

Filled with this great idea, Mr Bounderby came in to lunch, and sat
himself down in the dining-room of former days, where his portrait was.
Mrs Sparsit sat by the fire.

Since the Pegler affair, this gentlewoman had covered her pity for
Mr Bounderby with a veil of quiet melancholy and contrition. It had
become her habit to assume a woeful look, which she now bestowed upon
her patron.

"What's the matter now, ma'am?" said Mr Bounderby, shortly.

"Pray, sir," returned Mrs Sparsit, "do not bite my nose off."

"Bite your nose off, ma'am?" repeated Mr Bounderby. "Your nose!"
meaning, as Mrs Sparsit conceived, that it was too developed a nose for
the purpose. After which offensive implication, he cut a crust of bread,
and threw the knife down.

Mrs Sparsit said, "Mr Bounderby, sir!"

"What are you staring at, ma'am?" retorted Mr Bounderby.

"May I ask, sir," said Mrs Sparsit, "have you been ruffled this
morning?"

"Yes, ma'am."

"May I inquire, sir," pursued the injured woman, "whether I am the unfortunate cause of your having lost your temper?"

"Now, I'll tell you what, ma'am," said Bounderby, "I am not come here to be bullied. A female may be highly connected, but she can't be permitted to bother and badger a man in my position, and I am not going to put up with it."

Mrs Sparsit gathered up her work into its proper basket and rose.

"Sir," said she, majestically. "Clearly I am in your way at present. I will retire to my own apartment."

"Allow me to open the door, ma'am."

"Thank you, sir, I can do it for myself."

"Allow me, ma'am," said Bounderby, passing her, and getting his hand upon the lock. "I can take the opportunity of saying a word to you, before you go. Mrs Sparsit, ma'am, I rather think you are cramped here. It appears to me, that, under my humble roof, there's hardly opportunity enough for a lady of your genius in other people's affairs."

Mrs Sparsit gave him a look of the darkest scorn, and said with great politeness, "Really, sir?"

"I have been thinking it over, you see, ma'am," said Bounderby; "and it appears to my poor judgement – "

"Oh! Pray, sir," Mrs Sparsit interposed, with sprightly cheerfulness, "don't disparage your judgement. Everybody knows how unerring Mr Bounderby's judgement is. Disparage anything in yourself but your judgement."

Mr Bounderby, very red and uncomfortable, resumed:

"It appears to me, ma'am, I say, that a different sort of establishment would bring out a lady of your powers. That of your relation, Lady Scadgers's, now. Don't you think you might find some affairs there, ma'am, to interfere with?"

"It never occurred to me before, sir," returned Mrs Sparsit; "but now you mention it, I should think it highly probable."

"Then suppose you try, ma'am," said Bounderby, laying an envelope with a cheque in it in her little basket. "Take your time for going, ma'am; but in the meanwhile, it may be more agreeable to eat your meals alone, and not to be intruded upon. I really ought to apologise – being only Josiah Bounderby – for having stood in your light so long."

"If that portrait could speak, sir," returned Mrs Sparsit. "However, it has the advantage over the original of not possessing the power of committing itself and disgusting others, – it would agree that it has been a long time since I first addressed it as the picture of a Noodle. Nothing that a Noodle does, can surprise; the proceedings of a Noodle can only inspire contempt."

Thus saying, Mrs Sparsit surveyed him fixedly from head to foot, swept disdainfully past him, and ascended the staircase. Mr Bounderby closed the door, and stood before the fire; projecting himself in his old manner into his portrait – and into futurity.

But how far? He saw Mrs Sparsit fighting out a daily fight with the grudging, smarting, peevish, tormenting Lady Scadgers, still laid up in bed with her mysterious leg. But did he see more? Did he catch a glimpse of himself showing Bitzer off to strangers, as the rising young man, devoted to his master's great merits, who had won young Tom's place, and had almost captured young Tom himself? Had he any prescience of the day, five years hence, when Josiah Bounderby of Coketown was to die of a fit in the Coketown street? Probably not. Yet the portrait was to see it all out.

Here was Mr Gradgrind on the same day, at the same time, sitting thoughtful in his own room. How much of the future did he see? Did he see himself, a white-haired decrepit man, bending his hitherto inflexible theories to appointed circumstances; making his facts and figures subservient to Faith, Hope, and Charity; and no longer trying to grind that Heavenly trio in his dusty little mills?

Here was Louisa on the night of the same day, watching the fire as in days of yore, though with a gentler and humbler face. How much of the future might arise before her vision? Broadsheets in the streets, signed by her father, exonerating the late Stephen Blackpool, weaver, from misplaced suspicion, and publishing the guilt of his own son, were of the Present. So, Stephen Blackpool's tombstone, with her father's record of his death, was almost of the Present, for she knew it was to be. These things she could plainly see. But, how much of the Future?

A working woman, christened Rachael, after a long illness once again appearing at the ringing of the Factory bell, and passing to and fro at the set hours; a woman of pensive beauty, always dressed in black, but sweet-tempered and serene, who, of all the people in the place, alone appeared to have compassion on a degraded, drunken wretch of her own sex, who was sometimes seen in the town secretly begging of her; a woman working, ever working, but content to do it, and preferring to do it as her natural lot, until she should be too old to labour any more? Did Louisa see this? Such a thing was to be.

A lonely brother, many thousands of miles away, writing, on paper blotted with tears. At length, this brother coming nearer home, with hope of seeing her, and being delayed by illness. Then a letter, in a strange hand, saying "he died in hospital, of fever, such a day, and died in penitence and love of you: his last word being your name"? Did Louisa see these things? Such things were to be.

Herself again a wife – a mother – lovingly watchful over her children, ever careful that they should have a childhood of the mind no less than a childhood of the body. Did Louisa see this? Such a thing was never to be.

But, happy Sissy's happy children loving her; all children loving her; she, grown learned in childish lore; thinking no innocent and pretty fancy ever to be despised; trying hard to know her humbler fellow creatures, and to beautify their lives of machinery and reality with those imaginative delights, without which the heart of infancy will wither, the sturdiest physical manhood will be morally stark death – she holding this course as part of no fantastic vow, or bond, or brotherhood, or sisterhood, or pledge, or covenant, or fancy dress, or fancy fair; but simply as a duty to be done, – did Louisa see these things of herself? These things were to be.